I0838147

https://www.amazon.com/gp/profile/amzn1.account.
AFPPTTSP6QWIIHTWEQ4E4IWGYQXA/
ref=cm_cr_dp_d_gw_tr?ie=UTF8
5.0 out of 5 stars **Small Town Thriller**
Reviewed in the United States on November 13, 2011
A real page turner, especially if you are familiar with the area. In fact, I think that's what made it so interesting is that I never imagined something like that would ever happen in Padanaram. The author has a sense of humor as well and made for a very good read. I'll never think of the village in the same way again. I'll always be thinking if those joggers or Sunday cycilists that slow me down on my way to church are really just out for the exercise.

https://www.amazon.com/gp/profile/amzn1.account.
AGCH436CYA22SQCQM6DTXLV4Z3FA/
ref=cm_cr_dp_d_gw_tr?ie=UTF8
5.0 out of 5 stars **Good story and ends in an OK mood**
Reviewed in the United States on June 12, 2016
Keeps you waiting for the next shoe to fall. Good story and ends in an OK mood.

5.0 out of 5 stars **Well written story, believable characters**
Reviewed in the United States on June 16, 2015
Believable characters, good story, well written, moves along at a good pace.

5.0 out of 5 stars **Excellent read.**
Reviewed in the United States on April 2, 2016
I found the title curious.I loved the element of suspense.Love a book that is difficult to put down,you will like it.

5.0 out of 5 stars **Five Stars**
Reviewed in the United States on March 7, 2016
Good read. Had me worried and rooting for the protagonist (Rich).

Nov 29, 2020 **Shey Saints** rated it:

Padanaram Village: A Mystery of Sorts is a legal thriller by Jack Burbank. I enjoyed this book! This is the third book I have read by this author (and still counting), and he never fails to entertain. He doesn't like run-of-the-mill stories; he writes the most out-of-this-world scenarios that would make you keep guessing what in the world would happen now?

I love the client-lawyer relationship between Rich and Alan, the budding romance that Rich has with Gail, and came to appreciate Judge Santos whom I didn't like at first. As for Debbie, Tom, and Lafleur, they can all go to hell.

I'm giving this book 5 out of 5 stars. The author is my favorite when it comes to legal and crime investigation stories. This book has entertainment value and a story that is out of the ordinary. Readers who love thriller with a touch of humor will love this book.

See More at "Good Reads":

https://www.goodreads.com/book/show/26035548-padanaram-village?ac=1&from_search=true&qid=Ub6zVIfFVF&rank=1

PADANARAM VILLAGE

ONE LITTLE GUY
ONE **BIG** PROBLEM

JACK BURBANK

Primix Publishing
11620 Wilshire Blvd
Suite 900, West Wilshire Center, Los Angeles, CA, 90025
www.primixpublishing.com
Phone: 1-800-538-5788

Published by Primix Publishing: 07/08/2024

ISBN: 979-8-89194-183-0(sc)
ISBN: 979-8-89194-184-7(e)

Library of Congress Control Number: 2024911229

To Phil.

Who once proclaimed to me, "Anyone can write!"
I took him seriously, began writing and this was my
first piece.

CHAPTER 1

June, 1999
Early Monday

The silver 750iL BMW looked as much out of place driving among the dunes near Horseneck Beach as did the two men in it. They could hardly afford a bike between them, yet here they were in one of Germany's finest. The car sloshed its way onward with the two nervous drivers bug-eyed and breaking a slight sweat from concern over all the slipping and sliding.

"That sand can't be good for this paint job." Tony was talking to Marty, his eyes fixed ahead.

No response from Marty.

"There's the trees," he said to Marty, relieved to

be at the end of their wilderness trek. Now, get the job done and be gone. No response from Marty.

They pulled close to the shrubbery and trees. This early on a Monday morning they looked as alone and isolated as Crusoe and Friday. Doors opened quickly and both men were at the trunk. To Marty and Tony, this job was part of paying their dues. There would be better days ahead, or so it seemed on this beautiful morning. A large green plastic bag was hoisted out, shapeless and bulky.

Tony grunted, "We should'a cut this up smaller. Separate bags." Marty didn't reply. They dragged the bag together into the shrubs to a standing of trees.

"I'll keep watch, you go get the suitcases." Tony barked. Marty cast a bewildering glance. Still no reply. "And bring the pick-ax and shovel too."

Marty returned obediently for the last load - two large Samsonite "Voyager" suitcases and the tools.

Taking the pick-ax, Tony handed Marty the shovel and whacked at the ground a few then motioned for Marty to shovel.

"What if someone happens by?" Marty finally spoke.

"Pity the sucker does."

Marty kept digging, completely ruining his new, best suit. Kiss that hundred dollars goodbye, he thought. Tony watched. Rested.

With the hole dug, they dragged the plastic bag to the edge and slid it in. They stuffed the two suitcases down the sides. The two-tone, beige suitcases with brass and leather trim detail were clean and without a scratch.

"What a waste," Tony expressed, "look at them beauties of suitcases! Could'a used boxes. Anyway, we gotta cover it good, make it look normal and all."

"Uh - we? You got anotha shovel?" Marty asked.

The hole got covered and Marty dragged some large branches over to cover it. Tony let him finish the job, brushing the marks away. The job looked done.

They returned to the BMW, slammed the tools into the trunk and took a slow pan around, checking again that no one had witnessed what just happened. They tried to catch their breath.

"Rosie's for a beer?" Tony suggested.

"Some place closer, for a few?" Marty countered. It was decided, if there was a place that served beer this early, they'd find it.

The car pulled away with a fan spray of sand and gravel. Tony sensed the soft base under his wheels, gave it more pedal and overcame any notion the Beemer had about getting stuck. They fishtailed all the way out, spraying sand and debris along a wide swath, sandblasting a hummingbird's nest clinging to a scrub pine just off their path. As distance was put between them and the site, the ecological balance of the dunes quickly returned to normal.

Two startled Ruby-Throated hummingbirds hovered

around their house, unfamiliar with the form of disaster that had just shook their cottage by the beach. Hovering and turning, darting here and there, they spied the area sensing no further danger. The scene was serene as always, no predators or destructive storms apparent. Even their heightened senses couldn't detect anything abnormal just a hundred and fifty feet east.

Richard Lewis remained still and hidden, not a single leaf shaking out of sync as he lay camouflaged in his hunter's blind. He had fashioned the blind earlier in the spring and would often park a quarter mile away, quietly slipping into it at dawn. Lying prone in his hammock, even his six-foot plus frame was comfortable. He would spy for hours on the wildlife of the dunes through his 800mm Nikor lens and hardly have to budge. What he had just witnessed though, was something entirely unexpected.

With the car gone and the dust settled, Rich rolled out of his hammock and scooted out of the blind and up to the dig area, overcoming the soft sand of several dunes. He approached carefully. He took a three-foot long branch, broke off the small sidepieces, used it to break the ground apart, then used his hands. He worked harder and faster than either Tony or Marty, but with never a bead of sweat. You can always tell a jogger.

When he finally hit his target and scooped away enough dirt to peer in, a wave of anxiety rushed through him. The plastic bag loomed before him. Had he seen too many movies or didn't this have to be a body? And the suitcases. Drugs? Loot? Body pieces? "Just calm down, it probably won't be anything to get shook about." But it was. A body.

Middle aged man. No smell, no blood that he could see. This was fresh, maybe a few hours. Like he was really experienced in these things. He shook, a wave of the woolies passing through him in a second. He'd have to report this. But the suitcases caught his attention.

Heavy as it was to drag out, Rich admired the style. The cases were new, or at least looked it. Had the appearance of something from the thirties, for the real traveler type of the time, steam boating all over the world, sometimes hopping an airplane, a Pan Am something or other. These cases would suit a savvy and experienced traveler. But they were copies, fairly new Samsonites, capturing the colorful mystique and flair of that bygone era. He noticed the brass emblem with a single word, "Voyager" embossed in it.

They were locked. Rich took out his Swiss Army and tried the awl. He popped the first lock, then the second. He took a breath anticipating body parts, or maybe clear plastic bags of coke. Or heroin. Or whatever drug was put into clear plastic bags. He'd seen it a hundred times on screen, but couldn't keep up with which drugs are which. For an intelligent man, Rich could be very naïve in many ways.

He opened the case. Money. Lots.

Spread before him were thousand dollar bills! Stacks and stacks, nothing but thousands! Like a

Grover Cleveland family reunion. In all different condition, no consecutive numbers, it had to be millions worth!

Rich closed the case, then dragged the other one out. It was a duplicate of the first, all in thousands. Questions flooded his mind as he tried desperately to grasp the full impact of this find. Who? Why? How? His mind raced considering the possibilities. It had to be illegal, there's a body for crying out loud! Nothing could be legal about that. But why all thousands? How?

For a guy who never broke a law in his life, one speeding ticket that he didn't deserve, a strange thought quickly took shape. If the money's illegal, who would be hurt by taking it? Richard Lewis had never been in the trouble he was in lately and this money might just save him.

He locked the second case, grabbed the other and made for his Explorer parked three hundred yards away. He returned, first to his hunter's blind to salvage his equipment then tore the blind apart, scattering the pieces. He took a fresh scrub-pine limb and used it to sweep away his tracks counting on the ocean breeze to erase the slight brush marks left behind. He made sure to get all of his tracks, right up to the burial site. He stopped short of the original foot prints made by the two goons. The police should find something to follow, otherwise they might start looking too close and find only his trail. Let them spend their resources tracing the BMW and the goons.

Awkwardly, Rich carried his equipment back to his Explorer while brushing his tracks clear. He threw the branch to the side, hopped in and headed home.

Cruising north on 88, then east on 195, Rich reached for his cell phone and punched 911. But he stopped - cell calls are too easy to trace. He remembered a gas-and-go type place off the next exit.

He punched the 911 again. Dartmouth Police Station picked up, a woman's voice answered, warning that the call would be recorded, then asked how she may help. Rich disguised his voice, feeling silly about it.

"Just an honest citizen reporting that I saw a body being buried near Horseneck Beach, maybe two hundred yards east of Bridge Road, in the dunes. You'll find tracks." He hung up, then pulled away and headed home. Rich mused over his two new life's experiences: He had just reported a major crime and he had just committed one.

CHAPTER 2

Later Monday

Home for Rich was the second floor of a three-story tenement just off the highway, near downtown New Bedford. Captain Ahab would have thought the building old in his day. It was a far cry from the showplace he had recently built and lived in for all of one year. He tried to shake off the thought that she was enjoying all that now. As Rich pulled to the front he could see his landlady, Ellen, burdened with groceries heading from her car.

Gathering his photography equipment, Rich threw a blanket over the Samsonites. He nodded to Ellen, said his pleasantries, yes he did get some great shots, mostly birds but one deer, sure he'll be glad to show her the pictures, bye and up the stairs. He was nervous. But he was also amazed, getting by her while avoiding any reference to the overdue rent.

He dare not even think of moving the suitcases. With Ellen's three hyperactive kids and her nosy husband, he'd wait for lights out. He wondered how much money there might be. Three million? Five? But why speculate, he'd count later.

He needed to busy himself. He flipped on his computer, deciding to polish up some finish detail for the interior elements of his latest design. It was a sprawling tri-level, ocean front gem, with steep pitched roofs, multiple guest and servants quarters and featuring a real moat circling the outside porch and into the entryway. The arched bridge in the foyer leading to the main hallway was his piece-de-resistance, very chic and most worthy of the Wellington's, one of Padanaram area's most austere residents. Another ten or twenty hours and he could put this project to bed and collect his last installment.

For hours he toyed with scanned imagery of different wall covering patterns and tile selections. Rich couldn't keep his mind from wandering. An incredible amount of money was sitting in the back seat of his car. While part of his mind raced with ideas of spending and buying, another part was working as logically as ever, his trademark persona. Probably the Russian in him. If he were to start spending, it would surely be noticed. Somebody would be watching. Any movement of large amounts of money would raise eyebrows, especially the eyebrows sitting on top of some mob czar's beady little eyes.

Anything Rich wanted to do was possible now with all that money. But the money would stop him. Whoever would be looking would know how to track it, wouldn't they? He imagined there were ways to monitor traveling, banking and investments. Weren't there? He didn't know and thought it best to just hide it for now.

He got up, looking for hiding places. Hardly room for him, let alone to hide two bulky suitcases. Scanning the room for some overlooked area, the flashing red light caught his eye. The machine showed two messages bringing him relief - Bell Atlantic hadn't shut him off yet.

Rich pushed the "Play" button for his first message:

"Mr. Lewis, this is Bay State Gas Company calling. Please call our office at 508-555-5656 before noon time tomorrow. Thank you."

He smiled. If they'll break a thousand, he could pay them. Next message:

"Rich, Alan here. Look, they've filed a contempt charge. Not to worry, but give me a call and see if we can't work this out without involving Santos. They've expedited the matter and we've got to appear in two days."

Contempt! Debbie had been threatening a charge of contempt if he didn't keep up with the mortgage payments, or rather, her attorney was. But Rich couldn't believe they'd really do it. He was only behind a month or two. Or three. And go before Judge Santos! Santos thought Rich was the biggest hard-head ever to get a divorce in his court. An appearance before Santos had to be avoided if at all possible. He'd call Alan in the morning since he never stayed in his office this late. The fire had gone out of his career a long time ago. Knew his stuff, but Rich sometimes wondered if he should have hooked up with a younger, more aggressive horse. Maybe he wouldn't be in the mess he was.

—◆—◆—◆—◆—

A Dartmouth Police car was on the scene mingled in with two Westport Police cars, an ambulance, four television news vans and the channel twelve helicopter.

It was Westport's jurisdiction, but since the call had come into Dartmouth, a courtesy was extended and Dartmouth Captain Tony Hernandes took them up on it.

The body had been photographed eight different ways before being removed, the bag then carefully cut open length-wise. More photos.

The middle-aged male victim had not been beaten, hacked or maimed. No marks, no injuries, no messages, no weird chickens feet or bat's teeth. But there was also no wallet, so Forensics would have to be called for identity. Could be natural causes, but then why bury the body in such a covert manner?

Captain Hernandes was speaking with two

Westport officers and one of his own, Officer Humbolt. Desperate for some kind of clue or evidence, it wasn't looking as though there would be much to go on. Even the tire tracks seemed useless.

"Too sandy to be of much use. But follow them out to Horseneck Road or wherever they go. Near the shoulder you should get a clear enough print." One of the Westport officers on his two-way.

"Has to be new-boy mob," Officer Humbolt, second year servant noted, "who else wouldn't think to cover their tracks?"

"I've learned a long time ago to never speculate." Hernandes could almost agree with Hombolt, but wanted to be sage-like.

"Anything else turn up in the area?" the Westport officer inquired.

Hernandes looked up, rubbing his neck in frustration. "No. Nothing yet. Some funny marks going north, probably the caller covering his tracks. Poor shmuck probably thinks he'd be blamed for a murder just because he stumbled across a body being buried. Why can't people learn to trust us when they find things like this?"

Officer Humbolt let a few seconds pass, then corrected, "Or 'her'."

She earned a small grin from her captain. The voice had been disguised on the phone and who knew if it were a man or a woman making the call?

Tony and Marty were feeling like a couple of new men. Draining their fifth pitcher of Bud at The Harpoon Bar, they were regaling in the successful completion of their biggest assignment yet. With their careers launched less than a year ago, today's action should earn them junior executive status. Marty would need the bonus that would likely be thrown their way. The beer spills mixed with the dirt marks on his new suit were staining the wool content of the blend. The polyester would probably clean up, but forget the wool. That's the trouble with these expensive suits, Marty thought. Tony's suit had equally as many new stains from the day's activity, but wasn't as noticeable. The odd shade of pinkish gray hid a lot.

They had idled away the day shooting pool, drinking beer and feeding on nachos and popcorn. Tony, the "take charge" guy, had been checking on their boss, due to meet them around six. He ended his call and put his cell phone back in his pocket.

"Carlo should be here any minute," he drawled in his southern New Bedfordese to Marty. "He's left his home twenty minutes ago and's headed right over."

He was just a little pie-eyed as he studied the mostly empty pitcher. "Whata'ya say we do one more and if he wants us to go, we guzzle it down." He looked to Marty for approval.

"Guzzle it down if we stay, too." The ever efficient Marty.

"Karla babe, one more and a couple more popcorns." Tony caught her attention as she was reaching to change the station for the 6:00 news. He poured the last of the suds and held the pitcher high for her to see.

"Anyway, like I said," Tony was returning to their earlier argument, "I seen a guy do it four out of five times down in Providence. He had a break like a hammer, always nailed the front ball on the right with left follow english, and so help me, that eight ball would drop just about all the time."

"Not saying it can't happen. But nobody does it regular."

"I'm tellin ya. Five breaks, four wins. BANG. Pop, pop, pop, pop. Like a real artiste"

Marty looked unconvinced, shooting Tony a sideways glance through his slowly fading eyes.

"And how many pops've you had by then?" he asked sarcastically.

Tony started to retort, "Hey, I've been all around the state and ...." when in his subconscious, the words "body", "buried" and "Horseneck Beach" all rang and echoed around in his head, not making any particular sense as they hung there. Not knowing where they were coming from, he noticed Marty turning his attention to the TV above the bar.

Natalie Jacobson, long standing Boston anchorperson, was reporting and looking as sharp and knowledgeable as ever with her Farrah Fawcett hair style still looking good, an ageless wonder in the competitive, local television market. As Tony picked up on her trailing words, the view switched to on-the-scene video. It was a scary sight for them. Familiar. The sand and shrubs, the scrub pines, the hole they had dug… A nightmarish scene was being played out before them as they sat motionless, speechless, their jaws slowly dropping to their chests.

An on the scene reporter went on, "…following an anonymous tip placed from a local gas station. When Westport police arrived, the grave was already partially dug out with the green body bag exposed and a small hole torn in the bag that would verify the worst of fears - it was in fact, a human body! No identification has been made yet, and there were no visible bruises or wounds. But police suspect foul play due to the bizarre manner in which the body was disposed of and hope to make identification shortly. The body is that of a white male, approximately thirty years old, with no visible identification marks. He was fully clothed. No witnesses are available now, but it is hoped that the anonymous tipster will come forward as they may have very valuable information."

At the same speed, going down the same path of logic, Tony and Marty digested what they had just heard and began to puzzle out what they *hadn't* heard. Nothing was said about the money. In a flash of about three seconds both Tony and Marty arrived at the same conclusion: Somebody took the money.

Tony stared at Marty staring back. As he began to form a few choice words, he suddenly froze, a chill shooting down into his two-tone, beige, Thom McAnns. Marty sensed his chill and turned in time to see Carlo making his entry with three associates in tow. Both Marty and Tony recognized the associates. Tony and Marty were aiming for their jobs.

A sick, nauseous feeling settled into both of them, deep into the pits of their stomachs. And that was to be the *best* they would feel for the rest of their lives.

Rich managed each suitcase up the stairs separately. Closing all his blinds and shutting all lights out but the one in his bedroom, Rich placed each suitcase on the bed. He popped all four locks and flipped both cases open. Mirror images of each other.

His initial impression was confirmed. Nothing but $1,000.00 bills! He never knew they made $1,000.00 bills. The most he ever had were a few Garfields. Not that he was a poor man his whole life. His profession as an architect netted him a very good living, reporting over a quarter million in personal income several different years. That was one very good reason for his tax dilemma now. But his wife, ex-wife, did the books and handled all that. He'd get fifty a week for his wallet. So staring at all this cash laid out in front of him, well, it was truly inspiring.

He carefully lifted a few stacks. It seemed uniform throughout: Three stacks of bundled bills laid out in four rows of twelve. One hundred and forty four wrapped stacks of $1,000.00 bills. As he flipped through the stacks, he halted at seeing a bill that looked different. It was a thousand dollar bill, but different. It didn't have Cleveland on the front, it had Alexander Hamilton! He took it out and examined it more closely. The back was different too, sporting a bold eagle and boasting the thousand dollar figure even more proudly. Turning back to the front, he noticed the government seal was blue, not green. But it looked genuine and of United States issue.

Puzzled at this anomaly, Rich flipped through more stacks and found several more of these style bills. After comparing dates, he decided the Hamilton version was older.

Taking one stack out, Rich counted the bills. One hundred. One hundred thousand dollars! In each stack? He picked another random stack and counted. The same. Then another. And another. With eight counted from one case and three from the other, he knew it was all the same.

Final calculation: 144 stacks of $100,000.00 *in each case* equaling $28,800,000.00!

Rich was awash in the surrealism of this whole scene. His mind was going wild searching for an explanation that made sense of all this. The impact floored him, literally. He sat on the floor before his bed, two stacks of money in his hands. He reflected on his past two years: Debbie leaving him for their real estate man, cleaning the home out of most of their valuables, leaving Rich with only the furniture not yet paid for, then the court settlement awarding Debbie the house and demanding that he continue the mortgage payments, all because of a convoluted and distorted portrayal of their income situation. He thought of his fights to ward off depression and the impact it all had on his business, which was down the tubes and practically non-existent at this point. With no way out and no light at the end of the tunnel, his irresponsible decision this morning to take the day off, again, and grab some wildlife pictures has brought him unexpectedly to this point today

Maybe it was joy, maybe grief, maybe his reliving the sting of betrayal, but Rich gave in to his emotions. Sitting on the floor before this enormous wealth, he felt like a very small man. But he also felt like a new man. He curled up in a ball and fell fast asleep on the floor.

It was around 4:00 in the morning when Rich awoke. The faint glow of the morning illuminated the house just enough for him to set about his final task of the night. He slid a kitchen chair to the side, mounted it and pushed a ceiling tile up and over. About thirty trips and six ceiling tiles later, the money was safely hidden. He crawled into bed for a few more precious winks.

CHAPTER 3
Tuesday

"Alan, Rich."

"Rich, how are you doing?"

Alan had a special concern for Rich, beyond a normal attorney-client relationship. His messing up at the divorce hearing and allowing his client to get walloped beyond belief had a lot to do with that. Rich's patience in not firing him, or suing him for that matter, had a lot more to do with it.

"Did you say something about contempt?"

"Ahhhh," Alan's voice trailing slightly. "We were served notice of a Motion to Compel and a complaint for Contempt on your court ordered settlement. Evidently you're what, a month or two behind on your mortgage?"

"Try three."

"Three. Okay, well what's the bank saying? Are they threatening foreclosure?"

"The words came up a few times, but I think I have them at bay. I explained that I'm finishing up a project and my last installment check should be in this week." Rich smiled to himself knowing that these problems were all behind him now. If he wanted to, he could buy the bank.

"Well, why don't you go to your bank, get them to write you a letter as to their intent and the understanding that you have with them and we should be all right. But the hearing is scheduled for Thursday and like it or not, you are in contempt if the payments are behind."

"Alan, I had no money come in for three months. What can they do?"

"Well, I'm more concerned about what you can do. Like, ninety days for starters." Alan wanted to impress upon Rich the seriousness of his situation.

"How can they send someone to jail for not paying a bill that he has no way of paying? I thought debtor's prison was abolished with the country's independence!"

"Rich, you know Judge Santos. He already thinks you're hiding money and trying to stiff Debbie. He sees you as a professional with proven credentials, perfectly capable of supporting your end of the order. If you show up Thursday with the house in danger of foreclosure, for sure he'll send you up the river."

"So you're serious. Jail is a real possibility because

I fall behind on a mortgage, and for property I don't even own any longer? Who goes to jail for falling behind on a mortgage?"

"Evidently, Judge Santos's guests." Alan had seen Santos in action enough to know to warn Rich.

The point was made. "Let me come over and we'll talk," Rich implored of Alan, "I'll come with my letter from the bank. And I've got to talk to you about another matter that's come up."

"Can we do lunch? Say at Freestone's, 1:00?"

"You'll have to pick up the tab. I haven't been paid for the Wellington project yet." It cut Rich to have to ask. He was always the one to pick up the tab. Always.

"That's not a problem. You know I keep the receipt and add it to my expenses anyway. It'll show up on your bill."

They hung up, both smiling to themselves about the lunch tab. Only attorneys can make a show of picking up the bill at dinner, tip heavily, and then turn right around and bill the client every penny of the meal, tip, consultation time, and the trip back and forth to their office, which would include car expenses and their time. The postage stamp on the envelope will be included along with a $ .09 charge for copying the receipt. And if you dare call to complain, you get whacked with their hourly rate as they listen to you complain. At $240 an hour, they can put up with a lot of complaining.

But Alan might be Rich's only friend in the world right now.

⸻⬩⬗⬩⬗⬩⬗⸻

First Federal Bank was directly on the way to Alan Levine's law office. Rich popped in to talk with Michelle, his friendly mortgage representative.

"Michelle!" Rich was always happy to see her. Though she might be initiating the foreclosure of his home, or his former home, Michelle had a way of making you feel right at home while the rug was swiftly being removed from under you. Special person.

"Hi, Rich. Are we getting caught up today?" She looked quite professional today in her double-breasted, light gray suit.

"Two or three days more. I had cash, but didn't think your bank would know what to do with it, so I have to deposit it, wait for the cash to clear, then I can write you a check against the funds." Bank rules were getting as distorted as Massachusetts probate laws. Anyway, Michelle appreciated the humor and was satisfied to know the payment was imminent.

"But I need a letter from you to keep out of jail."

"What are we playing, Monopoly?" Michelle thought he was still joking.

"More like 'Risk'. Debbie's attorney got wind of my being behind on the mortgage and filed a contempt charge. My attorney says to either get a letter from the bank or bring a toothbrush."

Michelle paused for a moment. "You mean for jail?"

Rich nodded affirmatively with a look of disbelief. Michelle obediently went to her keyboard and started typing.

"That home is so beautiful. You must miss it." Michelle had seen it for inspection and closing and felt for Rich.

"Well, yeah. But to know that the two of them are so happy there makes it all worth it." And he didn't crack a smile.

"I've seen a lot of one-sided settlements, but yours ..., I wouldn't have dreamed it. Debbie and her husband have both called a few times asking about the status of the mortgage. Even her attorney, what's his name?"

"LaFleur."

"LaFleur, that's right. Anyway, he called a few weeks ago trying to get heavy. I told him he had no right to that confidential information and if he were much of an attorney, he would know that. He backed right off."

"He probably didn't know. He couldn't even tell Debbie when she was officially divorced and able to get married again. I had to go to the Clerk's Office and get the document so she could prove to the guy that she was marriage material. Can you imagine a piece of work like that, a divorce attorney that couldn't even tell his client when she was divorced? And I let a guy like that best me in court! Whatever I can say about his intelligence level, I've got to look in a mirror and say it twice to myself."

Michelle smirked with him and added, "And your attorney. Don't forget to blame him."

"He's not so bad. Let this one get away from him though."

Rich took the letter, thanked Michelle and proceeded to Alan's office, three blocks south.

Alan's office was on the fourth floor. Not the commanding penthouse station that he once occupied in Providence, but more than satisfactory for the twenty hours or so that he liked to work now.

"Mr. Lewis. How are you doing today?" Marge, the receptionist, was her same polite self, impeccably dressed in a navy blue suit that took ten years off her real age. "I have you down for lunch with Mr. Levine at 1:00. Is that still on?"

"Absolutely. I wouldn't miss giving Alan another billable hour for lunch. But I'm a little early."

"I'll let him know that you're here." Marge disappeared down the short hallway. She had been with Alan almost from the beginning and the two were like a well oiled machine by now. She was back in a flash and led Rich to Alan's office.

"Hey, Alan."

"Rich, come in, come in." Alan was a content sort of man. He'd done what he wanted, had a loving family and was ready to retire but just had no need to do so yet. So he worked a few hours weekly, probably half pro-bono. Rich wondered why he still charged for copies and postage.

"I didn't think you'd mind me being a little early."

Alan probably hadn't gotten mad at anyone for fifteen or twenty years. You would think in a profession like his that he'd have a lot of controversy, but it was all just a job to him. Nothing personal. He could tear a witness up in court or berate an opposing attorney, chopping him up in little pieces for the courtroom rats to feast on at night, but if he bumped into him the same evening he'd buy the same witness or attorney two drinks and dinner. Far from being two-faced, Alan was a sincere professional and had a court record that Alan Dershorwitz would be envious of.

"First, here's my note from the teacher." Rich handed Alan the letter Michelle had typed.

Looking it over, Alan called Marge in to fax a copy to Debbie's attorney, Mr. LaFleur, along with a cover letter to the effect that the contempt hearing would be moot as the mortgage would be up to date within days and the bank was happy. Out of a thousand lawyers, probably nine hundred and ninety five would quickly acquiesce and drop the charge under the circumstances. But with LaFleur, Alan would bet against it.

"You're really serious about doing jail for this? Falling behind in my mortgage?"

"Rich, it's not just a mortgage. It's a court order. A settlement. It's like not paying alimony or child support. By law, you're obligated to maintain the payments on Debbie's property until we can get the order modified."

"So I'm like a 'dead-beat dad'? Will my picture make a milk carton?"

"Well, maybe an evaporated milk can."

"Alan, I can't even pay a six hundred dollar rent. My phone and utilities might be shut off any day. I never even got cable, didn't have a TV worth doo-doo anyway. But I'm obliged to pay a $1,500.00 a month mortgage for a wife who runs off with a real estate guy?"

Alan just looked at Rich. He had explained everything many times in the past, but Rich couldn't accept it. In a no-fault divorce state, it doesn't matter who did what to end the marriage. Someone wants out, they're out, and assets theoretically get split down the middle. But if one party was largely responsible for supporting the other, they're expected to continue support for a reasonable period of time. How simple these things sound in the halls of justice, where legislators dreamt up easy ways for the system to work after their two hour, three martini lunches, far away from the annoyances of real life.

Rich raised his hands in surrender. He'd been over this before and knew the problem had come from being unprepared at the divorce hearing. Alan had thought the case to be a slam-dunk, so never asked Rich to bring all the records needed. LaFleur blind-sided them by making allegations and misrepresentations he had never hinted at before. Alan admitted being bettered but explained that such tactics usually only happen in criminal cases. He had never seen such ruthlessness in probate. He never imagined LaFleur even had it in him.

"Let's change the subject. I'm fried with the divorce until you work your magic with the modification. Enough said?"

Alan smiled, understanding the frustration. "Done. What else is on your mind?"

Rich settled back, a little uneasy now.

"Alan, as my attorney, can I tell you anything related to my life and know that it will remain confidential?"

"If I didn't learn that in law school, I'd know it just from the law shows on television."

Another TV addict, thought Rich.

"Because something happened, unrelated to the divorce but something that will certainly have an impact on my situation."

There was a knowing nod from Alan, not suspecting what was about to come.

"Did you watch the news last night?"

"Never miss it. Get some of my best clients from those reports."

"Well, one of your clients all but made the top story. You see the story about the body?"

Alan sat back. Rich definitely caught his interest.

"Around Horseneck Beach area. Certainly."

"I was the caller. The tipster."

Raised eyebrows. Alan would rather a good criminal case over probate any day.

"I was out shooting some pictures in the scrub pine and was hidden away the way I do. All of a sudden I see this car come barreling down in a cloud of dust and what looked like Mutt and Jeff get out, drag things out of the trunk and bury them. I went over to look after they cleared out and couldn't resist taking a peek. I found the body."

"Well, it was good of you to call it in. And so fast! The news report said they'd like to talk to you, and I can see why. Rich, if you're worried that you'll fall under suspicion or that you waited before coming forward, don't worry at all. It's been what, less than twenty four hours? And now you're talking to your attorney before coming out? You're protected under law. You have every right to consult with an attorney."

Rich took a deep breath. He turned to see that the door was shut. He still had doubts as to whether he should do this, but who else could he turn to?

"Alan, I don't think that day will ever come."

"What? Telling the police?" Alan was still confident Rich would do the right thing.

Rich nodded affirmative.

"Rich, don't be foolish. You have nothing to hide, but it's a crime not to report a crime. And a man's body for crying out loud! Report it and report it today. I'll be right by your side."

Again Rich just stared. He took a deep breath and studied Alan's expression carefully. Here's the man that let a simple divorce settlement get away on him and now Rich was in the deepest financial crap of his life, yet he was about to trust the same man with his biggest secret.

"There was something else in the grave."

The silence could be cut with a knife.

"Two suitcases. They dragged them out of the trunk after dragging out the body, then put them all in the pit and covered the whole thing over. When I went, I dug down and checked out the bag first, then the cases. Wouldn't you?"

Alan shook off his bewilderment. Wouldn't he? He wouldn't ever have been there! Not in the sticks, not shooting pictures of birds and certainly not digging up graves.

"Anyway, there were two. I checked them both out. They were the same."

Ten seconds of silence.

"And…?" Alan was about to go spastic.

"And I came into some money."

"You came into… Meaning it was money? And you took it?"

"Little ol' me." Rich smiled innocently.

Alan shot up out of his chair and walked away shaking his head. Rich sat still watching him through the corners of his eyes.

"You're a felon if you don't report everything and turn every bit of the money in."

"I may be. But I'm dead if I do." He shot a cold stare at Alan.

"Dead. Don't get carried away. It may be intimidating to have seen what you saw and then walk away with some money, but once you do the right thing, it will all take care of itself."

"You mean even if it was like two or three million dollars that someone was out?"

"Two or three mil…," Alan's surprise was obvious. He regained his composure, then added, "Yes. Even two or three million dollars. Did you really get two or three million dollars?" There was no pause between the two sentences.

"Oh, I got two or three million all right." Rich paused briefly. "In fumes."

Alan stopped, startled.

"What do you mean, 'in fumes'?"

"Alan, I've got twenty eight point eight million dollars hidden away. Never saw so much money. You wouldn't believe what that looks like just lying in one place."

Alan rushed to his chair to sit back down. He looked out the window a bit. Then he glanced at Rich. Then he stared at the wall hanging.

"Twenty eight eight?"

"In thousands. All thousands. Did you know they made thousand dollar bills?"

"Yes." Alan was in disbelief. Then he added, "But not that many of them."

"And they're not counterfeit, near as I can tell.

These are all different serial numbers and in different grades of condition. They're real, I know they are."

"But it's not yours! You can't keep it."

"Alan, maybe I shouldn't have taken it. But I did. Before I knew how much was there. Didn't take the time to count it on account of I had to get out of there. There was a body giving me the woolies and I was gone." Rich was trying to justify things but Alan was still looking doubtful.

Rich continued, "But now that I know how much money I took, how could I turn it in? You know it has to be serious mob or drug money. We're not talking some huckster that picks pockets or breaks into homes at night. Whose ever it is, they're big time. And I get the feeling they'd be pretty ticked-off to learn I had it. Don't you think, maybe?"

Alan was more serious than Rich had ever seen him.

"Rich, as your attorney, I have to advise you to come forward, turn everything in and tell the authorities what you know. As your friend, and I hope that's what we've become to each other, friends, as a friend I tell you…," he paused, stuttering, then had to admit, "I don't know what I tell you. I think you're right. You're in some real deep stuff here."

"At two forty an hour, what did that brilliant piece of advice just cost me?"

That brought the mood back to normal.

"Richard, what do you care? You're a twenty-eight-millionaire!"

"Yeah, well, I want to stay a twenty-eight-millionaire. Somehow when attorneys get involved there's always a shifting in the tides of fortune."

"No worry here. I can't get involved. If you're not going to come forward, and I can't say that I blame you, I can't be involved. What you told me is more than I need to know. Now if you want another attorney to handle this situation, I'd understand. I can still represent you in the divorce settlement, but I'm not touching this, this, this gangster thing. Not unless we're calling the police this afternoon."

A smirk on Rich's face. "Well, we're not calling the police this afternoon. We're going to go have lunch at Freestone's. But I'm glad I got that off my chest."

"And on to mine. Rich, I think you should think this through more."

Rich wanted advice and had dumped it all on Alan because he respected his opinion. But he'd been thinking it through and regardless of how honest or legal he'd like to keep things, if he spoke up, he'd be a gonner.

Alan turned to Rich and in a quieter voice said, "You know they're not making them any longer?"

Rich shook his head slightly, not understanding. "What?"

"Thousand dollar bills. Clevelands. They're calling them all in, taking them out of circulation." With that said, Alan wanted no further part of any discussion about the ill begotten booty. He signaled a note of finality to Rich.

"Let's go eat, Alan."

"Certainly. And now that I know you can afford it, it's on you."

"Sure, if they can break a thousand."

Alan cringed, putting his hands up as a shield. He didn't want to hear any of it.

Dartmouth Police Station is an aging, red and tan brick building as if someone couldn't make up their mind on the color to use. Captain Hernandes was sitting at his desk in a rare moment of solitude. It's not that Dartmouth was all that busy with crime or incidents, but with all the summer activity, largely an overflow from surrounding town beaches and attractions, they never pumped up their staff that much, so it was a busy time of year. And though the body was found in Westport, his brief, token involvement with the case had piqued his interest.

Tony Hernandes was studying the photographs that had just been sent over from Westport as a favor to him. At first glance they didn't seem too promising as nothing unusual jumped out at him. But after a while, when he was finally trying to ignore them, one of them caught his eye. A particular photo taken of the original scene before anything was touched, bore an image of an interesting mark in the gravel at the side of the body. Hernandes looked closer and could discern a gap between the side of the body and the gravel where the mark seemed to originate. He could imagine the marking as a track. He could imagine the gap as a place where something else had been.

The four block walk to Freestone's was purposely devoid of any further mention of the money or crime scene. Alan seemed serious about not getting involved. Who could blame him? Disbarment and jail after such a successful career would be a real bummer. And if Rich didn't play his cards just right, he'd be tomorrow's lead news story.

Inside the restaurant, Rich asked for a private table and they were led to the back section. Though it was much quieter, it was less private because everyone could hear. He apologized and asked for a table in the thick of the noisy crowd and sure enough, they had all the privacy they could ask for. They could hardly hear each other, no chance of anyone else hearing them. One of life's little oxymora.

The martinis arrived without them even ordering. Gail saw them come in and was chilling their glasses before they were seated, shaking the Bombay before their waitress ever arrived. They nodded their appreciation and Gail shot them a big friendly smile. A former model smile. Beautiful woman still, jet dark hair, bright shiny, toothy smile, with dimples!

Great figure. With two years of divorce behind him, that was all Rich needed to completely melt. He felt his arm go weak and forced himself to divert back to Alan.

"You know, Rich, the court notice of contempt wasn't the only matter I had to handle yesterday for you. It just seemed the most urgent."

"What else happened? They asking for lethal injection?"

"No, I.R.S. and Mass DOR problems. Both, within an hour of each other. They don't usually work together, but in your case, they've teamed up."

"So they need money. Can they break a thousand?"

"From the figures they're talking, it wouldn't matter. You'd probably just have them keep the change."

Rich took a long, slow sip of his Bombay Sapphire. If it was any colder he'd be re-enacting the Dumb and Dumber movie scene on the ski-lift with the frozen tongue.

"It gets bigger by the day. The tax bill, that is."

"Well, they called me because they're getting serious. If you had property, it would have been gone a long time ago. Maybe it's good that Debbie got the house, at least one of you keeps it."

Rich looked up slowly from his drink. Anyone else and them would be fighting words.

"The fact that you're genuinely broke now," Alan was sticking to his story that he knew nothing about any recent 'find', "might allow us to negotiate some sort of settlement. We could never do that if you owned property." He would leave it there until he could make more headway with the tax representatives. "How did you ever let your tax liability get so far out of hand? You're a professional!"

"It's so simple to explain, but hard to understand. The last few years together, Debbie must have been taking a lot out of the business because my reported income was just incredible! We paid most of those taxes, but the year we built the house, we put off in excess of $100,000.00 in taxes to get the house finished. Debbie agreed it was worth paying the fines and interest the next year and promised to get more involved in the business. We could have cleared it up easily. But with the house built, she met this real estate guy and you know the rest." Time for another sip. Two.

"But they're looking for almost twice that. And it's from your returns in later years, not your last joint return." Alan had never pressed Rich for any explanations on tax issues since he had enough to catch up on regarding Rich's business and finances.

"Well, the next year I was forced to file individually, but paid off most of the taxes for our last joint year. $175,000.00 in one check! Biggest check I've ever written in my life, and it still didn't cover the whole thing, but close." The thought of it brought up the stem glass again. Bottoms up! "Anyway, taxes aren't deductible, so that went down as income to me. Add the forty or fifty thou I legitimately earned and I had to report almost a quarter mil in income. Filing single, no deductions, you know what the new taxes are? Almost a hundred thou! So I'm back up way over my neck again. Plus the fines and interest on the unpaid balance. Next year, same thing. And the next. After three years I've paid more taxes than the combined national debts of most free world governments. And it all looks like income on my returns, thus my wonderful divorce settlement which Judge Santos based on my *apparent* income."

Now it was time for Alan to hoist the glass. He knew this part of the story. Rich's tax returns were honest and straightforward, but in the divorce hearings all that was coming through was the incredible income Rich reported. Alan had been called in late, failed to do his homework and simply wasn't prepared for the attacks from Debbie and Attorney LaFleur that Rich was raking in profits. Judge Santos could only see dollar signs and in ten minutes it was all over: Rich got the failing business, failing because all the funds had to be drained for the taxes and bills left behind, and Debbie got the home that the tax money bought. Rich had to continue with the mortgage because it seemed reasonable to the judge under the circumstances. Alan blew it and he knew it.

They placed their orders including a second round of martinis.

Alan started. "If they can't get the full value out of you, they're prepared to press for prison time."

"Let's hope Bubba never asks what I'm in for.

Could prove embarrassing." Rich still couldn't believe they were seriously talking about jail.

"Well, it's a real problem." Alan only had to visit three of his clients in jail in his thirty-seven years of practice, none as innocent or well meaning as Rich. He'd hate to come to the end of his career and not be able to help Rich, but these were serious situations.

"Obviously this isn't going to be a problem now, considering my little windfall."

Alan dropped his chin, put up both hands as a guard, and rolled his eyeballs. "No, No, No. I don't want to hear the 'windfall' part. I'm no part of that."

"All right, then let me just say that I think I could handle the tax problem. Give me a month or so. If jail becomes imminent, give me two hours." Rich would move a few ceiling tiles around if it meant avoiding jail.

The second round was delivered and more waves to Gail. Another photographic smile from her, dimples even deeper, and Rich went even weaker. This time he didn't turn away so fast.

"Will your check from the Wellingtons cover a good portion?" Alan asked.

"It should cover all current bills and a little for taxes, but no, nothing substantial." Rich had only this check to look forward to before yesterday and it clearly wasn't going to be enough.

"Well," Alan said with finality, "As long as you know how serious all this is. You're a good man, Charlie Brown. Hate to see the system do you in."

And that would be the final word. The rest of the meal they talked about the Red Sox and their series chances and going tuna fishing. Neither would likely happen, but over a two-martini lunch, hope springs eternal.

As Alan settled the check, Rich checked his tip. Twenty five percent, the usual for an attorney reimbursed meal that would be charged back to his client.

"Let me just leave a thousand for Gail," Rich quipped. "Unless you have something smaller."

"I'd stay away from Gail in your condition," Alan offered, quietly.

"What condition, two martinis?"

"No," Alan smirked, "Two years," referring to single life.

Rich agreed and they smiled politely as they waved goodbye to Gail, making their exit. She smiled back. Dimples. Rich's knees began to buckle.

They walked along the cobblestone street, Alan deep in thought about something. Rich was absorbed in his own thoughts about his incredible situation. Threats of jail, bankruptcy and possibly even mob killing, but enough money in his possession to buy his way out of anything. Should he be happy or scared?

"Rich." He paused. "Rich. If you were to come into some money for any reason, you know, *unexpectedly?"* Alan was not incriminating himself. "You'd want to be careful. Your ex has shown herself to be a bitter, vengeful adversary. She'd love to see you put away. The I.R.S. and Mass DOR? They're not the most compassionate of adversaries either. If they sensed, or worse, if they could prove that you had money, they'd claim you had hidden it, and they'd go for the throat. You know that, don't you?"

"Oh, I'll be careful. If I were to come into something, *unexpected*, I'd be very careful about my spending habits."

"Especially in your case, not having had anything for the past few years. Any spending now would be obvious." Alan reflected on his years of experience with very well-to-do clients, and some not so. "You know, it's easy to hide money once you have money. After a million or two, who notices? Who can tell if your suit is a two thousand dollar tailored piece or only a thousand? Who knows if your European trip cost you fifty thousand dollars or twenty? But until you get up in that bracket, coming into big money is usually quite obvious."

"After a million or two, who notices?' Can I quote you on that?" Rich smiled at Alan's homespun logic.

"Sure. Quote me all you like. But I'm concerned Rich. This group will go for your throat. Every one of them."

The throat. That's where they all had him and now he desperately needed to find a way out. Alan was right in observing that by hiding the money, getting caught with it could be the worst scenario possible. There would be no way to prove where it came from. Debbie, LaFleur, the IRS, the DOR, some mobster or drug lord and even Judge Santos, they would all nail him for their particular "evasion du jour", whatever charge each would try to make at the time. There would be no way to prove that all this money just fell in his lap by accident. And even *that* was illegal, so there would also be the police to deal with, both the State and the Feds, on a rainbow array of felonious matters. The trick was in not ever getting caught.

"Alan, I know that. But you know what?"

Alan was listening.

"All of these adversaries, they all went for the throat. Everyone is ready to press me to the limit. They've left me with nothing. Literally nothing. And you know why that's not too smart?"

Alan raised his eyebrows in a "No, why?" sort of a way.

"Because they left me with nothing to lose. And no one is as powerful as when they have nothing to lose."

Rich returned home around four o'clock and set about printing out his final design proposals for the Wellingtons. Then he called them to confirm his appointment the next morning. A check would be waiting, and it was money he could show.

He grabbed a beer and turned on the six o'clock report, wondering if any new information was available on the Horseneck beach body.

Natalie led off referring to last night's lead story, but adding that today, yet another mystery was unraveling as fishermen reported bringing up body parts in their nets. As an on-the-scene report came on, the camera zoomed in on two or three body parts caught in the net. One captured Rich's attention. It was a man's calf and foot, a leg severed from the knee down. But the clothing was still wrapped around the leg; a cheap grayish, pinkish pant leg and a two-tone beige shoe on the foot.

CHAPTER 4
Wednesday Morning

Wednesday morning started early for Rich. Up at five, half hour of jogging, shower, latte' and down to business. He had to package the final plans and specifications for the Wellington's for his meeting with them, yielding the final $25,000.00 check, as elusive as the holy grail lately.

It was a sobering morning. Rich couldn't quite shake the feelings he had the night before on seeing the news report. It underscored his logic. His life wouldn't be worth spit if there were any trail leading back to him. The two men he had spied burying the loot didn't last twenty four hours after botching the job and Rich knew he could be next.

He printed out a final invoice on his stationery and

by nine he was out the door heading to Padanaram via The Java Bean for his second latte' and a newspaper.

The front page carried the story and overnight the identities had become known. Antonio Perreira and Martin Gomes. Two small-time felons loosely connected with the Mafia. The report indicated they were low members in the Carlo Bartelli family, Carlo being rumored to be the Don of the entire New England operation and possibly exerting power in New York.

Rich knew Carlo Bartelli. Not well, but they had met a few years previously. Rich had quite a reputation as an architect in the Padanaram Village area, a picturesque, old fishing settlement built on a scenic peninsula just south of New Bedford, in the Dartmouth Township. Rich designed more than a dozen homes, among the finest in and around that area. While supervising their construction through the various stages and trades, it dawned on Rich how much the General Contractors were raking in for just lining up trades people to ply their skills. He set up his own contracting firm and made his wife Debbie it's president. Their income tripled and Rich Lewis Design, Inc., became "the" design firm of the area.

When Bartelli purchased choice, ocean view land on the southern tip of Padanaram, most of the finish work got awarded to Rich, with Debbie as the front person. So Debbie knew Carlo well, Rich a little. Now came the first hint that maybe Carlo had some connection with the body and money.

A second article covered details on the first body that was discovered and finally identified: A Richard Fowler. No known mob connections, but a history of drug dealing and rumors of his trying to make a move to the big time. Then Rich read the most startling piece of news, cause of death: Heart attack.

Rich finished his latte' and headed to the Wellington's, a few miles south-east of Padanaram, with just one quick stop at a bank to break a thousand. He needed spending money.

It was a beautiful day, especially around the coast. With the temperature hitting eighty degrees already, clear skies and puffy cumulous clouds forming along the shore line, this was a picture perfect, New England poster type day. The kind of day that had Rich wishing he had bought a Z-3 instead of his Explorer.

Cutting through Padanaram Village for the scenic route, Rich came to a blocked detour. The road was under repair with a detour pointing right. But Rich knew that if he went left, less than a mile down the road would bring him by "their" home, his "dream" home. Small, as most homes in the Village were, but well designed, giving a spacious, airy feeling from any of the six rooms. Three rooms boasted an ocean view, the most impressive being from the Jacuzzi room which had a 120 degree panorama of the shoreline from Clark's Cove with Fairhaven and Sconticutt Neck across the bay, through Apponagansett Bay, and south almost to Round Hill Point.

Rich slowed as he approached the property. He

had to swerve to avoid an empty garbage can that had blown into the street. Tom's red Porsche was parked in the driveway, indicating that he was home again. Rich often wondered if the only house Tom Cochrane closed on in the last two years was the sale of his home in Swansea.

As the deck came into view, Tom and Debbie could be seen. It looked like breakfast on the deck, after 11:00. But even from this distance, there was a tension between them that Rich could feel. It looked like Debbie was yelling, but it was impossible to tell. Tom had a kind of schoolboy-in-the-Principal's-Office look about him. They passed out of view as Rich swerved to avoid a second trash can. Trash day in Padanaram.

❦

Rich tooled through his old neighborhood enjoying the quaintness of the tiny village and catching up on changes to the hamlet. There were none that he could see. There never are. That's part of the lure of the Village.

An old New England fishing village dating back to 1652 when it was purchased from the Wampanoag Indian tribe, Padanaram grew slowly and stubbornly. It resisted change, starting out as a fishing village and remaining as such until today. It had even become quite a whaling center for a period in the late 1800's, no doubt spurred on by the neighboring whaling city of New Bedford.

Although the yuppies discovered it in the eighties, the typical tourist shops and bistros never seemed to follow. A handful of shops, not particularly upscale, took root along with only a few eateries, but nothing ostentatious. The village kept its mystique and ambiance, attracting cultured and well-healed residents while continuing to be a major center for fishing and boating. Local folks kid that maybe the name keeps people away. Who can pronounce it?

It's actually a bible name. Not that much biblical has ever happened here, but back in the early 1800's, the village was dominated by industries and financial ventures of one, Laban Thatcher. From his bible reading, Laban Thatcher related to an obscure figure in Genesis named, appropriately enough, Laban. He was the father of two daughters, Leah and Rachel, who wiled their way into Jacob's life and became his wives. Both of them. Don't ask, it's a biblical thing. Anyway, Laban of the bible was also an entrepreneur, and wasn't beyond pulling a shrewd deal on a victim if given half a chance. Laban Thatcher related to the whole story and since their names were the same, he dubbed the old fishing village after bible Laban's area, 'Padanaram'.

Anne Wellington greeted Rich at the door. There

was no doubt that they could afford servants, but Rich knew they objected to the exorbitant going rates for such help these days. They'd think nothing of having a $150.00 breakfast, then drop only ten dollars in a tip and expect it to be appreciated. They'd accept whatever rate their designer ran by them if he was well credentialed, but heaven help the painter that expected to make more than $100/day.

"Mrs. Wellington," Rich greeted her as she opened the door, resplendent in her gold trimmed, forest green oriental robe. "If I didn't design this house myself, I would be gushing all over with superlatives and praises, but modesty forbids."

In her sixty-one years on earth, Anne Wellington had never learned to pick up on when someone was blatantly flattering her to get on her good side. Or if she did, she learned not to object.

Laughing at the much appreciated adulation, Anne greeted Rich, "Well, you don't have to be so modest. All we get is praise for this house and we have you to thank for it."

Rich entered and Anne started in. "It's been such a hectic day, the Shattuck's have filed for divorce. I always saw it coming. His traveling and drinking, the two never mix well, you know. And her running around trying to get an acting career off at her age." The word, acting, enunciated two octaves higher. "But they filed yesterday and I just don't know what that will do to the neighborhood. I hope someone buys their house and knocks it all down and starts over. Maybe hire you to design a new one."

"Put a word in for me. I'm game."

"Mercy, we also just heard that Mr. DiGerolomo was in a bad accident up in New Hampshire. Something about a gasoline truck and a motorcyclist, but he got banged up pretty bad. Terrible news."

Rich didn't know DiGerolomo, but usually the explanations led to more detail than he'd ever want to know, so he simply nodded in understanding.

"And oh, that Tom Cochrane. I'm sure there's no love lost between you two, lord knows, but that Tom is heading for trouble."

Rich looked intently at Anne for this one, for now she had piqued his interest.

"Well, you know he jogs every morning. Early too, as soon as the sun comes up. And at that hour he always sets off Joseph and Mary." Her two greyhounds. "John has called him several times about changing his route and Tom just ignores him. I'm not surprised that he's caused you so many problems, he's trouble, he is."

Rich couldn't imagine Tom Cochrane running every morning. Rich runs three times a week and has to flog himself. But it fits. Tom can be driven in selective areas, and anything to do with his body would be select enough. But why so far from home? The Wellington's lived about five miles out of Padanaram, though they acted like they owned the Village.

"Well, I stay out of their lives," Rich offered. "Didn't even know he was a runner."

"Every morning." Anne punctuated her reference, unknowingly rubbing it in for Rich. "Even in the rain or cold. So every morning, our two babies get startled and wake us up."

Rich let Anne go on for about ten minutes with the latest gossip of the area. It was a ritual he had learned to respect. If Anne had no one to share her gossip with, what would be the use? And if she couldn't gossip, she might decide that life near Padanaram was boring and tell John to sell their summer cottage here and go elsewhere. That would never do, at least not until Rich was fully paid.

After the obligatory ten minutes, Rich turned Anne's attention to his purpose in visiting.

"I've got the final selections. With your approval, I can have the wall covering and tile overnighted and with a little luck, have it all completed by Saturday."

"Oh Rich, I wish we had planned the party for next month. It's been just so hectic here."

"We'll make it. Besides, no matter when we planned it, there would always be last minute details that would take us right up to the last second. That's life." Rich had enough experience with these things. "This way, your house is done in June and you have the whole summer to enjoy it."

Ann shook her head back and forth in frustration. It was all just too much for her.

"And remember," Rich continued. "The deadline

was set back in March because if *'Architectural Digest'* couldn't do their initial shoot next week, you would have missed out. Waiting for the next year is always chancy. They might find another property to feature."

"Oh, I know. It's just that there's so much to do. The florist had to cancel the birds-of-paradise because of a shortage and I have to decide on the alternate later today. And the caterers say there may be a shortage on fresh Dover sole, so we may need to substitute that too."

Crisis hits the Wellington's. Will they survive?

"Well, let me show you my suggestions. If they're acceptable, we can call it a wrap and you can rest well tonight."

They poured over the elevations and product samples. Anne had a million questions and concerns but all were deftly allayed by Rich's patient and understanding replies. After about an hour they were satisfied that the project was completed. Rich called the suppliers, scheduled early A.M. delivery and lined up the trades people.

Enter John Wellington, shuffling across the kitchen floor in a beeline for the bar area. The secondary bar, in case he couldn't make it to the main bar twenty feet into the next room. Like today.

"Hello, Mr. Wellington."

"Hello."

"John," Anne turned to him. "Dick Digerolomo had an accident up in New Hampshire. He's in the hospital. Don't know what the extent is, but what a terrible thing!"

John's half smile faded to maybe a quarter smile out of concern. But as the bar came to within reach, he returned to his normal half-smile. He poured a vodka and tonic. Didn't even have to shake it as his perpetually shaking hand was just enough to do the job naturally.

"And I told you about the Shattucks, right?"

"Who?"

After his updates, Mr. Wellington was drawn into the final decision process on the decorating, or at least the staged decision process, the real decision having already been made by Anne. But this humoring of John allowed him the dignity that he deserved for inheriting such wealth, which had allowed Anne to amuse herself all these years with whatever projects that fancied her, while creating the illusion that John was involved.

The formalities all completed, Rich took out the final invoice. Going through the motions of handing it to John out of respect, he knew full well it would be diverted to Anne and she would be the one to write the check. Then have John sign it.

"I'll get you a check right now." Anne smiled brightly as she asserted the claim. Prone to argue over any bill placed before her, Rich had overcome her pettiness by lining up *Architectural Digest* to do a spread on their new cottage as well as landing a prized New England design award that got the Wellington's a silver plaque for their dining room. The perfect conversation piece.

"If we don't see you sooner," Anne said handing Rich the check, "Two o'clock on Sunday. You're our guest of honor."

"I'm flattered and looking forward to it." Rich would never be invited to one of the Wellington's catered affairs, but this was a house warming party to celebrate their new cottage and editors of several design journals were going to be there to consider the possibilities of featuring the cottage. Having the designer present to expound on the architectural details and structural problems overcome could only help their chances.

Rich said his good-byes and was escorted out by Mrs. Wellington as she filled his ears with three more tid-bits of Padanaram goodies.

It was just before one o'clock as Rich pulled in front of First Federal. Taking a chance on the already expired meter, he went straight to Michelle's office and was glad to see that she had no one else inside.

"As promised," smiling as he held up the check.

Michelle smiled back, "I knew you'd come through," raising her hand victoriously in a fist.

"Why don't I just deposit this," said Rich. "When the funds clear, take out what you need for the mortgage and save me a trip."

Michelle looked at the check. "From the Wellington's? Consider it cleared. Do you want the change?"

"No." Rich was surprised they would cash it just like that. "No, deposit the balance into my checking account. I should be able to keep ahead of you for a while now."

The paperwork got done and Rich asked for one more letter addressed to Probate Court affirming that he had done his duty.

As he left Michelle's office, he darted around the corner to the last teller's window, out of eyesight from her office.

"Can you break these?" Rich handed over three, one thousand dollar bills.

⸻ ❖ ❖ ❖ ⸻

No parking ticket. Things were definitely turning around. Ready for lunch, Rich had no choice to make. He drove a few blocks to Freestone's, a pair of dimples awaiting.

"Hey!" she said as he saddled on up to the bar.

Rich smiled and raised his eyebrows in a greeting fashion. She was easy on the eyes. Gail's fair Cape Verdean looks had landed her a brief modeling career in her younger years. Even did a bit of support acting. But the camera knows first when one is beyond prime, so now she plies her looks in a bartending career that, coupled with her vivacious personality, has her at the top. She's had opportunities to own her own bar or restaurant, but ambition never drove Gail, people did. And here at one of New Bedford's most popular watering holes, Gail was in her element and life didn't get better.

"The usual?" she asked.

"You know, I think I'll do a beer today. How about a Sam Adams on draft."

"What! You always do Bombay martini's and I make it my business to learn my customers. After I learn to make them just the way you like them, you're going to change on me?" Each syllable was enunciated as clearly as the Queen intended. "Now what if I saw you parking and had the Bombay already shaken? I'd have to shake you, you Palanga!" Firm, authoritative, but smiling widely, boring the dimples deep into her cheeks, driving Rich crazy.

Shrugging his shoulders, Rich could only plead for forgiveness. "Shake me. Please shake me."

Although they had known each other by sight for a number of years (who didn't Gail know?) it was only for the last few months that she seemed to give Rich more than the usual attention. And that was hard to discern because Gail was a great bartender making everyone feel at home and giving everyone more attention than they really deserved. Her tips proved just how good she was.

As Gail sauntered away to pour the brew, Rich looked around the bar, casting for familiar faces. None here. He had missed the blackboard specials, so he left his stool and walked the few steps to the front dais and read them off. While there, he took a quick glance into the dining area and did a double-take. Alan! Rich was pleasantly surprised and thought of going in to say hello, but noticed another party at the table and didn't want to disturb them. Rich studied the man's back. Large man. Well dressed. Then the man turned sideways and Rich stiffened: Carlo Bartelli.

His heart sank. His mind was ablaze with alarms. Visions of Alan ratting out on him, letting Bartelli know who had his money and maybe expecting a reward for the info. He thought of bolting.

But another thought occurred. He should stay and make certain that they would all meet. If Alan were connected with Bartelli, surely there would be some sign. Between Alan and Carlo, one of them would surely send a sign if Rich was on the "Out" list. Rich returned to his bar stool planning to meet as Alan and Bartelli leave.

"Gail," Rich shouted. "Don't pour that Sammy. I'll have the martini after all," thinking he might be in for a stormy one.

Gail threw a play tantrum. Even in his concern, Rich cracked up at her antics as did half the bar patrons.

With lunch over, Rich kept his eye on the exit area.

He motioned to Gail for his tab at the same moment Alan and Bartelli appeared. Rich spied them through the corner of his eyes but gave the appearance that he was absorbed in the drink menu. If Alan didn't notice him, he'd change his tactic and call out at the last second.

"Rich!" Alan's voice - it worked! "What's this, Freestone's again? Must be some kind of a habit?"

Rich turned to greet Alan, acting surprised, then stood to reach out for Alan's hand. This would force a few steps between them, bringing them closer.

"Hey, Alan! What a surprise! You must have the same bad habit though." Rich couldn't detect any outward sign of betrayal on Alan's face.

"My habit's the food." Alan had lowered his voice. "Not the bartender." He nodded in Gail's direction, now deep in a discussion with another patron, probably an attorney, on some of the latest news about the courtroom buzz. Lawyers, judges, fishermen or garbage men, Gail was equally at ease with them all. That's what Rich liked about her. No, that's what Rich loved about her.

"Martini's. They're my habit. And I know who makes them best, so I come here." Rich turned to Carlo. "Mr. Bartelli, Richard Lewis. Don't know if you remember me."

"Of course I do. How're you doing?" He seemed sincere. No daggers. No kisses on the cheek.

"Is this your normal watering hole?" Alan asked of Rich sincerely.

"It's a frequent stop. But, today I'm celebrating. Finished the Wellington project."

"Oh, that's great news." For Alan it was, it meant he'd be getting paid. With honest money.

"The Wellington's!" Carlo Bartelli was impressed. "They the one's that just built that new estate on Slocum River, by the bridge?"

"Cottage. They call it their summer cottage." Rich couldn't get over it either.

"Aye, Paisano! We should all have it so good."

Carlo was Italian. That was his way of announcing it. Rich still sensed no hostility. But it could be a cover. Then again, maybe Alan doesn't even suspect that Carlo might be connected to the money. Rich made the connection based on the newspaper. Maybe Alan hadn't read it.

They made small talk for a couple of minutes then said their good-byes. Rich was momentarily relieved. He could detect nothing outward that would indicate to him that Alan was dropping the dime on him. But it was still a surprise that the two knew each other and that they were dining together a day after Rich had confided in Alan about the money. It was just too odd that the one man Rich confided in is dining with the one man that may be cutting people up for chum in order to find the money.

Gail brought him the check, lingering more than usual. Rich resisted the temptation for a third drink, paying the twenty-two dollar tab with a fifty and leaving. Smoothly, Gail worked into her good-bye the fact that she works two shifts. She's here every evening until one.

Rich headed for home, but with three detours. Three bank stops to get some smaller "change".

CHAPTER 5
Wednesday, Mid-day

His first stop was a small, local bank. At Slade's Ferry he would only change two. But the other banks, Bank-Boston, Citizens and Peoples, he'd do three each.

He first noticed the car on his trip between Bank-Boston and Citizens. He didn't think much of it at first. A light blue Ford of some kind, nothing special. But when he saw the same car three car lengths behind him turning into the People's Bank lot, Rich was uncomfortable.

He continued driving out of the lot pretending that he had just driven in to make a turn. Whoever it was, he didn't want them to suspect that he had bank business everywhere. Rich headed home.

Though barely discernible in his rear-view, he spotted the blue Ford pulling to the side a few blocks away as he parked in front of his apartment. Rich locked up and went on to his apartment. He looked out the window and spied the car.

About a half hour later, Rich saw the car pull closer, across the street. Two more minutes and the doors opened, two men in suits. He readied himself for them, not imagining they could be mob. Too clean cut and conservative in dress.

After three raps on the door, Rich counted to ten and opened, chain still on. He had a bat within reach if the door suddenly exploded.

"Richard Lewis?" they asked.

"Yes."

"IRS Agents." Badges flashing. "We'd like to talk with you."

"Well, I own nothing that you can take, so I guess you're more than welcome." Rich was trying to diffuse the tension.

"Mr. Lewis, we've already spoken with your attorney, Mr. Levine. Are you aware of the seriousness of your situation with regards to some overdue taxes?"

"I've got three shoe boxes full of letters from you and with each new letter, the amount I owe is bigger and the consequences more foreboding, so yes, I'd say I'm aware of it."

"Well, Mr. Lewis, we were sent to assure you that our department stands ready to assist you in any way we can. But also to let you know that it is our duty under law to bring this matter to a conclusion. It can't be ignored. We understand some of the problems you've experienced in your personal life lately, but taxes are every citizens' responsibility."

"I'm not going to argue with you." Rich was going to try to placate. "I owe taxes and I'm not trying to dodge anything." There was only modest comfort in thinking of his newfound treasure.

"Mr. Lewis, this department has received a number of promises from you in the past and we've always taken you at your word. But the fact is you've paid only a small fraction of the amount owed for the last three years. Frankly, we can't wait any longer."

It was the taller, older one that did all the talking.

"I hear you. And I apologize. What did my lawyer say?"

"That he can't save you."

"I doubt he'd admit that. For what I pay him, he'd better never admit that." Again, trying to diffuse a tense situation.

It was obvious to Rich that he'd be off the hook today. They would have served papers by now if they were taking him away or seizing property.

"Frankly, I've just completed a project and received payment today. I went to a few banks to arrange a substantial payment to you people very soon." He thought this would explain the bank stops, having no idea how long they had been tailing him.

"When might we expect that substantial payment?"

"In a week or so I can sort things out. With this

payment today and a few other deals in the works, I might be able to secure a loan from a bank and pay off the entire amount." Bull, thought Richard. No bank will touch me.

The agents threw a few more standard intimidating lines at Rich, but all in all they seemed settled. They excused themselves and promised Rich ten days before they would go into the "red" zone, whatever that meant. The tall one said goodbye, the smaller one nodded.

The flashing light caught his attention again. Only one message:

"Hi Rich, Alan. It was good running into you at Freestone's. When I got back to the office I had an important message regarding the contempt charge. Give me a call. If you miss me at the office, try home. It's urgent."

The last word was not a good word to hear from an attorney. Rich dialed him immediately.

"Urgent?" Rich led off, "Didn't I tell you about using that word? Can give a man my age a heart attack."

Alan was glad to see Rich in his usual form. That was likely about to end.

"LaFleur's not dropping the charge. He still wants the hearing tomorrow and makes no bones about the fact that he'll be pressing for seizure of assets, fees and jail." Alan waited.

"Assets are a joke. I have none left. What do you mean, fees and jail."

"Well, he'll want all his attorney's fees reimbursed for this matter, and by law, he'll get them if you're found in contempt. Let's hope the Judge accepts the bank letter."

"Not to worry. The bank did me a favor today and accepted the Wellington check as cash. The mortgage is up to date and I have my note from mommy to prove it." Rich was disgusted at all the rigmarole he had to go through to keep Debbie in her home.

"Well, that's great news. Then jail will likely be avoided, unless we get Santos and he's in a bad mood."

"You're still serious? Jail! Even though I'm up to date?"

"Well, not likely. I think you've appeased the court by paying today. But that will be the judges' decision."

There was silence while Rich grimaced. He wanted to lash out, but what good would it do.

Alan continued, "But back to the fees. By going to court LaFleur is running up fees. You'll likely get tagged for them."

"How much we looking at?"

"My guess is two or three thousand."

Even if he was sitting on top of 28.8 *billion* dollars, Rich would hate to have to pay LaFleur a single cent. But he knew enough not to shoot the messenger.

"Thanks Alan. What time tomorrow?"

"I'll meet you at the courthouse at nine. I imagine we'll be called early, but be prepared to spend a few hours.

"And Rich, I'm sorry. LaFleur should have just dropped this and maybe gotten us to agree to a thousand or so for his time. Like I said yesterday, they're going for the throat."

Rich understood. He thanked Alan and was about to say good-bye when he thought better.

"Alan, eating with Carlo Bartelli! You two know each other?"

Alan laughed. "I've done real estate work for Carlo for years. It's like a hobby of his, always grabbing any land deal that he thinks is a bargain. He has one philosophy: 'Land, they're not making any more of it.' So he buys! I imagine he may be all what rumors say he is, but in my dealings with him, he's never been anything but a gentleman."

"His name was in the paper this morning." Rich was fishing.

"Oh, in that article about the thugs. Who knows." It was a statement, not a question. There wasn't the least bit of tension in Alan's voice. Alan wasn't the coolest of men, not easily able to hide his emotions unless he was in court, excitable and worrisome everywhere else. Rich thought he could trust what he was hearing.

"Well, we'll talk more tomorrow. See you at nine."

They hung up and Rich pondered the day's developments. He was somewhat more relaxed about Alan's relationship with Bartelli, but not a hundred percent. He was glad the IRS didn't slap him in jail or seize his car, but that was only a temporary delay. He didn't like having to go to court again, and as for writing out a check to LaFleur, he'd rather get AIDS. Finally, he couldn't stop thinking about the apparent connection between the two dismembered thugs and Bartelli. The more Rich thought it through, the more convinced he was that it was Bartelli's money. But he forced his concerns into some deep recess. Then he replayed some of the lighter events of the day. The gossiping Mrs. Wellington, and Tom Cochrane being on the Wellington's bad side.

A thought started to nip at him as he considered the whole convoluted scene: His tax troubles, divorce troubles, lawyer troubles, judge troubles, mob troubles, all of them seemed to be centered in one way or another in the Padanaram area. He thought of his ex and Tom arguing over a late breakfast on the deck, no doubt over money. The mob boss Bartelli who's searching desperately for whomever took his money.

The thoughts played over and over in his mind like a looped tape as a realization began. Then Rich shot up, alert and awake from the nirvana-like state he had almost drifted into. There was something here. He walked in circles around his small kitchen talking with himself. Stopping now and then to puzzle out a particularly sticky problem, but there would always be an answer. By three in the morning, Rich had a new outlook on life.

And a plan.

CHAPTER 6

Wednesday - The Cochrane's

Debbie Cochrane was being more stern than usual with LaFleur. She had met him at an all time low in her life, having just left her husband of fourteen years for a younger man. Social mores have come a long way, but even in her conscience, she had sunk below what could ever be accepted.

Enter attorney Robert LaFleur, Esq., who made her feel good about her decision, supporting all of his consolations with Commonwealth Law as he was able to proclaim and prove to a legal certainty that she was not at fault. Every move of hers had been right, proper and fair. He became her guru in both a legal and moral sense, lending dignity to her affair with Tom and the breakup with Richard. Trusting him entirely, LaFleur had surprised her with the fabulous settlement that he pulled off, assuring her that the laws of Massachusetts were firmly behind her. He was worth every bit of the $25,000.00 bill he had run up by then.

But his bill continued to climb. When LaFleur was fighting for support and the house, he was worth his bills. But now, his hourly rate is the same, yet the take has evaporated.

"But Bob, if it's paid up, what's the point? I'm afraid if he goes to jail he'll just give up and let the house go into foreclosure next time." She never used to argue with LaFleur and the frustration of the mixed feelings that it raised in her was almost unbearable.

"Debbie, *we* don't put him in jail." The emphasis on we. "It would be the judge who sends him up." LaFleur always seemed to be able to lead Debbie to any conclusion he wanted. Lately she was becoming fiesty though. Why do all his clients eventually give him such trouble?

"Think of it," he continued. "Why would a judge throw him in jail if it wasn't deserved?"

The mixed emotions welling up in Debbie were putting her in a real fit. Yes, she enjoyed giving Rich a hard time, but why does it have to cost *her* so much? LaFleur's making more than his share now and it's got to stop soon.

"Debbie, don't worry about the money. I'm almost sure we'll get sanctions and your share will be nothing compared to what he'll pay. Have I ever let you down?" Said so smugly.

"But I still get enough of your bills to choke a cow. And now I have to be in court tomorrow." Frustration, anger and a little bit of guilt swirled together.

"Please come." It would be his final plea.

"You say it's at nine o'clock?"

"Nine. Right in New Bedford, what's the big deal?" Then it occurred to him to add, "Dress appropriately."

"All right, Bob. I'll have someone cover the gallery."

Debbie's gallery in Newport wasn't the rage she had hoped, so not covering wouldn't really hurt. But it seemed a fitting statement as she hung up.

"What's the verdict?" Tom Cochrane had been listening to Deb's half of the conversation, but knew he was missing some things, like the logical side. Sitting across the umbrella'd table on this beautiful June morning, Tom popped the last of his croissant into his mouth.

Irritated already, Debbie really didn't want to have to explain everything all over again to Tom. He had it so easy back then, just having to walk out on his live-in. Wasn't even his house anyway, so he had nothing to lose and no complications. He walked out paying virtually nothing to his ex-live-in and now he's free.

"Bob still wants me in court and I really don't have the time. Frankly, I think he's pushing Rich a little hard."

"Hey, if the law requires him to pay regular, let him keep up. If he's going to put us at risk like this all the time, jail the guy and teach him a lesson." Tom had an understanding way about him.

Debbie rubbed her head, trying to ease away her tension headache.

"Even though LaFleur thinks the judge will sanction Richard for most of his expenses, there will be some charges not covered. I can't believe how much he's making on this whole deal. Bob didn't *give* me a house, he got me what was rightfully mine by law. Why does it have to cost me so much?"

"Hey," offered Tom, "Rich probably spent more than you did for legal fees and he got crap out of this. Look at the bright side."

"Rich got his business." Said with an air of a jealous schoolgirl. "That's all he cared about anyway. So stop making it sound like I got the prize. We split down the middle and this house was on my side."

Tom was willing to drop it. He could see the frustration building in Debbie, and he was anxious to turn the page to one on his own agenda.

"I won't be home this evening until nine or so. Got a showing out in Mattapoisett." He could see daggers forming already. "I should offer them dinner at the Inn, so I may not be home till late. It could go ten, eleven."

"*Another* evening that you have a *showing!*"

For all the hours she works, and the few Tom

works, why does he always choose the times they could be together?

"It's the nature of my work." Then, in his most caring tone, "That's why I want to get my own agency. I'd have enough staffers to do all the showings in the evening. Then I can just run the office and take the showings that come up during the day." Tom should have left it at that, but being the man he is, he went on.

"I let you put the money into your gallery, remember? That could have started my agency, but I'm giving you first crack."

The steam could almost be heard. Seething, she replied through clenched teeth, "First crack! You mean, with *my* money, you *let* me have first crack?"

"Your money. Deb, we're married. It's our money."

Deb hit all alarms. "You came into this marriage with a five hundred dollar a month note on your car, some Italian suits and a broken down living room set. That makes it '*our* money'?!"

"You know what I mean." Tom was trying to bring it down a notch. "Sure, you had more than I did and I don't want to take any of that from you. But we both agreed to work our businesses and whether we invest it in yours or mine, it's ours. We didn't do the pre-nup thing, remember?"

"You dare bring up the pre-nuptial agreement that *I* decided not to force? That worked to your benefit, not mine." Debbie, turning crimson. "I did *you* a favor."

Debbie poured a final glass of orange juice to cool

down. Then she speared the last melon wedge to top off the outdoor breakfast. The anger inside of her wasn't going to subside easily and she wished Tom would pick up on the hint and just go away for now. Her lawyer is milking this case for everything he can get, her husband thinks he's entitled to any of her money that he can grab and he doesn't appreciate the long hours she's investing to make her gallery work.

Debbie's temper was blocking her other senses as she was too distracted to notice the champagne colored Explorer passing by, swerving to avoid their trash cans in the middle of the road. But her anger was obvious even to the driver of the car from that distance.

***

Debbie arrived on Thames Street in Newport and pulled down the tight alleyway next to her gallery, honking at some tourists partially blocking her way as she turned in. An out-of-state car was in one of the two spots reserved for the staff of her shop, leaving one open for her. Her only help didn't drive, so she just needed the one. She noted the license of the offending car and would call it right in.

"Jules, how is it going?" Debbie's one and only employee, Jules Agnacia. He was gay, in college and a lover of art, so for minimum wage, Jules thought helping to run a gallery in Newport for the summer was a dream come true. It beat returning to Montana for the summer, where some of his persuasions weren't always appreciated.

"Oh, I'm just in a frenzy!" Jules was excited. "The 'Curtis's' arrived but there was a big gash right through the package. I didn't notice it until the driver had left and I've been trying to call U.P.S. all morning. I just can't get through, oh, I don't believe it!"

"Were the paintings damaged?"

"Well, one of them had a cut right through the ballerina's foot. Oh, I was so destroyed! Can you just imagine?"

"Big cut?"

"Oh, I don't know. Maybe this big," fingers spread to less than an inch.

"I think we can repair it. Curtis isn't exactly a Picasso." Debbie figured it could be fixed with a piece of tape to the backside. "But keep calling U.P.S. and file a claim. Full retail value."

Debbie thought Jules was worth the minimum wage that he agreed to work for. Not so much for the work he did, but for the clientele he attracted. His friends alone would rave about her place and that would generate some business, some of his friends actually having money. He earned his keep in the long run.

"Styles called and said he'll be bringing someone by to look at the Weymouth painting. He's pretty sure he'll buy, sight unseen." Jules was excited, contributing to their yet and future success.

"I decided last night to raise the price on that

piece by three hundred dollars. Could you take care of that for me?" Debbie had a fast mind.

Debbie got on the phone and reported the out-of-state car in their space. Yes, her partner was waiting for the space. That would bring them right down.

Jules volunteered to take the Curtis in the back and try a repair. While he was gone, Debbie took the ledger out of her leather Chanel briefcase and exchanged it for the one behind the counter. She had made the adjustments that she needed to at home and now could exchange again. She would be thankful next April.

Jules returned proudly displaying his "behind the cut tape trick" that took all of two minutes and looked it. Debbie okayed it and went on to her own business.

"I have to appear in court tomorrow. Probably won't make it down here until one or so. I know it's your day off, but any chance of you just coming and hanging around?"

Jules didn't really mind, not having a lot of places to go anyway. "Sure," he volunteered.

"Since you won't really be working, I won't be able to pay by the hour, but I'll make it up to you with a few hours off later." It seemed perfectly fair to her.

Tom Cochrane arrived at the Century 21 office by six o'clock. His "trainee", Judy, was already waiting and he no sooner got out of his Porsche than the perspective buyers, Pat and Bob Thompson, pulled up. With pleasantries aside, Tom offered Judy's car since there were four of them, but the Thompsons were all too happy to offer theirs for the twenty minute drive to Mattapoisett. Then it struck him that they would all have to come back this way but he and Judy had another appointment later that evening in the same area, so would they mind following him? Of course not, so Tom and Judy hopped into his Porsche and the Thompsons followed.

Judy wasn't really a real estate agent, or a trainee for that matter, but was a young housewife Tom had met last Saturday while having lunch. When Tom mentioned that he was an agent, she expressed that she had often thought of getting into real estate, so why not come with him for a showing? She'd see how the whole process worked then he could debrief her and she'd have some valuable experience.

The house got shown, rather quickly. The Thompsons went their way and Tom and Judy headed for the Mattapoisett Inn for a debriefing, as Tom called it.

"So what did you think? Easy enough, wasn't it?"

Judy, 24 yrs. old, was really impressed. "Absolutely. At least the way you handled it. You really know a lot about construction. It would take me a while to learn all that."

"That's why you go to the classes. You'll learn fast enough."

"And you seemed to know a lot about local laws and code. Is that hard to learn?"

Actually, Tom thought it was, but why worry her? "Nah, you'll catch right on."

They arrived at the Inn and were quickly seated. Tom called the waiter over to place their drink order wanting to get an early start.

"You know, when I get my agency up and running, I'll need an office manager." He was smooth. "That might be a good position for you while you're in school."

Judy loved the idea. She thought it was quite the outstanding offer from someone that she had just met. She looked at her watch, commenting that she needed to check in with the baby sitter. When she returned, she announced that all was fine and that the baby sitter assured her not to worry about the time. Separately, and unseen by each other, they both slipped off their wedding rings, making for a more comfortable evening.

⸻ ❖ ❖ ❖ ⸻

Eleven thirty. As Debbie waited for Tom to return she poured herself a glass of wine and headed for the Jacuzzi. It was a moonlit night so she was able to appreciate the ocean view in the moon glow by turning off the lights and just lighting a few scented candles. She relaxed, thought about what court may bring tomorrow and lamented that she was turning so much harder since her divorce. Richard and Tom were to blame. Suddenly she could hear Tom pull up and into the garage.

"Hi honey, I'm home." Tom waited to hear where she would be.

"I'm in the Jacuzzi, Tom."

"Okay dear. I'm heading to bed. Had a long evening and have to get up early."

Frustration racked Debbie's entire being. She slowly sipped her '92 merlot, watching the moon gradually pass out of her view on it's way to set on the western horizon. As she emptied the bottle and the jets shut off again for the fourth time, she knew that she had been in the tub for two hours. Three times Debbie had to interrupt her comatose meditation by getting out to reset the half hour timer. She had exceeded Massachusetts Official Jacuzzi Zoning Time Standards by an hour and a half. But she needed it.

CHAPTER 7

Thursday, Early Morning

Waking at 4:00 A.M., Rich bolted upright. He would force himself through the moves until his body woke up. He showered, dressed for court and skipped his latte', heading straight for Padanaram at 4:30. He parked his Explorer away from Debbie's home worried at not seeing Tom's Boxster on display, but sprang to life when the garage door rattled up and the roar of a Porsche, mid-engine roadster was heard. Three seconds later, Tom Cochrane emerged confirming Anne Wellington's tale.

Rich had a hunch that Tom didn't start his running from Debbie's home. If he did and his route took him by the Wellington's home about five miles to the south, with the return trip, he'd cover more miles than an iron man. Tom wasn't a marathon type runner. Rich doubted Tom did more than two or three miles. So why drive so far when Padanaram was fine for running?

About five miles out, Tom pulled over to a side of Potomska Road, the quiet country road the Wellington's lived on. It was a scenic spot just before the waters edge, the Wellington's cottage just in view. So far, so good, thought Rich. It was very private, devoid of any other runners or traffic, just what Rich had been hoping for. And if Tom always runs the same route past the Wellington's, he must be a creature of habit. As he watched Tom lock up his car and go into a good five minutes of warm-up stretches, he grew confident that his plan could work. Tom took off in the direction of the Wellington's.

Rich wasn't so interested in the route Tom would take, although he could pretty much guess it now as there weren't many roads around. Tom must run in one direction, then double back. Rich thought it strange that he didn't pick a loop somewhere, but the last thing he'd ever do is seriously try to figure Tom out.

About a half hour into the wait, Rich could hear Joseph and Mary barking for the second time, indicating Tom was returning, probably five more minutes away. Rich calculated it to be a four mile route. Not bad. Rich would have to increase his route.

Rich made a beeline for the Java Bean thinking he might check up on Tom's routine one more time, just to be sure. He had too much riding on this to rely on Anne Wellington's piece of gossip.

At the Java Bean, Rich ordered a double latte', a cinnamon roll and the "Standard Times".

The "Times" carried some updates on the original two murders, but nothing special. He almost skipped a secondary lead story, but something drew him back to it:

ASIAN LOTTERY WINNER FOUND DEAD

The story told of a Fall River man from the Philippines found murdered in an old warehouse near Battleship Cove. He had been tortured before being done in by some ghastly method. The poignant thing about the story was that he had just recently won over five million dollars in the Massachusetts State Lottery. Friends and family weren't aware of it because he had arranged with the Lottery office to collect as anonymously as possible. Smart of him considering the countless hounds that come out of the woodwork trying to woo the money away from these new millionaires. So Marco Fernandes collected his first check without fanfare.

Was Rich just being paranoid, or could it be that Marco's coming into money attracted the wrong attention? He read on. Mention was made by close friends that Marco had just purchased a new Lincoln

Town Car and a new motor boat. He was also shopping for some real estate and it was a shame that he was cut off at this time in his life. Friends wondered where he had gotten the money. All week long, Marco Fernandes had been the talk of the community with his mysteriously newfound wealth.

Sipping the last of his latte' Rich felt terrible for Marco Fernandes. His suspicion of the mob looking for people coming into sudden wealth was proving valid and he was feeling partly responsible. His one comforting thought was that Alan Levine wasn't a rat. He couldn't have told Carlo Bartelli about the money because it had been almost twenty four hours since Alan and Carlo were together and Rich was still alive.

———————————

There were three banks Rich knew of having branches that opened at 8:00. He hit all three, changing three bills at each. He didn't like how slow this was going, but until he could find more time he had little choice.

———————————

It was earlier than Captain Hernandes liked to report for duty, but last night's killing had him wondering. After getting the run around on, Fall River Police divulged that the new Filipino body had some similarities to the other murders, but that he should check back later, a hint to stop bothering them.

Hernandes didn't know what he was looking for, but something bothered him. His juices were flowing and it felt good.

CHAPTER 8

Thursday, Late Morning

By 8:50 Rich was passing through the security check at Bristol County Probate Court. A hellish building that bred depression, animosity and heartbreak. A building dedicated to the art of divisiveness. Rich had lost his shirt here in episodes past. Today he might lose more.

Alan arrived a few minutes later and ushered Rich downstairs, into a private conference room.

"Are you feeling all right today?" Alan was asking because there was a genuine concern. Rich had been through the ringer and may well face a bitter session today. They were docketed before Judge Santos.

Rich hunkered down low, and in an even lower

voice said, "For a man sitting on top of almost twenty nine million dollars… No."

Alan didn't smile. Rich was always joking, but not today.

"Well, I think things might start looking up." Alan unbuckled his two-buckle leather case. He removed several folders.

"I've been pouring over your tax returns for the three years leading up to the divorce and the financial statements of both yours and Debbie's," Alan continued, "and something's not adding up. Did you and Debbie dine out a lot?" Alan asked, hoping for the right answer. "I mean, like a lot?"

"Sure," Rich shrugged, "most nights, I'd say. I spoiled her pretty good. Isn't that why they leave?"

"Most nights, but not all? And not every meal, like breakfast, lunch and dinner?" Alan had a hopeful look in his eyes.

"Nah, we were too busy. Generally just dinner at night. A few nights we'd stay home. Order pizza or do a cheese plate, simple stuff."

"How about expensive hobbies or past-times. Did you or Debbie have any indulgences?" Alan may have been hinting at coke.

"No. Nothing like you might be getting at." Rich was amused at the thought. "Debbie liked the spas, but that was about it for 'indulgences'".

"Trips? Travel? Did you spend a fair portion traveling the world?"

"Not really. My business took us around for

seminars or occasional projects. Like the big one I did in Hawaii. But our clients always paid for travel, we only put money in for some souvenirs or a few days extension." Rich looked at Alan. "Why? What are you getting at?"

Alan grimaced and shook his head.

"It just doesn't add up. The personal income reported the years leading up to your divorce was almost two hundred thousand per year. Yet your mortgage and other expenses just weren't that high. Neither financial report shows that kind of cash or assets lying around."

Rich leaned forward. "And you are getting at..." His voice trailed.

"Somebody took a hunk of money out those years. And maybe the years before. They must have. You paid the taxes on it."

"I wouldn't really know," Rich said, shaking his head, "Debbie kept the books and did all the banking."

"You mentioned Hawaii. What about Hawaii?"

"Six or seven years ago. A client from Newport wanted me to design and supervise the construction of their home on the Big Island. I put my bid in at ten percent of the project cost plus expenses, a little high but, you know, it would consume most of my time. It was a nice surprise when I got it. The project cost started out around five million, but finished around ten by the time it was completed. We had to be flown out quite a few times, first-class, and always got to stay at the greatest places. That was all covered and

I probably made the biggest fee of my life!" Rich was beginning to see the light. "But Debbie kept the books. I couldn't tell you exactly how well we did."

Alan shot Rich an incredulous stare. "Rich, you're a great designer and architect. Don't architects need to know math?"

Rich shrugged. Actually, no. Computers, calculators. What's to know? But there was an image to maintain.

"Yeah, sure," Rich offered. "Why?"

"Because your fee for the Hawaii project alone was about a million dollars. Did you ever see a million?"

Rich stared off into the courthouse air.

"If that was six or seven years ago, that would be five or six years before the actual divorce," Alan continued, excited. "We were only concerned with the previous three years leading up to the divorce, so I never saw those records."

They stared at each other long and hard.

"Rich, I think Debbie might have squirreled away a small fortune from your prosperous years. I'm not saying that she had intentions of leaving you, but as she drew closer to the decision to leave, she probably withdrew the funds for herself."

"Don't investments and bank accounts get reported to the IRS? How could she hide things like that?" Rich no longer had a hard time believing that Debbie would stiff him. He just had his doubts that the system wouldn't uncover her plan.

Alan shrugged. "There are ways. Lock boxes, cash accounts, overseas banking."

"What you're getting at is possible. I never checked on the money during our whole fourteen years together." Rich stared vacantly.

Had he really been taken? Was Debbie sitting on a gold mine that she hid from the divorce proceedings?

"Rich, when we're before Judge Santos today, we'll handle the contempt matter and the mortgage. But I'm going to raise this issue. We may be out of line and Santos may not hear us, but we have to try."

"The worm turns." Rich said this as he was pondering if this could really be true.

"If she cheated you," Alan continued, "and withheld disclosure of assets, we've got a whole new ball game and she'll have two strikes against her before coming to the plate. And next time, I'll be throwing my best stuff."

⁕ ⁕ ⁕ ⁕ ⁕

They sat on the hard wooden benches watching Judge Santos make or break people's lives. Rich had to sit and watch LaFleur in action as LaFleur tried casually to destroy another mans life. If LaFleur had his way, the man would be leaving with only his socks and shorts and would have to send them in later. After he got checked into the shelter.

As the battle ensued before Rich's and Alan's eyes, Alan leaned to Rich and quietly asked, not really expecting an answer, "What's LaFleur on? Look at him constantly twitching his neck, his runny nose, his hyper-activity." Rich had no idea, but one of his friends had asked the same question at an earlier hearing while observing LaFleur's demeanor. They both shrugged their shoulders and let it ride.

With Santos far from finishing the first case, it was Rich's turn to lean toward Alan for discussion. Speaking through the side of his mouth, Rich mumbled, "I think the money belongs to Bartelli."

Bombshell.

Alan turned slowly, a look of concern, then the hands went up. Rich recognized what they meant.

"You had lunch with him and were talking with him," Rich explained, "You better know what we might be into."

"*We?* We, as in what Tonto said to the Lone Ranger?" Alan's lips never seemed to move.

"Okay, if you don't want to know. But when I'm tortured, the name 'Alan Levine' can come out even if I'm gagged."

Alan folded his head into his hands. He couldn't believe what he was hearing.

"Spit it out," said Alan. He knew he'd better hear this.

"It was the two chum guys I saw burying the body and the money. The same two guys the paper said worked for Carlo."

"So..." It's amazing how calm Alan sounded keeping his voice so low.

"Alan, why would they be chopped up? They get sent on a turkey run to bury a body and a fortune. Less than twelve hours later the body is on the six o'clock news and the money's gone. Another twelve hours and fish are spitting out polyester blend suits. Put it together."

Alan shook his head in disbelief.

"How do you know those bodies were the two guys you saw? They only found a few parts!" It was a struggle to talk so softly.

"I saw the parts clearly on TV. It was a leg, or part of a leg, from the knee down. The pant leg was a weird pinkish gray color and the shoe was a two-toned beige job. That's exactly what the taller one was wearing. Mutt. Or is it Jeff that's taller."

"That's it? You draw your conclusion from a pinkish gray pant leg and a two-toned beige shoe?" Alan wasn't quite buying it yet. "It's a good thing you don't work in homicide. You'd be declaring President Clinton dead every time a corpse came through with a blue suit on."

Rich thought Alan was being ridiculous now.

"No comparison. A lot of guys wear blue suits."

"My point exactly," Alan retorted.

"A pinkish gray suit and a two toned beige pair of shoes! Alan, how many guys wear that?"

"In New Bedford? Plenty." Referring to the large Portuguese population.

It was obvious to Rich that Alan was in denial.

Bartelli was a good client and Alan didn't want to lose him.

"Alan, it's Bartelli's money. You wanna make a bet?" They'd be betting with their lives, Rich figured.

Alan gritted his teeth as he nodded ever so slightly. Alan could see one and one adding up, which meant Rich was in deep trouble and that placed Alan there too.

———————

"In the case of Cochrane vs. Lewis, all parties stand." The court bailiff called them to attention.

"All parties, raise your right hand ..."

The two attorneys stood at attention beside their clients while Rich and Debbie did the oath thing. Debbie wore a simple dress, with less jewelry on than Rich had ever seen her in public. Also with less make-up than usual, doing her best to look as waif-like as possible. LaFleur's idea no doubt. Rich thought how nicely dressed they all were. Too bad they couldn't be enjoying dinner at the Candleworks rather than trying to tear each other apart in Probate, then they could all leave feeling good about themselves. That never happens in this building.

"What's going on now?" Judge Santos decided to dispense with the formalities and cut right to it. He seemed to know everyone so well by now.

"Your Honor," LaFleur dug in. "As you read in my complaint, we have knowledge that the defendant,

Mr. Lewis, has been purposely neglecting the paying of the mortgage payments on my client's property as ordered by this court. This places the property and home of my client, Ms. Cochrane, in serious jeopardy and thus I called for this emergency session. I believe ..." Santos cut him off.

"Is this true Mr. Levine?" Santos's eyes looking sternly at Alan. "Is your client in breach of his obligations?"

"Not as of yesterday afternoon, your Honor." Alan said the whole thing while releasing an audible sigh. "I have a letter from First Federal, the Mortgagor, confirming that Mr. Lewis paid them in cash yesterday promptly after receiving a substantial payment for a project he had been involved with for quite some time. The letter confirms that the account is current and secure."

"Furthermore, your Honor," Alan was now showing irritation, "Upon receiving notice of this complaint I immediately contacted Attorney LaFleur to inform him that Mr. Lewis had everything under control, the bank was not initiating foreclosure and there was no need to waste the court's time with these frivolous charges. I further ..."

"Frivolous charges!" Interrupted LaFleur. "My client's very welfare is at stake, her home and property are subject to bank seizure. Mr. Lewis is displaying open defiance of this court's order, and Mr. Levine thinks that to be frivolous?"

He was indignant.

"As I was saying," Alan calmly went on. "This letter was sent to Mr. LaFleur's office, both by mail as well as a facsimile transmission. This was all done the very next day after my being notified of this action and two days before this hearing. Your Honor, it is my opinion that this action is unconscionable and frivolous on Mr. LaFleur's part."

"Mr. Lewis had fallen behind *three* months, your Honor!" LaFleur was fast. Not a moment passed from the last sound out of Alan's mouth to the first syllable out of his. "My guess is that Mr. Lewis keeps pushing the limits to see what he can get away with in this court. He certainly came up with a tidy sum of money quickly once we blew the whistle on him."

LaFleur's eyes looked down, he was very satisfied with himself.

"My client is a professional designer." Alan felt obliged to respond. "His paychecks come from fees which are typically structured over extended periods of time. Since he left the marriage with virtually no savings, it's not always possible for him to pay every bill on time. These last few months have been full of pressures for Mr. Lewis as he's had to put off virtually all of his bills until he received a large fee just yesterday. Furthermore, when Mr. Lewis received his fee, the mortgage at First Federal was the very first bill he paid. He no sooner had the check in his hand than he was on his way to the bank."

Judge Santos handled a hundred cases a month, but what he remembered of this one was an impression of a husband seemingly hiding assets. This embittered Santos and he wasn't about to be duped by some amateur con-man who thought he was above this court.

"So, until yesterday afternoon, and certainly at the time that Mr. LaFleur filed on this contempt action," Santos was interjecting, "your client was indeed in contempt of this court's order?"

"Technically, yes. But he…"

"Even his own attorney has to admit it, your Honor," interrupted LaFleur, ecstatic now.

"But my client acted prudently and in good faith, your Honor. The facts stand for themselves."

LaFleur didn't miss a beat. "That's my argument, your Honor. The facts speak for themselves and there are two distinct facts. One, Mr. Lewis withheld payments obligated by this court and, two, there were means to keep up with the obligation, being the well known and successful professional that he is."

"What means?" Alan was frustrated. "My client is broke! He's been financially ruined by the unfair burden of this settlement."

The Judge interjected: "Mr. LaFleur makes an interesting point in that he came up with the money pretty quickly once the complaint was filed. As I recall, that's not the first time he's saved the day in the nick of time."

"Your Honor," protested Alan, "Are you going to castigate my client because he's lucky? I know his situation very well and I had my own doubts as to whether he was going to make this payment, but he hung in there and did it. Are you going to hold that kind of tenacity and good luck against him?"

The judge wasn't impressed. "If Mr. Lewis is so close to the edge when it comes to his financial life, then he is placing Mrs. Cochrane in jeopardy. The court has to look at the whole picture and rule accordingly."

"With all due respect, your Honor," and Alan knew he was taking a chance on this one, " the 'whole picture' would have to take into consideration the emotional effect this divorce has had on my client as well as the lopsided split of assets that we have been contending from the beginning concerning which we have filed a 'Motion to Modify'."

"Well, that's not before me right now." The judge knew where to draw the line. "An issue of contempt is before me now and unless you're able to tell me something that I don't know in the next minute, I'll be making a finding of civil contempt. Now is there anything else?"

LaFleur knew enough to keep quiet even though he was salivating to be heard again. Alan sighed, trying to think fast.

"I stand by my belief that contempt, civil or criminal, has not taken place. But if the court disagrees, then I respectfully want to address the issue of jail, since Mr. LaFleur has made it clear that he is pressing for this."

"There will be no jail, Mr. Levine." Judge Santos

wanted to expedite matters so he took charge. He went on, "Let me address the defendant, Mr. Lewis, directly." He turned slightly to face Rich.

"Mr. Lewis, I find you to be in civil contempt of this court's order and direct that a finding of 'guilty' be entered on this matter. There would have been jail time had you not purged yourself of this charge by bringing the mortgage current before coming here today. Let there be no doubt that if you appear before me on this matter again and your payments aren't current, I will find you in contempt and put you in jail. I don't like to do that, but I will."

"Now, because you have been found to be in contempt, I further order you to pay restitution of fees. Counselor LaFleur, what are your charges at on this matter?"

"Three thousand, five hundred, your Honor." Somebody should scrape him off the ceiling. He was just too high with the ruling obviously going his way.

The judge did what almost looked like a double take. Out of respect, he held his tongue and put his head down for a quick moment.

"All right, well, I'll have to approve of them first, of course." That was a surprise coming from Santos. "Submit your charges to my office for me to examine and the defendant shall be notified by mail as to the amount owed. Mr. Lewis, these charges will have to be paid within thirty days. Do you have a problem with that?"

Does Rich have a problem with that? His lips began to form the words…

"That will be fine." Alan knew to interject

"Then let the order be entered." Judge Santos to the Court Clerk. "Is there anything else then?"

Now normally at this point, both attorney's would bow out gracefully with the winner thanking the judge, then both quietly make their exit. Normally.

<hr>

"Yes there is your Honor." Alan spoke confidently, LaFleur taken by surprise.

"I realize this is a little unconventional, but upon reviewing the documents that were submitted by the plaintiff during the discovery period for this action, I've come across some apparent discrepancies."

"Your Honor!" Shouted LaFleur in disbelief. He needed to make a showing of outrage.

Santos raised his hand to calm him down and then cast a hard grimace to Alan. He motioned for him to continue, with a look of, "This better be good."

"The fact that we never received all of the discovery documents requested and were …"

"Objection!" LaFleur screamed.

"This matter is not before me," Santos went on, "and besides, it's a closed docket. I'll sustain that objection."

Alan wasn't easily deterred, especially in a matter of fraudulent discovery practices. Little in law was as sacred as rules of discovery. It formed the basis of all that could be fair and just through the remainder of the legal process and playing fast and loose with it would jeopardize the entire case. A judge had some leeway in how they ran their court and if they began to suspect foul play in the discovery stage, amazing things could happen.

"I've already filed a Motion to Modify, scheduled for early July. But in preparation I would ask the court's support in helping us to obtain what we had every right to from the beginning."

"This objection was not raised at the trial." LaFleur needed to press.

"To the contrary," Alan countered. "It's in the transcript," holding up a stack about an inch thick, "but the objections were ignored - twice. In addition, evidence has surfaced that I am not at this time prepared to argue, but which I intend to introduce at a future hearing. Your Honor, this new evidence will put an entirely different light on the equity of this settlement."

"Objection! Your Honor!"

Santos raised his hand as if to hold LaFleur in abeyance. "I can't have you making issues of points that have already been fully adjudicated. Mr. Levine, you know the rules of evidence perhaps better than anyone in this room including me."

"My client almost went to jail today. I think he's entitled to a little consideration."

"Nevertheless," Santos was obviously bringing the

matter to a conclusion, "You've filed for modification, until then this court will not entertain any colloquy on matters before their time. I will conclude by cautioning Mr. LaFleur to cooperate with the production of any meaningful records that Mr. Levine requests. If you have nothing to hide, there's no reason not to. If there is something to hide, all the more reason to," looking at them threateningly. "We are dismissed."

The crack of the gavel brought them all to attention. As Santos exited he was mulling over what Levine had just said. For the first time since this matter came before him, he was beginning to have doubts as to Debbie's character.

<hr>

The four filed out of the courtroom in an almost military manner. Rich observed Debbie taking jewelry out of her purse as they moved swiftly down the hallway, putting it on as quickly as possible. She was headed for the ladies room where she would paint on mascara and lipstick. Life would then return to normal for her.

As Rich and Alan passed down the hallway, Alan was reassuring his client how wonderfully it all went.

"So we avoided jail. But you see that Santos was ready. I knew he had it in him."

Rich couldn't care less. Knowing that he had to write a check to LaFleur upset him far more.

"And, I'll bet we got Santos thinking." Alan was

truly relieved and optimistic. "There has to be some seed of doubt planted."

Rich was glad to be leaving this nightmarish place.

Rich and Alan stopped at the end of the walkway before the sidewalk. Alan put his hand on Rich's shoulder, looking puzzled and frayed.

"What was all that about Bartelli's money?"

"Alan, you should know." Rich felt bad, remembering the innocent Asian killed. Now Alan's life may be endangered. "I'm sure the money came from Bartelli's organization. Whether it's his or the Organization's, I'm convinced he's on the hook for it."

Alan didn't miss the import. "So I guess I'm involved after all," Alan admitted. "I don't doubt you, Rich. Everything you've said makes sense."

They looked at each other with as much empathy as either had ever felt for anyone. A brotherhood was definitely forming.

Alan continued, "You know, I've thought about your situation a lot lately. What you did in taking the money wasn't legally correct, but who can blame you? You're not an attorney, and even so, most attorneys I know would have done the same thing. And you're right, you really can't come forward now." He paused momentarily before adding, "Just like I can't."

"I'm sorry Alan. I never meant to implicate you."

Alan waved it off. He not only understood, but at this point, he was rooting for Rich.

They lamented their situation for a while, wishing they had a beer to cry in. As they were about to split for the day, Rich put into motion another piece. A piece that was not without risk, but Rich had discovered a newfound confidence in his plan and his ability to execute it. What he was about to ask of Alan would have seemed insane to him at any other time.

"Alan, I need you to do me a favor."

Alan reacted suspiciously.

"You say Carlo Bartelli loves snatching up real estate deals. Do you have any land you can sell him right now?"

"There's always land to sell. What are you getting at?"

"I need you to call him today. Tell him there's a parcel of land, any piece you can come up with, that may be available for a song, but that he'll have to move fast when it's ready."

Alan was a puzzled. "Well, I have land to sell, but nothing at a bargain basement rate."

"Alan," Rich implored, "Take any piece that you can close on and offer it at twenty or thirty percent of its value. I promise, I'll make up the difference personally."

"With the money that I'm thinking of?" Alan could see it coming. "Then I'd really be in deep stuff."

"I'll get clean money. I'll have at least twenty thousand from the Wellington's, I could..."

Alan stopped him. "I'm already implicated, don't worry."

The money source was the least of Alan's concerns. Toying with Carlo Bartelli, that was a mega-concern. But Rich was up to something and if Alan owed anyone a break, it was Rich.

"If I can pull this off," Alan offered, "we'll straighten out the details about payment later. But Rich, why are you doing this?"

Alan sensed it was a useless question, and maybe he would be better off not knowing. As crazy a proposition as this seemed, was it any crazier than Rich staying with Alan after Alan had messed up the settlement so badly? Trust begets trust.

"I can't say just yet. But I need you to call Bartelli, set him up by telling him there's at least one other interested buyer, and if and when the time comes he'll have to move fast. Maybe within hours. Can you do that?"

"No problem. I'll call him this afternoon." Alan would do just about anything for Rich by now.

"And one more thing." Rich knew this would raise questions, but it would be explained later. "Mention to Bartelli that the other interested party is Tom Cochrane. Tell him he called you just this week looking for any good land deals because he was ready to buy."

Alan was beginning to feel more like a real estate agent than an attorney, but the scenario was credible. Cochrane would know that attorney's could be one of the best sources for leads on properties before they become public knowledge. As bizarre as it seemed, Alan was ready to help. He stood there, uncharacteristically calm. To the best of Alan's recollection, this was the first time in his career that he fully trusted a client of his.

With acceptance indicated, Alan asked Rich if he needed a ride. Rich thanked him but told him that he was parked just two blocks south. They shook hands and departed. Rich walked four blocks southeast. To Freestones.

CHAPTER 9

Thursday Afternoon

Debbie's problems in court were as far from Tom Cochrane's mind, as was the appointment at work that he was forgetting about at the moment, which he would simply blame on the office manager. Tom was enjoying his lunch with a window view table at the Riverhouse Grille at the foot of the Padanaram Bridge.

From his vantage point he could take in a healthy panorama of the Padanaram Bridge and the Apponagansett Bay. The harbor, teaming with sail boats and pleasure craft mixing among the working fishing boats and the quahoggers, dotted by hundreds of lobster trap markers, all made for an idyllic setting.

Tom chose this table not for the view, but for

the proximity to the next table where three bubbly and attractive young college girls were sitting. Tom enjoyed a good conversation. Munching a lobster roll and raspberry iced tea, Tom listened in laughing along and throwing quick glances their way when appropriate.

"Would you know what's in a cosmopolitan?" The brunette was asking.

"Vodka, cranberry juice, Cointreau and lime." Tom knows these things. "And to be technical, it should be Ketel One." Vodka that is, but everyone in this crowd knew that.

"See, I told you," the shorter blonde taunted. They all had a laugh on the brunette who thought it was grenadine instead of cranberry juice, but she didn't really care.

"Great drink," offered Tom.

"Oh yeah, but do they ever sneak up on you!" The taller blonde was rolling her eyes as the others were nodding in agreement. It was obvious that they all had some kind of recent experience with the great cosmos.

"Oh, my head is still throbbing." So it was last night.

"Two aspirins before you start drinking." Tom was wise. Old men usually are, and at thirty-four, he was old in this crowd. "You didn't know that trick?"

"No. Two aspirins? It works?" The taller blonde.

"You'll still get your buzz, but you usually won't wake up with a head banger. If you do, it won't be bad."

"Where were you last night when we needed you?" The shorter blonde was holding her head now too, evidently all of them having overdone it.

Tom wouldn't miss a beat. "Well, if you had only called, I would have raced right over. Where were you all?"

"Freestone's." The brunette.

"Freestone's! I know the bartender." Though not as well as he had wished.

"The brunette? Real friendly?" Shorter blonde.

"That's her. Makes the best drinks around." Tom would know.

"Oh, she was great!" They all agreed. "She was Portuguese, wasn't she?", the shorter blonde asked.

"Cape Verdean." The Portuguese brunette knew. Though the two cultures were often considered related, nothing could be further from the truth nor goad either of the two more.

The chairs swiveled towards each other. Tom was home free. As they lamented the effects of too many cosmos, the tall blonde, the most statuesque of the group, complained, "Don't know how I'll make it to work tonight."

Tom: "Work! What would that be? I took you all to be college girls, maybe on vacation or something."

Tall blonde: "Oh we are. But I teach aerobics three or four evenings a week."

Tom: "Really! Certified?"

Tall blonde: "Most definitely."

Tom: "You girls local, or just visiting in this area?"

Tall blonde: "Very local. I live in Fairhaven, attend U.R.I."

Tom: "That's interesting. I was thinking of opening an aerobics studio on Route 6. All I need to make it happen is a good manager. Would that interest you? …"

———————

Rich had finished his lunch and was just sipping some no-name sparkling spring water with a lime. The crowd was thinning out so Gail was finding it easier to hang in his area and talk.

At the moment, Gail had engaged Tommy, a thirty-six year old Downes Syndrome afflicted regular, in a conversation with a Brown University professor who was sitting two stools down from him. Tommy was laughing uncontrollably, obvious that this was one of his best moments. The professor, initially slow to get involved and displaying subtle signs of discomfort, was by now enjoying the shtick about what Tommy's little black book might be worth. Gail was saying if they put it up for auction, the price would probably go off the scale. The professor had taken out his wallet ready to bid. Tommy was "The Man". As Gail left them to check on other patrons, the professor had loosened up enough so that the banter between him and Tommy continued.

Rich smiled at this precious gift Gail possessed. It's doubtful she even knew how valuable the gift was.

Back to Rich now and in a more intimate tone, she picked up where they had left off, "So you designed that entire house! You ought to be proud of yourself. That's one of the most impressive homes I've ever seen, especially in this area."

"I'm glad they had the money to follow through on my suggestions. Not everyone does." Rich was trying to down play his role.

"But, oh, that setting! The way it just comes up on you out of nowhere! I was driving with my roommate the first time I saw it, and whoa! I had to stop the car and just gape."

"The inside is just as impressive. I could go on forever describing some of the details. Like the moat."

"The moat?" Gail hit the words, sharp and emphatic. Two notes, like a reverse doorbell.

"Mmmm. We tied into the water around the house and graded the land to form a small waterway. Then we had it pass through the foundation and into the entryway. As you come in, you enter the tiled atrium area, then you go over a slightly rounded bridge to the hallway." Rich was smiling proudly. "It's impressive."

Rich was under her spell. Before he knew, without thinking it through though, his mouth was speaking.

"I'm invited to their housewarming party on Sunday. Should be a nice gig - everyone who's anyone should be there. I could probably bring you as a guest."

Her eyes froze wide on him. Big smile. Dimples.

Gail shook her head with a girlish cutesiness and practically sang, "Okay!"

"And I probably just set the record for asking you on a cheap date." It occurred to Rich that all he needed was gas money.

"Oh, I can write the book on cheap dates." Gail laughed at the very thought. "No, this will be nowhere near that. Are you kidding? A catered buffet at the Wellington's?" She threw her head back and rolled her eyes.

"I don't like dropping names, but a couple of celebrities and some senators will be there." He wasn't bragging, but thought she should know what to expect.

"Oh. Did the Wellington's tell you that?"

"No, I saw a guest list on the counter when I was there a few weeks ago. Very impressive." As Rich was saying this the names came back to him and he grew a little queasy. He remembered seeing the name of Carlo Bartelli. It meant nothing to him at the time, but now it did.

"You know, Gail," Rich thought he should broach this point for everyone's good, "My divorce kicked me in the backside. I don't want to mislead you; I'm rebuilding my life. I've struggled just making a living these last few years. Don't have much to offer at this point but trouble and worry."

Gail scoffed and brushed it aside with a gesture of her hand and a blow of air like she was blowing away a fly. Money didn't impress her.

"Hey," she said with a voice of authority, "You and I are going to have a good time. So forget your problems, let's enjoy Sunday." She knew just what he wanted to hear.

"Thanks." She had put him at ease. Rich finished his water and said he had to get to Providence before the city closed. She reminded him that she worked until one that night.

The phone rang at the Wellington's as John Wellington was returning to his deck chair, vodka and tonic refreshed. He picked up the phone.

"Hello" he spoke quietly. "Who?"

Anne picked up the extension from the living room and cut in, "I have it John. You can hang up now."

John hung up, still half smiling, never recognizing who had called, and settled in to his deck chair facing the open Atlantic.

"Hello Richard," Anne spoke. "Yes, yes, the tile and wallcovering both arrived and the installers are working around each other. They have a lot to do by tomorrow, I hope they make it."

"They will Mrs. Wellington," Rich assured her.

"Well, it just looks like so much work to me. Did you hear about the Caswells, Richard?"

"Yes, I think I did," faking it, "but I don't have time to get into that. Terrible thing though."

"I'll say," Anne responded. Evidently Rich guessed right.

"The reason I'm calling, Mrs. Wellington, is to ask if it would be all right to bring a guest on Sunday?"

"Oh, why certainly Richard." Anne was a very gracious person and Rich had anticipated no trouble at all. "We would love to meet her." Anne was a throwback to the days when a man would naturally mean that he was bringing a woman.

"Well, I appreciate that very much and I'll look forward to seeing you then." Richard was ready to hang up.

"Yes, well did you know that the Dover Sole is not going to be available? There are some local fish that might do as well, but…"

"Mrs. Wellington, I'm getting out of range. We're breaking up, but thank you. Thank you very much." Rich smiled and pushed "end". The Wellington's were all right in his book.

<hr>

It was two thirty when Alan Levine finished up with his afternoon appointment. Calling to Marge, Alan pressed the intercom button on his phone.

"Marge, try getting me Carlo Bartelli, please?"

"Yes, Mr. Levine." Thirty seven years and it's still "Mr. Levine." Only the two of them in the office, yet rules of decorum are strictly followed.

About three minutes passed and Carlo's rough

voice crackled on Alan's speakerphone, "Alan. What's up?"

Alan picked up. "Carlo, sorry to disturb you, but something's come up that might be of interest to you."

"I'm listening."

"It's a little land deal out in Russell's Mills. Some farm land that has great potential. Anyway, a client of mine may need to ditch it, and real low."

Carlo was attentive. The only thing he loved more than buying land was buying land low. It was the only honest way Carlo had ever made a dollar in his life, even if some of them were forced.

"Well," Carlo spoke softly, "You know I love a good land deal. What are we talking?"

"Nothing's firm right now, Carlo." Past the first hurdle, Alan thought. "But if it happens, it will happen soon and you'll have to move fast. I mean real fast, like maybe with only a few hours notice."

"That's a strange one. What's with it?" Carlo was puzzled.

"Well, I'm not at liberty to disclose details or who my clients are, but they're sitting on a small parcel that's been in their family since dirt was made. They want to unload it quickly for confidential reasons. But first, a couple of other things have to fall into place, so officially, it's not on the market." Alan was making it up as he went, a new experience for him. "So if these other matters iron out, and I think they will, the parcel will go on the market and go fast. But I can call you before it becomes public."

"I like those words. But how much we talkin?" Carlo had recently lost a substantial sum.

"Standard appraisal, probably around two fifty. But, and I know you'll buy me a drink on this one; they'd let it go for around one eighty! If it could be done that day."

"That's pretty fast. Is that possible on your end?"

Alan really had him going! He had surprised himself. He'd worry about the consequences later.

"Oh, my end is the easy end. I've already begun the paperwork, searches and all that. We'll be ready."

Carlo mulled this over. One eighty in immediate funds. That normally wasn't much of a problem, but in Carlo's world, it wasn't money that was power, it was money on hand that was power. Maybe he should let this one go. There would be other deals.

"Oh, I should tell you, there is one other buyer that's ready to go."

Forget letting this one go. Carlo doesn't lose very easily.

"Oh, I'll be ready. Who's the other buyer?"

"You remember bumping into Rich Lewis yesterday at Freestone's?"

"Sure," Carlo responded, thinking about the little weasel. Who does he think he is, trying to ace Carlo Bartelli out of a land deal? The little grunt, he thought to himself.

"Well, it's not Rich," Alan said, "It's his ex-wife and her husband. You know the Cochranes?"

What weasels, those Cochranes! Rich was back

in his favor. Now it was the Cochranes he hated. Carlo grimaced and wanted to spit. Those low-life Cochranes!

"Yeah, yeah. I know Debbie pretty well," controlling himself. "She did some work for me on my house, or, you know, her company did."

"Well," Alan continued, "Just a few days ago, Tom called me to ask me to keep an eye out for him on any good land deals. He's in real estate, you know."

"No, no. Had no idea." Carlo was hating this guy more by the second. What was he trying to pull? Big-shot real estate man. Carlo had probably bought and sold more property in his life than Tom could ever dream of, and Carlo just did it as a hobby.

"Well, he's just an agent, to my knowledge he's never been a buyer. All of a sudden, he and his wife want to buy." Now for the big set-up, hoping this is what Rich had in mind: "Said anything, any size, they wanted to buy! Imagine that. Like suddenly they can buy anything."

"Well, you gonna tell me first, right?" Carlo's mood changed very fast.

"Absolutely. That's why I'm calling you." Alan continued, "I want to make sure you can move on a moment's notice."

"Sure, sure. I'll be ready." Carlo wouldn't let this one get away now. "Any idea when?"

"Within days, I imagine." Alan was so confident, believing in himself. "I'll call you. You'll be around?"

"Let me give you my cell phone number. Don't give it out to nobody." And he meant that.

They hung up knowing they would be in touch very soon. Any time, day or night, Carlo would be ready. Alan was pleased with himself. He didn't know why, but he knew it meant a lot to Rich and it was about time that he could start coming through for him. Now, he had to take care of other pressing matters for him. He pushed the intercom again.

"Marge, who are we using for private investigation now? Anyone that knows Padanaram and Newport? Good at financials."

Marge replied, "I'm not sure. Let me look into the files."

"When you find out, place the call and relay it to me. I'll hang around until I can talk to them."

Carlo hung up and went back outside to his bocce' game. He was glad for the news. It was going to be a good deal.

But something was gnawing at him. The kid, Tom Cochrane, had better not try to take any deals away from him down the road. Who does he think he is, trying to get into land right in Carlo's backyard, and why all of a sudden? Debbie was the one with the money from what he saw. Did Debbie have so much that she could start investing in serious land?

Carlo threw his bocce' ball and it went sailing way

too far, bouncing out of the court and over the cliff edge to the sea. He was in a fit.

Thames Street, in Newport, never saw such a spectacle. Debbie's slate blue Mercedes SL600, honking and blaring in an attempt to clear bumper to bumper traffic on a road that had exceeded its capacity fifty years ago. On this perfectly sunny summer afternoon the clear blue skies drew droves of tourists from the restaurants and shops. Having the top down allowed Debbie to communicate freely with the countless pedestrians, sending expletives generously through the air, laying on the horn if she got blocked. When the horn failed to do the job, Debbie aimed her roadster for the sidewalk, scattering out-of-towners like a bag of beads bursting on a hard tiled floor. As she came up to a pole or sign, she'd attempt to wedge in between them and the buildings, but soon figured that would never work. So, repeating the blaring horn method, she'd change direction and aim toward the street again, forcing cars up on the opposite sidewalk. Who would have ever thought it would actually work? But it did, and Debbie made continual, spectacular progress down to her gallery where she buzzed into the alley scattering two families who would have preferred remaining closer together.

She parked in the spot meant for her neighbor's store as both of her spaces were taken up. She keyed the offending cars as she passed by and got out her last expletive as she kicked an old cat crossing her path.

"Jules, keep a watch on things for a while more. I've got a call to make."

She laid in as soon as he was on the line. "Bob," LaFleur, that is. "What are they up to?"

"Calm down Debbie. They're just blowing steam." LaFleur loved this kind of action. The hours he could bill out in a situation like this were just incredible! "They had a lot on the line today, and as you saw, Richey boy almost went to the slammer. They had to blow some smoke. That's how desperate lawyers defend their losing clients."

"Levine didn't seem to be blowing smoke to me. He had records and documents, he was holding them up."

"We don't know what he had. He might have been holding up his last years American Express bills for all we know." LaFleur knew better but he had to allay fears.

"Bob, the settlement is over and I did all right for myself. But you keep pushing him and pushing him. I knew something like this would happen." Debbie was beside herself, visibly shaking and reaching for some pills. "I asked you not to push. Now he's getting desparate."

"If we didn't stay on him, he probably wouldn't be paying your mortgage, then the bank wouldn't be so understanding and where would you be?"

"So what do you think Levine was getting at?

What did he mean, 'they didn't get all of the records' that they requested. Are they missing something?"

LaFleur had never actually spelled it out for her, but he may as well.

"They kept asking for your '97 returns. At first I thought it was a joint return and that they already had it. When I finally realized you had filed individually for the first time that year, it was a little late to get to them." Then he thought he better add the real reason. "Besides, you had quite a bit of income from some of the things you had sold off. And the interest on savings and gains on investments you reported were a dead giveaway to the size of some of your accounts. Believe me, it was for your good."

"Well, what if Santos makes a big deal of it next time? What kind of worms will be in that can?"

LaFleur took a deep breath and sat back in his leather high-back. It was Debbie that had done all the misdeeds. She was the one that hadn't disclosed all of her assets or reported all her income. The most he had done was not provide one tax return, a mistake that could be easily remedied.

"Don't worry Debbie. So far, everything has gone our way. Santos didn't seem very moved by Levine's antics today. Just let it play out."

She downed her pills and waited for them to kick in.

"Listen, Debbie," he said, much slower paced now, "Levine has an almost impossible job. First he's got to get Santos to even listen. Santos has it in for Rich, plus he hates to go over ground already covered. He won't be easily persuaded to retrace his steps over past financials. Levine had plenty of opportunity to address this when he was supposed to."

"Levine was in La-La Land when we had the hearing. I think he woke up and now he scares me."

"Look, do you know how hard it will be for him to get anything solid on you? We can't even find out when the mortgage is paid or isn't, and we know who his bank is for crying out loud. Now, imagine trying to find out something like that if you didn't know the bank! Well, that's what they're up against."

Debbie just didn't know. LaFleur made sense, but Levine was sharp and had a reputation far beyond the level of what LaFleur had earned for himself. They agreed to talk again next week. If anything came up, LaFleur would call, day or night. For the umpteenth time he assured her of his deep and most sincere concern for her welfare. As they hung up he noted his phone timer: .8 hours. But rounded off, because Debbie *didn't* have a timer, that would be one hour, or one hundred and eighty dollars.

Debbie hung up her phone, clicked her stopwatch, jotted down .8 hrs., composed herself and stepped out of her office.

"Jules, I'm all set now, thanks. Tomorrow then?"

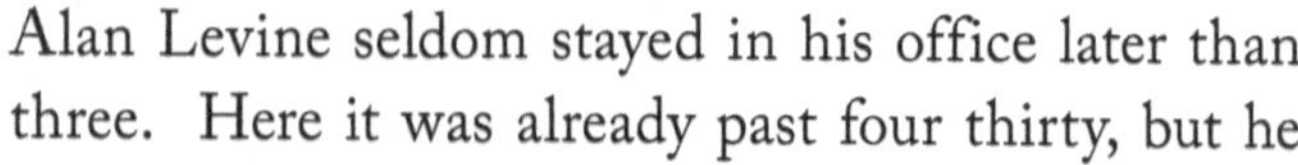

Alan Levine seldom stayed in his office later than three. Here it was already past four thirty, but he felt obliged to help Rich in any way. Marge finally paged him.

"Alan, I have a Jim Phillips on the line. He owns the 'I.C.U. Private Investigating Firm' and has done some work for us in the past."

Alan pushed his leather chair back over to the phone and picked up rolling to a stop.

"Thanks a load, Marge." He pushed the phone button. "Mr. Phillips, hello. This is Alan Levine."

"Hi Alan. Been a long time."

"Yes, yes. It certainly has." Alan didn't have a clue. "So how have you been?"

"Good. Getting along just great. You know Jimmy's big now, you wouldn't recognize him."

That's for sure. "Jimmy! Really, well that's great to hear. Listen, Mr. Phillips..."

"... Jim."

"Yes, all right, Jim." So Jimmy must be little Jim. But he's big now and not too recognizable from whenever. "Jim, how are you at tracking financial records, bank accounts, maybe even tax returns?"

"You know, Al," sure, call me Al, Jim, "that used to be an area that I avoided at all costs. But now that I'm getting up in years, (he's 34) I can't take all the crawling and climbing that I used to for all that camera and binocular work. So a couple years ago, I went back for some training in just that kind of work. Been doing quite a bit of it for the last year or so."

They offer classes on that? "Well, that's good to hear, Jim."

"Yeah. I'm tied in on my computer and can do seventy, eighty percent right from my chair here."

"Good. Well, the situation here is that I'd like to check back as much as nine years on a certain person, ex-wife of a client of mine, and get to know what her financials look like."

"Shouldn't be too hard," Jim was confident, "unless she hides funds off-shore. That could be a bugger for anyone. What's your outside?"

Alan wondered. "My outside?"

"Your outer limit. You know, how much do you want to spend?"

"Oh," why didn't he know that? "Well, actually, I have no idea. What do you charge nowadays?"

"I get three hundred a day. That's a six-hour day on the clock, but whatever extra hours I put in to mulling things over and figuring new angles is thrown in. Plus expenses. I don't think you'll get more for less anywhere."

"Sounds very fair. What about tax returns? If we can't obtain what we need through the court, do you have connections?" Alan knew he was on thin ice by going here, but Jim was a no nonsense kind of guy.

"I've always gotten what I needed. I know the places to go and when to go there."

"If it works, that's all we care about."

"Well, I'm your man. Again, what's your outside?"

"Well, I don't know what to say. What am I expecting to pay? Maybe three, four thousand. Does that sound fair?"

"It's a good start, but who knows, we might be able to do it all for that."

"What's your time like?" Alan knew virtually any price can be met, but could Jim work fast enough?

"I'm ready. We hang up, I hit the ground running." Jim hadn't worked for three weeks.

"Well then," Alan settled in, comfortable that he found his man, "let me fill you in and you can get started."

Alan briefed him and Jim outlined a plan of attack promising to be back in touch by mid-week, if not sooner

"Too bad that I contacted you so late in the week. I guess you'll have to wait until Monday to really get going."

Jim smiled at Alan's naiveté. "This is the age of computers, electronic banking, the Internet. Like I said, seventy, eighty percent gets done right here from my chair. And as for tax returns, the weekends are best! You know, weekend crews, cleaning crews, security crews."

Alan wished he hadn't heard that.

⚬━⚬⬥⚬⬥⚬⬥⚬⬥⚬━⚬

Heading east on Route 195, Rich started seriously pondering his situation with Gail. With flashes of the recent killings, he knew he had better be careful. Now he's got her coming with him Sunday. Just how much would he involve her? It would be best to keep his distance, but there was something about Gail that made that hard

Maybe he should back out cleanly. Make an excuse, tell Gail that Anne Wellington wouldn't be able to fit Gail in as a guest on Sunday. As he exited 195, five minutes from Freestone's, he considered his dilemma.

It was clambake night, so Rich skipped the martinis and kept the Sam Adams coming through all four courses. It thinned the butter he figured. Gail would pick at his clams and lobster whenever she had a break, but it was hopping tonight. Rich got to eat almost all of it, which she quickly noticed on her return.

"What? You didn't leave me another clam?"

Rich looked at his plate and thought of a dozen good lines. For guys. Not lines you'd use on Gail.

"I'm sorry." It was the best he could muster.

Gail frowned and swatted at the air. She was only kidding. But her eyes remained in a half squint as they stayed fixed on Rich's. She was losing an edge too, like maybe she didn't know quite what to say, a new experience for Gail.

"Desert?" she asked.

"No, I'll pass tonight." Then, after thinking, "Well, yeah, maybe one more?" holding his empty mug.

If he were going to tell her, this would be the time.

"Gail." He was going for it. "About Sunday."

"Yes," she drawled slowly, knowing full well something more was coming.

"I won't be taking you away from work?"

"Thank goodness for weekend help! Sunday's my day off." She smiled, flashing her dimples. Rich's knees began to weaken along with his will.

"You sure? It will last all afternoon, maybe longer. And I'll be kibitzing with some magazine editors and whatnot. I'll probably be neglecting you."

"What! Am I getting stood up already?" She said it loud enough for the whole room to hear. It was a mock disdain, and she played it well. "You just made the date a few hours ago and you're standing me up already?" Several octaves higher, she obviously wanted to go. There would be no getting out, not if Rich wanted to leave a whole man. The attention of the entire room was centered on him now, poised as the man standing Gail up. If he didn't change his mind, the crowd would get restless. They weren't about to let Gail get hurt.

"I'm just checking." Rich was bailing out, but glad to do so. "I thought maybe you just accepted to make me feel good." The whole bar breathed a sigh of relief, as they were all glad that the dufus standing Gail up came to his senses. Rich would walk away tonight.

CHAPTER 10

Friday

The alarm blared at 4:00. Although he'd made it home somewhat earlier, he hardly slept because another surprise had awaited Rich when he got home. A surprise that he'd take to Alan, hoping he'd gotten a good night's sleep.

Today, he would have his latte'. He fired up his Pavoni and began his morning ritual of grinding fresh espresso beans, steaming milk and pressing the ethereal concoction. He mixed everything into his Starbuck's stainless steel thermal travel mug thinking he should have been born Italian.

He arrived on Potomska Road twenty minutes ahead of schedule. He chugged down the last three sips from his Starbuck's stainless steel thermal travel mug and exited his car to see what would unfold.

There were no surprises. Within two minutes of yesterdays arrival time, Tom's Porsche could be heard almost a mile away in the still of the morning. He pulled up to the exact spot he had come to yesterday, got out, stretched, pulled, pushed and warmed up for his run. Then he was off. Rich scanned the site. Everything was fine for his plan.

After hearing Joseph and Mary go off for the second time, Rich piled back into his Explorer and headed straight to Alan's. It was 6:00.

<hr>

"I'm on the lam!"

Rich got the words out as Alan was opening his front door, surprised that someone would have the nerve to be ringing his bell at such an ungodly hour. He was also surprised that someone would use the front door. But when he saw it was Rich, he opened the door wide.

"You're on the lam?" Alan was still in a stupor. "What do you mean?"

"Mass. Electric. On a check fraud thing. I got home late last night and there was this notice from a constable on my door." Rich handed Alan the warrant for failure to appear in Taunton Probate Court. About the same time that he was getting his tail waxed in front of Judge Santos in New Bedford, he had been ordered to appear in Taunton on this other charge.

Alan read the warrant in detail, his hair looking like Alfred E. Newman's, but otherwise quite dapper in his navy blue silk robe and doeskin slippers.

Rich continued, "So many things happened this week, I completely forgot about this thing. My check for the electricity bounced. Twice. They issued a summons and I was supposed to be in Taunton yesterday. I just forgot!"

Alan was relieved. It was nothing, just a few phone calls that would need to be placed.

"Rich don't worry. We can handle this it's no problem. Can you pay this thing today?"

"Alan, I'm heading to New York. I'll be gone all day. But the money's no problem, you know that." Alan didn't put his hands up this time.

Alan stroked his chin as he walked backwards to his leather stuffed chair, still reading. He sat down and motioned for Rich to do the same.

"Let me make a few calls and I'm sure you'll be all right by the time you return." Alan was glad to help. "I've got your cell phone number, I'll call you if there are any problems." Then the real surprise, "If they can't wait until Monday for funds, I'll advance them. I know you're good for it... and then some."

Rich was floored. He had known Alan for ten years or more, and he never put up his own funds to help a client.

"Alan, thanks. The tab's only $369, plus whatever

fines or penalties the court adds. Here's a thousand to cover it all. Put the balance toward my account."

Alan stared dazedly at the thousand. Was Rich going to go through life now handing out thousand dollar bills for every problem? But he was also rewarded. For the first time in his life he had offered to float a loan to a client and here he was getting it paid back before he even made it!

"One other thing," Alan said. "I took care of Bartelli yesterday. Did just like said, told him to be ready for a great land deal but that he'd have to move fast. He even gave me his cell number!" Then, lowering his voice two octaves to imitate Carlo, "But I can't give it to no one."

"So, you think he'll go for it? Rush out to sign the deal on a moment's notice?"

"For the deal I offered, he'd get on a plane to sign." Alan saying that in reference to a well published fact that Carlo feared flying and would never step on an airplane.

"Great." Rich was truly thankful. Perhaps that one favor made up for any damage that might have been done in his divorce. "How about the Cochrane name. Were you able to drop it?"

Alan shook his head proudly. "Mission accomplished. That might have been a brilliant idea too. I sensed just a little reluctance in his voice about the deal. But once I mentioned that the Cochrane's wanted to buy, Carlo was in and in solid.

"Rich, I don't know what you're up to." Alan was

looking fatherly, but it wasn't a put-on. "But be very careful in what you do with Carlo Bartelli. I've only seen his good side, but I don't doubt for a minute that he has a bad one. And no one wants to see that," he shuddered, "No one."

Rich somberly acknowledged the situation. Then Alan shooed Rich away so he might return to his bed. As Rich rose to leave, Megan appeared at the end of the hallway holding her Barney doll and rolling her big eyes toward her grandfather, ready to play. Alan wouldn't be returning to bed that morning.

Rich was relieved by the morning's events as he pulled out of Alan's driveway. Heading down Smith Neck Road, the Padanaram Bridge shone brightly on the horizon and the Village glistened to the right, sprawled out across the sparkling blue Apponagansett water. The day was starting flawlessly. Rich again wished he had purchased the Z-3 as he headed for the Big Apple.

Two Dunkin Donut boxes lay on Captain Hernandes desk, well picked over with only the plain and lemon donuts left. Tony Hernandes had begun the custom of bringing two boxes each morning when he found out the absentees seemed tied up at the Dunkin Donut in town, so if Mohammed wouldn't go to the mountain, Tony could figure out the rest. The briefing was over and he had asked three officers to remain.

"Neither Westport, New Bedford or Fall River are really helping me on this." Tony was referring to the dead-ends he kept running into with all three police departments whenever he would call for information on the bodies found in their respective cities. "They all say that because we don't have jurisdiction, I should read about it in the papers."

"I thought Jack was a good friend of yours. Even he won't help?" Jane Humbolt.

"Nah. He was trying to help at first but since everything seems to be mob connected, even NBPD isn't on the inside track. Fed's came down and practically took it away from them, except for the public image."

"Why would they link the Fall River slaying?" Bill Ryan asked. "Fernandes was just an honest immigrant family man!"

"Fernandes body was found in an old warehouse that's owned by Carlo Bartelli," Tony answered. "He was tortured in a mob style fashion. But I'm glad the Feds are tying them together. Pretty sharp of them."

"Have you contacted the Feds?"

Everyone smirked at Jane for asking such a thing and several groans were evoked.

"I know, I know. Sounds like a dumb question, but have you? You guys ever hear about moods? Or luck? You might just hit it right." Jane brought the women's perspective to the table.

There was a pause, each man looking to the other for any signs of acceptance of such feminine logic. It would only take one of them to break and the others would follow.

"I might give it a try later." Tony condescended and the others immediately approved.

Jane was probably the closest to the situation, having been with Tony at the scene out at Horseneck Beach.

"What connections do you see? Where do you think this can go?" she asked.

"I don't know. All victims in one way or another crossed paths with the mob, not by choice for the Filipino, but he ended up where he ended up." Tony had this gut feeling that wouldn't leave. The more he relied on his gut, the more cases he was able to help solve. "Somehow, I think the Dartmouth area is involved. Or will be. It all happened all around us."

"Three days, three incidents, four bodies," Steve offered. "It could just be one big coincidence, but it did all happened in only three days."

"There's one thing that I'll share." Tony took out one of the photos and flipped it on his desk for all to view.. Maybe one of them would be able to make more sense of it if they knew exactly where he was coming from. "What do you see?" he asked. "Anything?"

They all craned their necks, studying the Kodak from different angles. Each wanted to see something. Each wanted to be the sleuth Tony was thought to be. Each wanted to outdo the other. Each had to say no.

Tony didn't want to point it out. If they didn't

find it on their own, what good would it be? But if he could get just one of them to see, to believe…

"Nothing incongruous? Nothing out of place?" He gave them more time.

Jane thought she saw it. "The pattern of stones?"

"What pattern?"

"Where?"

"What do you mean?"

It wasn't much of a pattern. Just about a half dozen golf ball size stones that happened to form a crescent, kind of. Nothing more than a random chance happening of any number of geometric shapes that happens when rocks are scattered naturally, randomly.

"I Just don't see it." Steve was out, he was stretching, putting an obvious end to his concentration.

Bill was out next, shrugging his shoulders and flipping his hands in an "I've had it" kind of way.

Jane hung in there. She leaned closer, shutting everything else out.

"I think I see what you mean," in a low, serious voice.

Bill and Steve shot somber looks, first to Jane, but quickly then to the photo. They leaned in closer, still seeing nothing.

"Along the side, both sides actually. There's an unnaturally straight impression, like an edge, running up from the body bag. I get the feeling maybe something was there and dragged out."

Bingo! Tony broke into a slow and appreciative smile.

"That's it. That's what I saw and it's been bugging me."

Steve was still pondering the whole thing. "But so what? What are you trying to say happened here?"

"Something else was in that grave." Tony was surer than ever now.

"Okay," Steve, wondering. "But what? Is it a big deal?"

Jane took this one too. Her mind was racing. "Somebody witnesses this burial, follows up after the perpetrators leave and uncovers everything. An hour later, they're reporting the body, but nothing else. I'd say it probably is a big deal."

They bantered different ideas back and forth, maybe drugs, money, jewelry, even weapons. But why? Why bury anything valuable with a body? Nothing seemed to explain it.

By 10:30, Rich had made it to Greenwich, Connecticut, rumored to be the highest income per capita city in the country.

Walking into the Greenwich Bicycle Shop, he felt just a little foolish because he wanted an item and didn't know what to call it. Rich was a jogger, not a biker.

"May I be of help?" A clerk asked.

"Yeah, but I don't know what to call it. I need one of those mirrors that you wear on your head so you can see what's behind you." Rich thought that came out all right.

"A mirror. Sure. Right this way."

The clerk led him to the second isle and showed him a selection of four styles, from about twenty to forty dollars. For a one-inch-mirror.

"What do they call these?" Rich asked.

"Mirrors?"

"Yeah, the mirrors. What do they call them?"

"Mirrors." The clerk kept a straight face out of respect. Rich selected the thirty-dollar model that didn't require a helmet to attach to.

At the cash register, Rich angled his wallet to hide the thousand dollar bills he had taken. But as the clerk rang up the sale and the drawer popped open, Rich couldn't believe the money that was in there.

"Any chance that you can break a thousand?"

"A thousand what?" asked the clerk, reasonably.

A thousand mirrors, thought Rich. "Bill."

"Bill?" still sounding reasonable.

"I have a thousand dollar bill that's more trouble than it's worth. Well, not literally, but I can't use it for anything until I break it. I saw all that money and thought maybe you can help."

The clerk looked with a cocked head as Rich showed him the bill. He took it out of Rich's hand, still looking quite serious. Then he broke into a gaffe-like expression, "Shhhhooo, I never saw one of these before!"

"They're not making them any more. Calling them all in actually. It would make a great collector's item." Then Rich thought he'd go for it. "Might be worth something one day."

No laugh. The clerk held it to the light. Turned it over a few times, played it like a fast accordion and then declared it to be real.

"What would you like, hundreds?"

"And fifties, if you can spare them. Maybe Twenties, you know, ten or so." Rich was home free on this one. "And some fives."

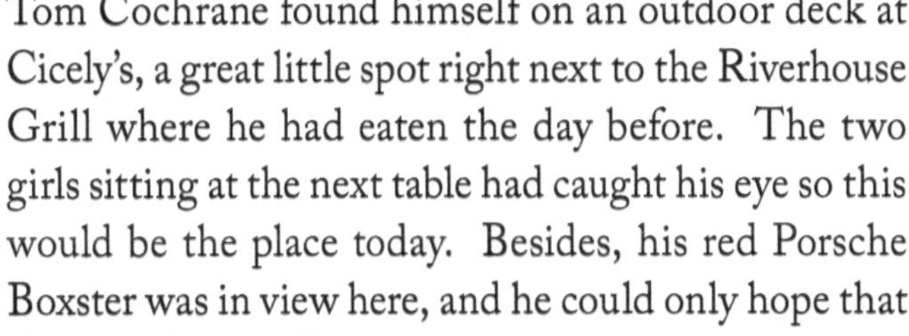

Tom Cochrane found himself on an outdoor deck at Cicely's, a great little spot right next to the Riverhouse Grill where he had eaten the day before. The two girls sitting at the next table had caught his eye so this would be the place today. Besides, his red Porsche Boxster was in view here, and he could only hope that they saw him pull up in it.

"That look's good." Tom was eyeing a chicken salad sandwich that the brunette was eating. "Would you recommend it?"

"Oh, it's just delish!" Said with mayonnaise on the corners of her mouth. "It's chicken tarragon salad. I'd definitely recommend it."

"Then that'll do me. I know a good dish when

I see one." The brunette wasn't sure about what she just heard, so let it go. Her friend, a brown haired, deeply tanned, cat-lover according to her T-shirt, had seen him pull up in his red Porsche.

"Nice car you have. Great day for it too!" She stared at the car, not Tom.

"Every day's a great day for that car."

"Four cylinder or six?" she asked.

Tom had no idea. "Six", he said. He thought it sounded bigger.

"Are you from around here?" the brunette asked.

"Padanaram citizen. Live a few blocks away, but what Padanaram citizen doesn't?" Padanaram was small.

"Oh, such a beautiful place to live! Are you from here originally?"

"No, just the last two years. Great place to be though."

The brown haired girl finally took her eyes off the Porsche and gave Tom a little attention.

"And just how big of a cat lover are you?" referring to her T-shirt.

She had forgotten she had even put the cat shirt on. Looking down to what Tom was staring at she realized what he meant.

"Oh, cats, dogs, hamsters, fish, birds. I'm an animal lover from day one."

"And are you two local?" Tom was fishing again.

"Fall River. But we never even knew this place

existed! We were lost and just happened to stumble across it."

"Fall River? And you love animals?" Tom was so surprised. What a small world, what are the chances? Why he was …

"I was thinking of opening a pet store in Fall River. But I would need people to work it, maybe manage it."

The three seats pulled closer together as Tom began his on the spot interview, one that he knew they would pass.

Business in New York completed at 5:00, but Rich was sitting in traffic at 7:10. He had made it out of Manhattan twenty minutes ago. From experience, he didn't expect to see open road through his windshield for at least another hour.

He had looked forward all day to topping the night off at Freestone's, but now he was looking at an ETA of around eleven, and he still had some important chores ahead of him. But he couldn't bring himself to skip seeing Gail. He held a vision of her dimples for the rest of the trip, pulling up to Freestone's at 11:15. The vision morphed into reality as he entered the restaurant.

Gail was engrossed in conversation with one of New Bedford's well-known judges and his wife. Long time friends, practically family. Involved with them in the discussion was Larry, a used car salesman who had probably run into the judge a number of times on the wrong side of the bench. Leave it to Gail to bring such diversity together. She spotted Rich as he entered.

Flashing a big smile, bright enough to shoot a photograph by, she motioned for Rich to take the empty stool next to the Judges wife. "Hey! Things go all right in New York?"

"Things never go all right in New York. But I survived."

Gail introduced everyone and then went off to mix Rich's drink. "So, tell me about your day." Gail spoke while she worked.

"Oh, there's not much to tell. Got everything done and sat in traffic for four hours afterwards." He turned to the Judge, "You know what they call that in New York, a four hour traffic delay?"

"Normal, probably." The Judge chortled, having spent enough time in the Big Apple to appreciate the truth of the statement.

"No word of a lie, the traffic reporter on the radio today called it, 'smooth sailing'"!

The Judge chuckled, then added, "One of the most useless things I've seen in our day is a traffic report. Any one ever hear a report that was useful?" He was asking everyone within earshot, looking around for a response. No takers.

The Judge went on, "If it's any good, you always just passed the last exit that would steer you away from the problem. If you should happen to have enough time to divert, you find out later that the jam was cleared a half hour earlier." He shook his head as others nodded in agreement. He was quite used to that.

"Yeah, and if you zip down the breakdown lane," Larry just being Larry on this one, "some pot-lickin' trooper pulls you over and bam, a hundred and twenty out the window."

Not the best comment to add to a Judge's observation, but then that's why he sells used cars, not new cars.

"What're you, a Palanga!" Gail yelled to Larry. "Only Palangas drive down the break-down lane."

Larry backed down, laughing at Gail's act. The Judge was glad to see the subject end. It was a small thing for any night of bar talk, but Rich noticed. He thought it was smooth of Gail to head off even the smallest of discomforts and keep everyone feeling good.

The group talked on, Gail being involved in at least two or three other conversations simultaneously as she was up and down the entire length of the bar fifty times. Gradually the group thinned out.

"I've really got to go." Rich knew there would be an objection. "I almost didn't stop tonight, I've got at least an hour or two of important work to do and I'm functioning on ten or twelve hours of sleep all week."

"Can't you stay and keep me company for just

a little while longer?" Looking very school-girlish again.

"Really, I'm ready to crash." He didn't know how he was going to do it, but he had one more morning to get up early.

They said goodnight. Rich sensed Gail was looking for a kiss, but he didn't dare. If he didn't pull off what he needed to, she'd be kissing a dead man. He smiled, nodded and left.

———— ◆ ◆ ◆ ————

In the ten minute drive to his apartment, Rich almost dozed off three times. His eyes felt like baked potatoes must feel when they're wrapped in foil and roasted. Trying to get his lids to flow smoothly over his burning eyes reminded him of trying to remove the foil.

Once in his apartment, he repeated the scene from a few days ago, pulling all the shades down, closing the blinds and shutting out all the lights except in his bedroom. He left his bedroom door open so some light would flow into the kitchen.

He took out two 33 gallon garbage can size, green plastic bags, then decided he may need more support, so took out two more and doubled them up. He dragged the kitchen chair over to the side and mounted it, then pushed a ceiling tile up and began the transfer.

After thirty minutes, the two bags were full, but

there was still a lot of money left. He doubled two more bags and completed the process.

It was an eerie view. Three green garbage bags loaded with cash. Like trash, ready to be discarded and crushed, but enough wealth to change someone's life, for better or for worse. He figured the money had changed his for worse. Now that he had Gail, he thought this would be best. If he could get rid of his most recent problems, he'd have to trust that his other ones would disappear too.

Rich was careful to hold back something for himself. His recent money problems made an indelible impression that he would not soon forget. Being broke in this world is a fearsome thing.

CHAPTER 11
Saturday Morning

With his alarm going off at 4:00 for so long now his eyes popped open at 3:56. They still ached, but were open. Rich's inner clock always adapted easily, but more likely it was the anticipation. This was the day!

Rich fired up his Pavoni again, a carbon copy of the previous morning. But he was even more tired, dead tired. He worried that by pushing it he might miss some detail and his entire plan become unraveled. Why did he stay so long last night?

He made his concoction, mixed it all into his Starbucks stainless steel whatever and finished dressing. He emptied the shopping bags from Connecticut, spreading the contents on his bed. He put on the oversized running pants and jacket, then laced up the Reebok ghetto jumpers that he would never buy in his normal life. He glanced in the mirror and confirmed that he looked like a new man. Who could recognize him? Finally he grabbed his new "Tweety Bird" hat and his mirror.

Two trips and he was loaded and out. He had a queasy feeling in his stomach as he left. Everything that life had brought him to through the years, everything he had become or would ever become, was riding on what would transpire within the next hour or so. He wanted to vomit. He sucked it in. He was on autopilot, because if he stopped to think about what he was doing, he'd likely bail.

The latte' was gone by the time Rich was turning onto Potomska Road. He drove to the area Tom would arrive a half hour from now. He pulled to the same spot he had hidden away in the morning before, well covered with trees and shrubbery.

Rich put his hat on. He hated hats. Then he hauled the three bags of money along with a shovel to the spot he had spied the last two mornings. His Explorer was well out of sight, but he had a clear view to where Tom had parked his Porsche the last two mornings. He dug a hole about three feet deep and now would sit and wait.

So many things could go wrong, not the least

of which would be Tom not showing up! Rich had planned this piece of the puzzle for today so that he'd have two days to fall back on if something failed, but this was the best day. And would he have the nerve again if it were to be delayed?

Within a minute of yesterday's timing, Rich heard the roar of the air-cooled, evidently six cylinder Porsche tearing down Potomska Road. Rich took out his mirror, small enough to not be seen from the sixty yards between them. He strapped it around his head. Turning his back to where Tom would pull up, he began digging.

Tom pulled up, revved the engine once and turned it off. Cool drivers do that. Rich heard the door open and shut and then captured Tom's image in his mirror. Rich tried to make a scraping noise, but it wasn't very good. He dug in hard and fast, trying to create a noise. In his mirror he still didn't see Tom notice him. Rich began to grunt slightly as he dug in hard with each repetition. Three grunts and hard shovel strokes later, Tom turned toward the curious noise.

Rich observed a shaky image of Tom in his mirror, the mirror shaking, not Tom. It was more difficult than he had imagined to keep Tom in view. But through the shakes and oscillations, Rich could determine that Tom's attention was firmly fixed on Rich's area now. Gotcha! Wasting no time, Rich threw his shovel down and quickly grabbed the three bags, throwing them into the pit. Confirming that Tom was still watching, Rich picked up the shovel again and started furiously covering the bags. By now Tom was almost out of sight. Rich thought he lost him, then saw Tom crouching low trying not to be seen. Rich watched as Tom's head would bob up and down, left and right, trying to hide but not miss anything.

Rich had been the curious one at Horseneck Beach last Monday when he saw the money being buried, yet he remembered how the scene had held his attention, had held him spellbound, fixated. If it had that effect on him, Tom would be swept into the intrigue of the whole scene as well. He couldn't help but be proud of his little plan, which was now working like the proverbial charm.

Rich had the hole filled in no time, then packed down the topsoil and pretended to look around, scouting for unwanted observers. Tom ducked down in what he thought was a cool, smooth action. Rich saw him duck and could see his image behind the well lit, inadequate shrub he chose for cover, but he knew Tom would think that he had been fast enough. Rich stifled a laugh, re-scanned the horizon and made a visible nod to himself like he was satisfied.

Satisfied that his plan was working, Rich took the shovel and skulked off to his vehicle. Rich knew Tom would never follow him, so there was no worry about his Explorer being recognized. Tom's attention was fixated on the dig site.

Rich went back to his Explorer, tore Tweety Bird and his mirror off his head, and was quickly out and down the road. About a mile down the road, Rich slowed, turned around and drove quietly back. Returning to the hidden cove deep in the woods he had just come from, Rich got out and quietly snuck back. He withdrew his Bushnell binoculars.

Rich was pleasantly surprised. He had never in his life manipulated anyone but it was all working just as planned.

He watched Tom running around trying to find some implement he could use as a shovel. He picked up a branch and dug in with such enthusiasm, Rich had to admire him. Rich had purposely left the dirt loosely packed so Tom wouldn't have any problems uncovering the bags. After a few minutes, Tom pitched the branch away and started in with his hands. He grabbed the first bag firmly and pulled it out. Tom was thinking this has to be either drugs or money, hoping it was the former. Body parts never occurred to him. As Tom tore the bag open and stared, Rich thought he looked like a Buddhist monk prostrating himself. Tom, squatting in an unflattering manner, froze as he beheld the sight in front of him. He was probably praying, thanking whatever god he could have believed in for the incredible luck that was turned in his direction.

Tom had hoped for drugs, but the money appeased him. After examining the first bag, Tom hauled up the second, checked it out, then the third. He shot glances in all directions, making certain no one was seeing him. With no one in sight, Tom made his move. He hauled out the three bags and in one sweep ran to his Porsche. He flipped the trunk open, fit one bag in filling the trunk to capacity. With no other options, he put the other two bags in the front seat and did one more glance around, super-sleuth style, then hopped into his car and tore off. He wouldn't be jogging this morning.

He tore past the Wellington's, and with his pedal down, all six (?) cylinders screaming, Joseph and Mary awoke, as did the Wellington's.

Rich was relieved. The first crucial part of his plan had worked like a charm. Then fatigue set in and he collapsed in his drivers seat. He wouldn't wake up for three hours.

———————

Racing home, Tom was at first so excited, he could hardly stay on the road. Visions of wild spending and partying blinded him to the real world curves and bends in the road. He thought of celebrating with Debbie and traveling and getting the big boat they always wanted. He was so proud to finally be a real breadwinner! He didn't know how much money was there, but even Tom could tell it was an incredible sum.

But thinking about Debbie brought up an interesting dilemma. Should he tell her? She was getting more and more protective with her money, arguing over where their money should be spent. She had craftily siphoned off a small fortune from her last husband without his knowing it, so maybe Tom should protect himself.

Then he thought of the good times they could enjoy together. Wasn't that why they married? They were just right for each other, like two pieces of a puzzle, they fit together perfectly. When times were good for Tom and Debbie, times were very, very good. No one knew how to party like the two of them. Like Yin and Yang. It would be the right thing for him to share this treasure with her. It would be the noble thing. Should Tom's nobility ever be questioned, let this be the stick by which he be measured.

Tom burst through the door, waking Debbie up, but standing so proudly. He sang out, "Debbie, we're rich!", holding out one large, doubled-up green trash bag stuffed with cash.

Debbie was startled. She took in the blurry view of her husband standing there holding a garbage bag and claiming they hit the lottery or something. Thinking he had lost his mind, Debbie recoiled just slightly as Tom came closer. But the words began to penetrate.

"Debbie, it's full of money! Tons and tons! Look!" Tom turned the bag over and emptied the entire thing out onto her bed, showering Debbie with bills galore. For the first time in days, Debbie smiled. Then she screamed and laughed heartily.

"Where did you get this? Where's it from?"

"It's from some sucker who's going to be kicking

himself black and blue the day he comes back for it."
Tom loves bettering people.

"But who? What?"

"Deb, I have no idea, maybe a drug dealer, maybe a crook, maybe some old eccentric who doesn't trust banks. I never even seen him very clear. But as I was doing my warm-ups this morning, I could hear this scraping and grunting from in the woods. I turn to check it out and I see this guy digging a hole. I was almost going to ignore it, then I sees him take thre... I mean this trash bag stuffed with something and toss it into the hole. Then he quickly covers it over, looks all around like he didn't want no one to see him, and then leaves.

"So I jog on over, get a stick and uncover the hole. Can you believe it? Do you have any idea how much cash must be here?" He picked up a thousand dollar bill, the crispest one he could find, and handed it to Debbie. They were wild eyed for each other. This was the magic they used to feel.

"And the best thing, Deb," Tom was panting, "it's all tax free! We don't have to report it!"

Tom was referring to a little known statute that said if you found money in green garbage bags that were buried underground and was obviously some one else's, the government would exempt it from all taxation as the schmuck who buried it would be considered to be a grantor of a gift and in fact, therefore, the party whereof and thereof to be subject to withholdings, state, federal, local, city and ignorance taxes. Something like that. Any accountant Tom would hire would know the rule.

They laughed and screamed and threw money in the air. Tom rushed to the kitchen, raided their KichenAid and grabbed a bottle of cheap champagne. Running back to the bedroom, shaking the bottle on the run, Tom undid the wire mesh and popped the plastic cork. Champagne everywhere, flowing over the bottle, onto the money, onto the sheets, onto Debbie. She didn't mind. She scooted up on her knees toward Tom and put her lips around the mouth of the foaming bottle, guzzling the erupting champagne until it seemed to subside. Tom licked whatever was flowing down the sides of her mouth, then licked her lips. Lapping at Debbie, he pressed her until she fell back, laughing and giggling. Tom took a swig from the bottle and passed it to Debbie who took two swigs.

Tom's sweats were soaking with champagne so he took them off and removed his beat-up running shoes. They spent the rest of the morning absorbing cheap champagne, money and each other.

❧

Rich awoke after nine. The sun was hot already, probably right around eighty degrees. Through the trees the road would show an occasional sign of other drivers, a jogger or two, even a biker, but traffic was very light.

After shaking off the cobwebs, Rich put the Explorer in reverse and backed out to the road. Cruising down Potamska, the Wellington's place loomed ahead like a castle in some fantasyland. The sun was glinting off the water stretching endlessly from their back yard. The bay they lived on was calm.

Past the Wellington's Rich could see some sort of roadblock. Three Dartmouth Police cars were parked to the side and four State Police cars were in the street. An F.B.I. car was parked on the front lawn.

Rich's first thought was of an accident. Could it have been Tom? Fear seized him. His whole plan would be down the tubes and the money gone, all because of Tom's fourth grade driving skills.

As he passed, he scanned the area for signs of an accident but detected none. A State Trooper directed him around and he could see all the action was at the house.

With his angle changing he could see the side porch and several groups of people, five or six in all. Each group seemed to consist of two or three law enforcement officers surrounding a handcuffed citizen. They were being questioned separated from each other. Then, just as he was about to clear the area, he saw two officers carrying out bales of clear plastic packages stuffed with what appeared to be white, crystallized powder. Rich recognized it from movies. Heroin. Or coke. Whatever.

Rich couldn't believe it. This should get Anne Wellington good and wound up for tomorrow's party.

With all those guests scheduled for tomorrow, the timing could not have been better for a neighbor to be busted. Rich was happy for her.

The Dartmouth Police Department had their hands full on this sunny, beach-perfect Saturday. The influx of tourists who swell the town's population on any given hot summer day, taxing the department's resources to the fullest every weekend, was only going to be the worse on this, the first perfect Saturday of the season. Adding to Captain Hernandes problems was the State Police Department's decision to choose today, of all days, for closing the trap they had been setting for the last few months.

For three months, State Police were working closely with the Dartmouth Police, keeping the home of Ricardo Montero under surveillance. Of Hispanic origin, born in Columbia, Ricardo could pass for a good-looking light Italian and had all but overcome any noticeable accent. Ricardo had an early brush with the law the first year after moving up from Long Island. It was just a minor disturbance matter, the result of a wild party, but then new Officer Bill Ryan handled the matter discreetly and helped Ricardo dodge a bullet.

By late winter, the Massachusetts State Police contacted Captain Hernandes with information that alarmed Hernandes and would keep his men busy for three months. Ricardo Montero was reportedly a rapidly rising kingpin in the northeast drug empire. Besides trafficking in some of the largest shipments ever seen in the northeast, he also pushed packets right out of his home, supplying to the white-collar society of Dartmouth, Westport and surrounding communities. He let the grunts push the high volume in the cities and slums, while he handled "direct retail" to a higher class of users at premium rates and wildly incredible margins.

Ricardo had bought the bungalow, modest for the area, but perfect in its location for his purposes. It was set on a quiet stretch of road and had no neighbors in direct view.

He used an old newspaper tube as a drop box. Each client was assigned a specific hour of day so as to avoid paths crossing. When the client wanted a pick-up they would send e-mail to Ricardo's secure site, simply stating the hour, no name, code or details, just the hour. At precisely ten past the hour, Ricardo or one of his people would walk to the tube and pick up the money. No money, no honey. If the money was in the nest a second trip would be made to plant the package. Ricardo's people would never be caught in a direct exchange. The pick-up was then the responsibility of the client. If they didn't show by half past, the package would be retrieved with no refunds.

One client stood out as they managed surveillance over the weeks, Dartmouth resident, Thomas

Cochrane of Padanaram. One of Ricardo's most regular clients, he routinely jogged by most mornings and always on Saturdays.

When Hernandes heard that the State Police wanted to pull the sting on Saturday, he objected to the drain on manpower. But the State Police assured him that Cochrane always made his pick-up around six o'clock and the whole affair would be over by seven or seven thirty, eight at the latest. Hernandes gave in.

Imagine everyone's surprise when Tom Cochrane didn't jog by on that perfect Saturday morning.

Confusion ensued as they all pondered what to do when Cochrane never showed. One officer, Jane Humbolt, was sure it was Cochrane she saw speeding by in his red Porsche at his expected pick-up time. Her superiors ignored her. The decision was made to hold position until the next client came by, whatever time that might be.

With Hernandes simmering in a slow stew, all twelve officers involved had to stay in their positions until another client surfaced. They were sure it would happen, but no one could tell when. On a hot day like this, it made for interesting sweat patterns on everyone's uniforms as they were forced to remain in tight hiding conditions throughout the grassy areas. By the time the first client finally made his pick-up at about eight twenty, it was a ripe and ornery crowd of law enforcement agents they would have to deal with.

Somehow through the din of partying and the blaring music, Tom heard the phone ringing and since it wouldn't stop in spite of his blatantly ignoring it, he picked up. Debbie danced on.

"Hey, Tom here." He recognized the voice, always good for the inside scoop. "Yeah, how you doing Billy? ... Say what? ... Busted?... this morning? ... Get out! ... No, No. ... No, I didn't!"

Tom was hearing about the bust for the first time, while it was still going on. Bill wouldn't be able to talk long. Tom's extremely good fortune in not getting busted was not missed by either of them.

"Bill, this is the first Saturday since I hooked up that I didn't pick up, can you imagine? Thought I might tick off Montero really big time after e-mailing him, but something more important came up. ... I can't believe it, the whole house? ... Montero wasn't? No fooling... He wasn't even there. Lucky pusher, I guess... No, no. Don't worry, I'll find us another."

Tom hung up in disbelief. Not out of concern for any of his associates now looking at twenty to thirty, nor for his counterpart, the poor guy who e-mailed for an eight o'clock pick-up and got nailed. Tom was in disbelief over his incredible luck!

His thoughts turned quickly to the other two bags of money he had stuffed in an empty trashcan in the garage. He would hide the bags in a more secure location when Deb wasn't around. Meanwhile, he was thankful to the powers that be for protecting him, cradling him, shielding him from harm. Yes, Tom was in fact chosen. The events of this day proved that.

"Who was that?" Debbie asking.

"Oh, just the office. I may have a closing Monday or Tuesday."

Debbie nodded, happy to see that Tom was taking his work more seriously, but more so because the spark seemed to be back. It wasn't the money; to Debbie it didn't strike her as all that important. She was good for over a million, even though Tom didn't know it. But it was Tom that she wanted back. She left a prosperous, contented, and yes, even a happy home for Tom and if he didn't get back to being his old flaming, passionate and vigorous self, what would the point have been?

Tom grabbed Debbie and danced a tango type step to an entirely inappropriate tune, but they were pretty well sloshed by now. They tangoed their way back out to the deck. Debbie and the Chosen One.

CHAPTER 12

Saturday Afternoon

With the morning's success, Rich felt surprisingly rejuvenated in spite of his missed sleep. Pulling to his apartment he ran upstairs, changed, and threw his sweats, cap and the mirror in the trash. He wondered if Carlo would be as easy. He was definitely a more formidable challenge than Tom, but the result today was encouraging. Rich could begin stage two.

Feeling the burst of energy he had never expected, Rich got involved in a few bachelor chores. His bills needed paying and he had squirreled away enough to attack them.

In the middle of writing his fifth check he became distracted by some odd truck sounds coming from the front of his apartment. Needing to stretch anyway,

Rich got up and took a look out the window and did a double-take. His Explorer! On the back of a tow truck!

"HEYYY! WHAT, WHAT'RE YOU DOIN?", he screamed.

A blonde, longhaired grease monkey in oily coveralls and no shirt looked up, grinning into the sun to where the sound was coming from. Needed a shave. And two front teeth.

"Got an order to tow her away." The monkey reached in his back pocket and waived a crumpled, black oil spotted, folded paper. It made sense. The installment loan was two layers further down in his pile of bills.

"STINK, MAN!!! DON'T GO ANYWHERE, I'M COMIN DOWN!"

He flew down in three seconds.

"Look," Rich was imploring. Begging, most would call it. "Please, please, please. I've got the money, just got it two days ago. I can write a check, pay cash, anything! You name it. I need this car. I need it tonight, I need it tomorrow." Tomorrow! Rich's heart sank. Tomorrow he has the date of his life! How can he pick up Gail without wheels?

"Aww, sorry man. I understand. Had two repo'd on me." He spit, in the manly way that mechanics and construction workers figure out. He could really relate. "Bummer. Sometimes I wonder why I even do this, but, you know, it's a job," he lamented.

"But I can pay! I've got the money! Why take it now? It will just cost everyone that much more."

The monkey laughed. "It'll cost *you* more, you mean. We all get paid and you're the poor stiff's gotta make it all up." But there was a sincerity, a camaraderie, from one dead-beat to another. "Look, you'll be able to get it back next week sometime. You'll have to cover the tow and storage charges, plus catch up your payments. Probably some legal fees, bonds and what not. But if you have the money, couple, few days, you're back on wheels man." He punched Rich on the shoulder.

"Look, I'll pay it. I'll pay it all now. I need the vehicle, BIG-TIME! Don't do this to me, please." Then he tried the calm approach. "Wha'da'ya say."

That should do it, Rich figured. Two guys bonding, each having had their troubles and tight spots, surely he'll understand and cut him some slack. Men are that way.

"I can't man. It's my job."

And so Richard Lewis stood a broken man on the shoulder of the street in front of his second story tenement that he could hardly afford, oil smudged court order folded in his hand, watching his Explorer wind it's way deeper into the belly of New Bedford. Insultingly being carried on the bed of "Joe's Tow" truck, it wasn't even afforded the dignity of turning itself in on it's own power. Humiliated on this fine, sunny, Saturday afternoon that had started out so promising.

As Rich turned to go in his eyes met the faces of Ellen and her family, one member per window staring out in awe at the sight that had just unfolded.

Two bottles of champagne and a few shooters of Grand Marnier and the Cochranes were ready for a little sack time. They would need to be rejuvenated for their dinner tonight, the official celebration dinner that would mark the passing of their "hard" times and the revival of their undying love for each other. Everything was right in the world today.

Debbie was on cloud nine seeing her relationship with Tom rejuvenated. How terrible it would have been if she went through all she had with Rich, only to have Tom ruin this relationship.

"Tom," Debbie called. "Come here, to bed."

"Yeah, Hon." Tom giggled back, a little tipsy from the champagne and shooters. "Let me make a couple of calls first. Be right there, babe."

Tom was in a dazed stupor listening to the ringing signal in his receiver. He shook his head rapidly, thinking that dispels alcohol. He'd have to speak as cryptically as possible in the remote chance that the lines were bugged, but Tom knew how to get a message across without spelling out every detail.

"Hey, Bobby. Tom here." … "Yeah, well listen. Something's come up." … "No, there won't be a delivery today. Serious problem." … "Calm down, calm down… I know it's Saturday, but when I say big problems, I mean big." … "Look, man, I need to locate another river." … "River. Man do I have to spell it out? Another source." What a dufus, not figuring that out. "Look, you can probably read about it, but the bottom dot is, I didn't pick up. You get it?" … "Well, I don't need your business anyway so pack it up and stick it where there's sunshine!"

Or something like that, it didn't matter. For the first time in his life Tom didn't need to make these connections, risking his life and freedom for a measly few hundred. This morning he became a free man.

Tom lay back in the plush sofa and hung up the phone. He was so tired from all the excitement today; he was beginning to come down feeling his whole body going limp. His mind kept drifting off to another plane. But Debbie waits. Down the hall. She waits. As Tom sleeps.

———❦———

If you want to see a pathetic sight, find a man who once had it all, happy wife, money, profession, respect, and who lived in a storybook house that he designed and built himself, but who's now living in a run-down, second floor tenement, broke, alone, in trouble with the law _and_ the crooks, and who's just had his vehicle repo'd before his very eyes. A lesser man would break.

As would Rich, but he didn't have the time. He had to get a car. For tomorrow, which meant today because tomorrow would be too late. And since he only had one friend in the world, albeit a friend that he paid by the hour for every conversation they had, it didn't take Rich long to figure out whom to call.

Alan was having a wonderful day. His daughter and son-in-law, who Alan actually liked, were visiting and the grand kids were warming the cockles of Alan's heart. These were the moments he lived for.

They were toasting marshmallows on the outdoor grill when the call came, Alan trimming sticks to spear the little things, showing the girls how to avoid spontaneous combustion by being a little patient.

"This is Alan."

"Alan, sorry to bother you at home like this. I hope I'm not disturbing anything." Rich was nervous.

"Hi Rich, well, you know, just playing with the grand daughters. This is what I've worked for."

"Wow, and what a great day for it! Are you having a barbecue?"

"Oh yeah. Perfect day for one."

"Really! That's great. Great." Rich was waiting for inspiration. "And how's your wife?"

"She couldn't be happier to have the family up for the week."

"Oh, that's nice. How long are they in town for?"

Alan looked at the phone. What's all this about?

"They leave Tuesday. It will be a week then."

"A week. Boy, that's great." A little pause. "That's great."

Alan put up a hand for his granddaughters,

signaling that he'd be just a few minutes. Then back to Rich.

"Rich, uh, what's up?"

Rich hung his head. There would be no smooth way to do this.

"They took my Explorer."

"Your Explorer! Took it? You mean, like in repossessed?"

"Right, right. Exactly like that." Rich gritted his teeth and rolled his eyeballs.

"Oh, Rich. Rich. That's terrible."

"My fault. Entirely my fault. I've had money since Wednesday, well Monday if you want to include..." Rich hesitated.

"Hey, I'm in." Alan conceded. "No reason to avoid the subject, but thanks."

"So I've had money since Monday. I should have gotten right on it. Would you believe, I was about five minutes away from writing their check when I hear this grinding noise out in front of my apartment. I look out my window to see New Bedford's version of Fabio reeling in my Explorer like it's the catch of the day."

Alan was in awe. How much more trouble can this guy take?

"Did you try to stop him?" Alan asked.

"No. I went down and washed and waxed his truck while he was reeling my Explorer in." Rich didn't mean to be sarcastic with Alan, it was meant

in humor. "Of course I tried. But, 'It was his job'."
Rich made an effort to sing "job" like Fabio had.

"Are you all right, Rich? Your voice sounds a
little funny."

"No, I'm not all right. I had one thing left in life
and God sent somebody to get it today!"

Alan did see the humor, but it seemed more
appropriate to dispense some fatherly advice and
consoling.

"Well, you'll get it back. It'll cost you a little
more, but you've got it."

"Yeah, but it shook me up." Then Rich asked
a stupid question. "Have you ever gotten a car
repossessed?"

Alan looked at the receiver. Then he said, "Rich,
I'm an attorney."

Stupid question.

"Rich, you'll get it back easily, you've got the
money. What's the big deal?"

"Alan, the big deal is tomorrow. The Wellingtons.
I'm supposed to be at their party."

Now he remembered. Of course, the Wellingtons
and "Architectural Digest", "Boston" magazine
and "Conde' Nast" and about ten other prestigious
publications.

"Rich, get a cab. There's nothing wrong with
that. Or better yet, hire a limo! Everyone does that
now, it would be a great way to arrive."

A limo. Now that was a possibility, Rich had never
thought of that. But he needed to do an errand or two

tonight, plus he'd absolutely need a car Wednesday and there would be no guarantee the Explorer could post bail by then. No, he needed to know today that a car was available.

"That's a good thought, Alan. But, without going into it, I need wheels. What am I going to do, hire a limo to go down and wash my shorts. I'm a bachelor, I've got a million errands to do. Alan, I need a car."

"I see your point. But I don't know what I can do." Alan wasn't trying to give Rich the brush off. He was really pondering what he could do. "If my family weren't visiting, I'd loan you my wife's Volvo. But they're using it every day. If my wife's not, my daughter is, if she's not, my son-in-law is, and if he's not, my grand daughters are". That was a good one for Alan.

"I know, I know. Alan, I wouldn't want to put your wife out anyway. I, I was thinking I should rent one."

"Well, great idea! Why didn't I think of that?"

There was a pause. Alan was trying to be so helpful, but just wasn't getting the picture.

"Alan, I can't do it on my own. Nobody would rent to me."

"Why not? You worried about your past credit record? Bring cash! Lord knows you've got enough." Alan thought that was funny.

"Nobody will rent unless there's a credit card."

"Yeah. So?"

"Alan, I told you. I lost all my credit cards this last year. I don't have one."

"Even your American Express? You were platinum for crying out loud!"

"That was the first to go." That hurt remembering how he lived on the card and lost a half million points when they took it.

"You mean they just take a platinum? They don't downgrade you gradually?" As wise as Alan is, he's still learning how some parts of it work. There was another pause while Alan pondered the situation. Surely there was something he could do. Rich had become like a son these last few months. Help him. Do something. Think of something.

"How about I rent a car for you?"

That's what Rich wanted to hear, but didn't have the nerve to come right out and ask.

"Alan, would you? I'd owe you my life."

"Well, I'll settle for my bill. Right now, it may be worth more." Only Rich would think that funny and not take offense. "Let me break away for an hour. What time is it now?"

"Two thirty."

"Okay, let me come get you and take you to a rental agency."

"Alan, what can I say? I'm forever indebted."

But that wasn't everything. Rich thought of his date with Gail tomorrow. He didn't want to be stuck in an Escort or a Neon. Please not that.

"Alan, one thing. You know I'm not a status seeker or an ego maniac, right?"

"No, not at all. Maybe just the maniac part."

"Well, you know me, I'd settle for anything. But tomorrow, the Wellingtons? I really don't want to show up in a Neon."

"I don't follow."

Rich hated to be so picky on such a generous offer of Alan's.

"I need an upgrade, something with a little style. Besides, I can pay you immediately, whatever you want."

"Oh, there's no need for that. But I really doubt that anyone's going to notice what you drive up in. Just tell them it's a loaner, everyone does that a few times in their life."

There was only one way to do this, Rich thought.

"Alan." Pause. "I'm taking Gail."

Rich thought Alan dropped the phone. He dropped something. There were a few seconds of jumbling and odd noises, followed by an equal time of silence.

"Alan, you all right?"

"Oh, yes. Yes. I just dropped the grill."

"The grill?"

"Yeah, no harm done." After a short pause, a warmer tone, "Gail?"

Rich smiled. "Somebody's got to mix my martini."

"Rich, that's great. Gail. She's a special one.

Don't know her well, but, what can I say, I'm happy for you."

"First date in sixteen years. Do you see why I want the upgrade?"

"No problem. Maybe a nice Contour or something. You know, mid-size."

A Contour. "Yeah, Alan, mid-size. Thanks for your help. You know where I live?"

Rich hung up a scared man. When you only have one friend in the world, it's nice when that friend comes through. But would he really be picking up his dream date in an Contour? Lord have mercy.

CHAPTER 13

Saturday at Carlo Bartelli's

This Saturday had started out so wonderfully perfect, it was hard for Carlo Bartelli to understand what went so wrong so fast. Like his week didn't start off bad enough, losing 28.8 million dollars of "family" money and not getting what he was supposed to. Then having to bury it, along with the stiff that stiffed him by dropping dead from a coronary. *Di male in peggio!* No, the week hadn't start out rosy at all.

But today was to be special for it was Saturday, the day for Carlo to traditionally cook and show-off to friends and family. He would simply wait until Monday to worry about the botched drug deal.

Rising at 5:45, like any other day, Carlo did his six

laps around the pool. As Carlo was exiting the pool, Cartello, his right hand man, street adopted brother, and top soldier passed him as usual. Cartello, or The "C", as he'd been known for forty or so years, would do thirty laps before calling it quits until his evening session of thirty more. At fifty years of age, The "C" was as fit as any man in his thirties, and as most in their twenties.

"Beautiful morning! I think today will bring progress in our search." Carlo didn't let little things like a missing $28.8 mil get him down for long. His anger would flare up when the moment was right, when they had their thief.

The "C" nodded his head in acknowledgment, then dove in. He never spoke. Never. Virtually orphaned at birth, and raised in the streets of North Boston, The "C" never had a lot to say. He was only nine when Carlo, seventeen, "adopted" him first into his genetic family and then into his other "family", gaining The "C"'s loyalty for life. Whether there was a medical reason for his muteness or a psychological one, no one ever determined. It really didn't matter. Judging from some of The "C"'s outbursts, the world was probably better off not hearing from him.

So leaving The "C" to his own designs, Carlo showered, changed and busied himself in the kitchen. Francesca, the maid, knew enough to stay well out of Carlo's way. If he ruled the eastern crime organization with an iron fist, the kitchen was ruled with a titanium one.

Today's fare would be his special home-made meatballs and sauce, which he had begun the evening before. And to distract him from his problematic week, his wife's favorite, Sicilian style Bracciole! Carlo kisses his fingertips every time he speaks the words.

This morning was sad because his wife, Carmella, would not be joining them. How seldom, if ever, had that happened through the last thirty-one years? Carlo adored his wife, loved her with all his life. They rarely were separated for an entire day, never a week! But considering the money lost, he would never put Carmella at risk. He sent her up to Boston to stay with family until the storm passed.

Adorned this sunny morning in his white apron with the words, "Italian Stallion" boldly emblazoned in orange across the front, Carlo was easing his special meatballs into the sauce when the first call came. It was only 7:45.

"Mr. Bartelli?" Carlo recognized the voice, it was Ricco Carlotti, from Chicago. Top soldier for the Capo D'Accusa, translated, "The Law", Vito Gentilianni.

"Ricco, how are you this fine, bright morning? Yes, this is Carlo."

"Carlo, Mr. Gentilianni asked that I place this call to you first thing this morning. I trust I did not wake you?"

"*Mio Manicomio!* Of course not. I am the stallion! I arise early with the sun!"

"Good. Mr. Gentilianni wanted me to inform

you of his departure early this morning for the New Bedford airport. Mr. Gentilianni would like to visit with you this morning and be your guest for a few days to make personal inquiry as to the nature of some diverted funds." Ricco actually seemed to be enjoying this.

"New Bedford Airport? Here? Today?" Carlo was startled.

"That is correct. His Citation is scheduled to arrive at 9:38 this morning and a limo will be waiting to take him to your residence. Do you have a problem with that?"

Carlo was confused and somewhat insulted. He and Vito had been very close through the years. Even earlier in the week, when Carlo informed Vito of the "temporary" loss of funds, there was confidence in Carlo's ability to recover the missing funds. So why this visit?

"No. No, that will not be a problem. I'll very much look forward to meeting with him. I would have been glad to meet him at the airport if you had only called and informed me."

"I'll contact Mr. Gentilianni and tell him that you're expecting him. Thank you."

Carlo couldn't help but wonder about the formality in Ricco's voice. Is Carlo Bartelli not to be trusted any more? Do they think maybe Carlo Bartelli is pulling a double cross? Perhaps they think the Stallion is ready for glue. If it were anyone but Vito, Carlo would be enraged.

The second call came in at 9:50, just as Vito's limousine was pulling into the driveway. Carlo was removing his apron in order to greet Vito as Francesca hailed him to take the call.

"Hello, Carlo here." The impatience in his voice was clear.

"Mr. Bartelli, this is Officer Ryan, Bill Ryan?" He waited for an acknowledgment.

"Yes, yes. I'm very busy right now. What is it?"

"I have to be brief anyway, but thought you'd want to know that the Fed's just pulled a raid on Ricardo Montero's house. Took out a truckload of drugs and made quite a few arrests. No Montero though." Ryan was nervous and rushing his words. "I've gotta be careful, tell you more later."

The news shook Carlo. Could Montero be having a worse week than he was? Did someone drop the dime on him? He would need more information. He shook off the questions and put on his stoical front as he went to greet Vito.

"Ciao! Fratello." The two Itlaianos embraced. Carlo was genuinely glad to see Vito, he went back as far as with anyone and had always done well by him, as evidenced by the two million dollar mansion serving as a backdrop for this reunion.

"Carlo, my dear Carlo!" Vito was smiling warmly.

"What a surprise! A very pleasant surprise," Carlo was gushing. "Only an hour ago I was informed of your visit and I ask myself, 'Such an honor! Why honor me in this way?'"

Accompanying Vito Gentilianni were two of his most loyal "becchinos" through the years, translated meaning "grave diggers". They probably never dug a grave in their life but the label was most appropriate as a description of cause if not action. Emilio and Valentine Sciacco stood quietly and respectfully observing the niceties and protocol of two long-standing friends and cameratas. They also observed The "C" standing in the doorway, quiet and respectful in his own way. The three had always wondered who might prevail should the winds of war ever blow against them. The emotionless stares between them perpetuated the question.

Exiting the limo, now that the driver had finally made his way around the front of the car and back the twenty feet necessary to reach the door, was an attractive, long-legged redhead. Dressed to the nines and displaying unabashed disdain for current fashion codes in her high stiletto pumps, she was anticipating a helping hand from the driver for the formidable task of standing up. Patience pays as the driver caught on three seconds later and assisted her up.

"Carlito, may I present my very efficient and very beautiful secretary, Jackie." Vito was beaming as he made her introduction.

"Jackie!" taking her hand and kissing it softly, "It is an honor and privilege to make your acquaintance. Welcome to my home. I wish you a long and happy stay and I insist, please, make yourself at home. My home is yours, your wish, our command." Carlo never trusted beautiful women.

With everyone honored and put to ease, Carlo ushered the group toward his home, onto the veranda and through the entryway.

"And where is 'La Cuore' (the heart), Carmella? Is she in good health?"

"Oh, yes, yes. Absolutely! 'Il Mio Cuore", is doing very, very well." Carlo swelled with pride just referring to her. "But a small family crisis has called her away to New Jersey."

"Tsk, tsk, tsk. What a shame, we will miss her." Vito couldn't remember Carmella not being home. Ever. It had never dawned on him until this moment, but any memory that he had of her in the last thirty-one years, the length of her marriage to Carlo, was always in their home.

It hit everyone the moment they passed through the entryway doors. The aroma of the sugo (sauce) throughout the house mingled in with the scent of herbs and veal slowly sautéing, blending with the smell of fresh bread baking and Sicilian style Braciole simmering, all wafting through the still air of the house. An occasional ocean breeze would gently usher the entire air mass into the farthest corners of the house bringing newer and stronger replacement scents with it. Carlo beamed with pride.

"And for how long shall you honor my home with your presence, Vito?"

"That depends. We must talk."

Carlo didn't like that. Having to talk had its own drama.

"Then let me have Francesca show you all to your rooms. Then you may relax and enjoy our facilities and the afternoon. It's going to be a perfect New England summer day! Enjoy. Get settled in and Francesca will get you all some wine."

With the chauffeur and Jackie bubbling away in the outdoor Jacuzzi and Emilio and Valentine running up the stakes in some sloppy eight-ball, Carlo knew that this might be his only opportunity to speak with Vito privately. He broke tradition and assigned Francesca the duty of watching the stove after teaching her the subtleties of separating the 'polpettas' (meatballs), *without* force. This allowed Carlo and Vito to stroll the back lawn and talk.

"It was smart of you to call immediately. Any hesitancy or delay would not have been interpreted very well." Vito was broaching the subject.

"It was not my money, but the family's. I was doing my job and had nothing to hide."

"Or to report?"

Carlo had to swallow on this one. "Or to report."

"That is not good news."

"Vito, it took a few days to spread the net and

prepare for the catch. But the net is now cast. We will not come up empty handed."

"Tell me what happened." Vito was pulling for Carlo and had only heard partially the distressing story of the missing fortune.

"You are aware of the deal. $28.8 million, cash only, in exchange for eight tons of pure coke, safely delivered to our shores and ready for pick up. But you know Montero. Nothing can be easy with him.

"It was set up for Monday. The money filled two suitcases, and that was only because we used one thousand dollar bills." At this point, Carlo studied Vito's eyes, hoping for some recognition of the enormity of the task. Carlo had to dig into his private trove of thousand dollar bills that had been passed through three generations of Mafioso family. The "organization" had a penchant for cash in the early days, and thousand dollar bills had been readily available back then. When Bartelli inherited the reigns of control for the northeast, he had all this money in his control. Nobody, not even the government, had that many thousand-dollar bills. Bartelli would never have used them if it weren't for the quirky demands of this Colombian dealer, Montero, who insisted on cash that he could carry. The only way to condense that much cash was to make the payment up in all thousand-dollar bills.

"We were to make the exchange with Montero's courier at one of my properties in Fall River. We were to receive a computer disk with our instructions for the pick-up. Montero kept his distance. If we all got busted, there would be no tracing anything back to him. Even the disk would be useless because a password was needed, which we would get from the courier only *after* the exchange was safely made."

Vito admired Montero's thoroughness. "Very smooth. Very smooth."

"I had the warehouse staked out with a small army, but the courier never knew. Never saw anyone but my two mules, Tony and Marty and myself. What *muscarados!* Anyway, this courier was kind of a pudgy guy, pale, sweaty, nervous. But formalities are formalities and we had to frisk him down. So Tony, the big guy, tries to act intimidating and for once in his life, did a good job of it. *Managela!* Of all times to impress someone he means business!

"All of a sudden, this courier's breathing hard, wheezing and looking even paler than when we first saw him. Next thing you know, he's falling to his knees, vomiting and hitting the concrete floor like he's had one too many Marciano cocktails. I couldn't believe it, Vito! Honest, the guy croaks right in front of us! And we didn't do a thing, you know? Nothing!"

Carlo had to pause while his eye rolled heavenly and then he needed to rub his temples and shake off the frustration he was feeling. He continued.

"So we're standing there at the location that _we_ had insisted on, with the people _we_ had insisted on, with all this cash and the disk, but the messenger is dead! You know what that's going to look like? Like we planned a double-cross! With the guy dead and the money gone, Montero's bound to think we beat the password out of him, so we're looking bad and Montero's fitting us for coffins!

"Montero can't be contacted because that's his M.O., it would take us days to make that connection again, but he was expecting two suitcases of cash within the hour or he'd be sending out the troops. Vito, it would have been war!

"So I thought of a place I use off and on when I need to hide something for a while. A stretch of dunes down near Horseneck that's well hidden, it's as good a hiding place as any. I've used it a dozen times through the years."

"Why not the warehouse?" inquired Vito.

"Too risky. Kids run through there at nights. Police stick their noses in, sometimes looking for the kids, other times looking for something on me." It seemed to satisfy Vito.

Carlo continued. "So I tell Tony and Marty to bury the money with the courier and the disk still in his pocket, it was no good to us anyway. This way, we're not holding nothing, the courier's got the money and the disk. What could anyone blame on us? The main thing is to make a show of the fact that we were ready to give the courier the money and we didn't do any funny stuff! Let Montero do an autopsy and confirm it was the guys ticker that done him in, not us.

"I gave explicit instructions to Tony exactly where to go and told Marty to keep an eye out. Even loaned them The "C's car, theirs wouldn't have made it out of town."

"A simple plan," concluded Vito, "that simply failed."

They mulled over the events and the attempts to find the person who reported the body and absconded with the money. Vito couldn't really fault Carlo on anything, but the bottom line was that $28.8 mil had to be recovered.

"Carlo, my friend. You have been like a son to me. But son or no son, we have got to recover the Family's investment."

Words that needn't be said.

"Time." Vito was resting one hand on Carlo's shoulder and talking very fatherly to him. "I will give you time. Until Thursday, that's five days. But Carlo, come Thursday I must be back in Chicago and, if there is no recovery, I'm afraid that you must return with me."

The Thought scared Carlo. In a jet?

⸺⬦⬦⬦⬦⸺

The final kicker came just after dinner. It was Officer Ryan.

"Good evening, Mr. Bartelli." Bill Ryan loved it when he could meet with Carlo in person. "I'm sorry for disturbing your evening."

"Nonsense, it's good to see you." Bartelli waved

his hand as if it were nothing, but thought this better be good.

Ryan noticed Vito, the old man, and figured him for a relative or some hanger-on benefiting from Carlo's prosperity. Ryan turned a shoulder to Vito as if to say, "I need to talk with someone important." He really should read the papers more.

"I wanted to follow up on our brief conversation this morning." Ryan anticipated a private meeting.

"Of course. I was expecting some sort of follow up." Carlo ushered Ryan and Vito into a private office. Ryan was surprised he had included the old man.

As they settled in different leather chairs, Ryan motioned with his eyes toward Vito. "It's all right to talk here?"

Carlo nodded his approval. "This is Vito Gentilianni. Vito, meet Dartmouth Police Officer, Bill Ryan." Ryan didn't recognize the name.

"Pleased to meet you." Ryan nodded quickly at Vito, then turned back to Carlo. "About the incident this morning, I was able to call Montero before the stakeout."

So, Montero had been home. He missed a bullet.

"That's good. Will he be tied into the operation?"

"I doubt it. He'll claim they were houseguests and deny responsibility. He'll claim he was never home, that always was the set-up." Then Ryan confirmed Carlo's suspicions, "He wonders who dropped the dime though."

"I don't blame him." Carlo was being truthful.

"That's the first thing I wondered. Does he smell a rat?"

Ryan shrugged his shoulders. "I tried to tell him it was a sting operation from the Feds, but you know Montero, always suspicious. Yeah, he smells a rat."

"Any suspects?" This was why Carlo kept him on the payroll.

"Actually, two suspects," Ryan loved this, "and both live right here in Padanaram."

Carlo sighed. One must be him, Carlo would think it himself if he didn't know better.

"Padanaram? Pretty small town to have two suspects, don't you think?" Carlo was hoping for some insight.

"Yeah, it's a small town. But we live in a small world." Clever for Ryan.

"Who does he think?"

Ryan smiled smugly. "You can ask him yourself."

That took Carlo back. "How?"

"Wants to meet with you Monday, privately"

A set-up for an ambush? "Where does he want to meet?"

"In Providence, up on the Hill. La Cantina at one o'clock."

"We'll be there." Carlo was surprised Montero chose Italian territory.

Ryan couldn't fathom why Vito was being included. He leaned to Carlo and said in a low voice, but clearly heard by Vito, "Montero wants the meeting alone. Ditch the old man."

"Bill, this is Vito Gentilianni, capo d'accusa. Where I go, he goes." Finally, Ryan knew he had blown it. "Please tell Mr. Montero that we will be glad to meet with him on Monday, at one o'clock."

Ryan was excused while Carlo and Vito continued alone.

"Montero thinks you double crossed him in the warehouse, stole his money and his drugs and then tried to set him up this morning." Vito was reviewing what there was really no need to. "Yet you are willing to meet with him on his terms? And bring me?"

Carlo had to laugh at the last part. "You wouldn't miss it for the world and you know it."

Vito also had to smile. At his age, the excitement far outweighed the risk.

As Carlo recapped the events of the day in his bed, he realized that his beloved Carmella would have to remain low for a while longer. Unless he could smooth things over with Montero, and make progress in recovering the missing money, things would be too hot around here. It pained him to have to sleep alone, but comforted him to know she was safe in Boston. He had told everyone she was in New Jersey.

CHAPTER 14

Saturday Evening

"How sure are you that it was Cochrane?" Tony Hernandes was asking Jane Homboldt, the only other officer on the scene willing to stay this late.

"It was him! I'd know his car anywhere. Few enough red Porsche Boxsters around, but how many with gold trim detail?"

Homboldt was certain it was Tom tearing down the street as they laid in wait earlier that morning. Most women in Padanaram knew who he was.

"He had to be tipped off." Hernandes wanted to nail Tom Cochrane in a bad way. Most men in Dartmouth, especially in Padanaram, have also heard about him.

"Or maybe he did the tipping," Homboldt suggested.

That was hard for Hernandes to accept. "What would be in it for him? He'd lose his supplier!"

"Maybe he didn't need a supplier anymore."

Jane thought it was implausible for Tom to be tipped off. Who on the force was Tom's friend? He was more likely the one to do the ratting.

"Maybe he found another source." Jane answered. "Blow the whistle on Montero and get rid of competition."

"That's a possibility," Hernandes conceded. "Let's leave it until we have more to go on."

———————◆—◆—◆—◆———————

Rich had called Gail and informed her he wouldn't be coming by tonight. His tiredness had caught him after Alan had picked him up and gotten him wheels. He had pulled off the stunt of his life this morning with Tom, hit the lowest point of his life with the repo, groveled to Alan for a car, and still had some work ahead of him tonight, making a sign. So after getting directions to Gail's house, and being called a Palanga for not coming by tonight, Rich turned on the six o'clock news for an update before tackling his sign.

The lead story was the drug bust. The report described the three-month stakeout, the overabundance of law enforcement officials involved, the surprisingly large supply of coke confiscated and the disappointment of not apprehending the main suspect, native Colombian Ricardo Montero, no warrant issued for his arrest yet. No tie-in to earlier events of the week was made, but Rich sensed something there was. No matter, he had more work to do and tomorrow would be crucial.

CHAPTER 15

Sunday Morning

Normally, Rich would cut his route at Court Street but decided to push it to Allen Street, then up Hathaway. This would give him the extra mile and he can start matching Tom's run. It bugged him.

On this sunny, hazy day, perfect for the Wellington's bash, the streets of New Bedford were vacant. Rich came across only one living stray cat and two street derelicts, life status questionable. Though not the prettiest route, why drive elsewhere to run? What would make Tom drive so far to run four miles? Then it hit Rich - the drug bust. Tom ran that route because he was a regular customer! Of course, it had to be. Light dawns on Marblehead.

Back in his apartment, Rich showered and threw

on some loose, clean sweats until he would dress for the Wellington party. He made a latte' and rested, studying his sign on which he had painted the background. Standard, D.P.W. orange, a hard color to find. His version was close enough. The latex paint had set up nice and tomorrow he'd do the black lettering. Latex kept the fumes down so his nosy landlady wouldn't be snooping around. The phone rang.

"Hello. Rich here."

"Richard Lewis? This is Jim Phillips. I'm a private investigator."

"I can pay the bill. It was just an oversight." It was instinctive.

There was a pause, then, "Pay what bill?"

"Whatever bill you're investigating."

"No, no," Jim had to laugh at this scenario, he had been there himself enough times. "I'm not doing collections. I've been doing some work for Alan Levine. On your behalf."

"Oh, all right. Yeah, Alan mentioned something about a private investigator."

"I.C.U."

"Now?"

"What?"

"Now?"

Jim was stumped on this one. "Now, what?"

"Do you see me now?" Rich wondered what kind of idiot this was?

"No, no. I don't see you. I meant I.C.U. Private Investigations! My business. The name of it."

"Oh! Well I'm glad to hear that. Could be embarrassing, you know?" Rich upgraded him from idiot, but was thinking he was still nipping at the edges.

"Well, you know, it sounded like a cute name when we started. It gets old though." Jim sighed. "I don't dare expand, you know, 'I.C.U.2'? That's even cornier."

The ice broken, Rich went on. "What can I do for you, Jim?"

"In a word? Hire me." Jim gets right to the point.

"That'll be two." Rich pointed out.

"Twoooo…?"

"Words. Two words. You said, 'In a word', and then you said two words."

"Oh, you're right! Sorry about that." Jim wondered, who counts these things?

"Why should I hire you? I thought you said you were working for Alan?"

"Well, I have been. And I've done a pretty good job for him." Jim spoke with pride. "Found a few accounts for your ex-wife that Alan had no idea about. Found three accounts she never disclosed, all going back seven or eight years."

Now this was news, Rich thought. Maybe this guy's not in the edges.

"Significant accounts?" asked Rich.

"A couple hundred thousand, total." Jim was beaming.

"Well, that's great! Sounds like you've done some great work, and in just a few days!"

"No, I've just done good work so far," Jim loved explaining this. "And it's all public and well worth Alan's money. But today I'm ready to do great work, and we need to get Alan out of it."

"I don't follow," Rich admitted.

"What I've found so far is all admissible and provable. Public records, just a little hard to get at for John Q. Public."

"So you obtained this information legitimately. Now, what, you're going illegitimate?"

Phillips hated words like that. "Let's just say that it would be better to keep Alan out of what I'm doing today and what I'm likely going to find. If we get what I'm expecting, we'll feed him bits and pieces. Discreetly. But we don't want him being party to the investigation."

Rich didn't know how to take this. "What do you mean about finding out today? Today's Sunday. What can you find out on a Sunday?"

"Oh, believe me," Jim said, "I do some of my best work on Sundays. I'll be going up to Boston, the Fed Building. Sunday's the best day for me up there."

Rich was assuming there would be some breaking and entering involved and rolled his eyeballs thinking of it.

"Are you getting me in trouble?"

"No, no, no." Jim was better than that. "I know how to get information through unconventional methods, not necessarily illegal, and there's a big difference. Alan will be able to take what he wants and introduce just enough into the court records to stir up the waters. It's a strategy game. Even if Alan can't use all the information, he simply puts enough out there to raise doubt and suspicion."

Rich didn't know quite what to make of Jim, but he knew he needed a break. Maybe this would be it.

"So what's the difference if you're working for me or Alan? Why are you saying I should hire you."

"Technicalities. There are certain things that can be introduced in court even if there's suspicion about how it might have been obtained. But if the attorney were directly involved in the gathering process, it would likely be thrown out. It's a game."

"What's my exposure?" Rich cringed as he prepared himself.

"None. Absolutely none. But that can change if you keep asking a lot of questions."

Maybe this guy really did know what he was doing.

"Okay. What's the next step?"

"Tell me I'm hired. I'll tell Alan."

"You're hired." Then Rich thought to ask, "How much?"

"I'll give you a bill tomorrow. We'll be meeting at Alan's office then."

Rich was amazed. This guy seemed to already know what he would find. Maybe he found it already.

"Again, how much?"

"My bill will be six thousand, three to you, three to Alan, but he just passes that on to you. If you don't think my information's worth it, you don't have to pay. I'll walk away with my files and you can fight your battles without it. Fair enough?"

Rich was nodding affirmatively to himself. "Fair enough. Now, what about Alan's office? How do you know he'll be available?"

"Already spoke with him. We meet at ten thirty tomorrow morning."

Rich had to smile. He had underestimated Mr. I.C.U.

Gail rose at 10:00. Early for the bartender world, but this was a big day, gleaning a date from the man she had admired from afar and was now getting close to. She had come into his life at a time most men would have given up, gone recluse or turned bitter, but Rich had hung on. With most single men falling over themselves for her attention, and some married men, she couldn't seem to get noticed by Rich. He heard her, was sensitive to what she would say, but never seemed to see her. Until now. She set herself to preparing so that what he saw would keep him coming.

If there were two things in life Gail did well, it was bartending and making herself up. Rich had sampled the former many times. Today he would mainline on the latter.

Rich appeared by noon, feeling awkward holding one rose and picking up his date like a high schooler. It was too many years and too many changes in etiquette. He had felt foolish buying the one rose and now thought of ditching it just as the door swung open.

He forgot about the rose. He beheld a vision. Her cheeks dimpled, his turned red. She greeted him, he stammered.

"I… I never imagined…" he got out.

Gail pursed a smile and shook as if she didn't know how to respond. That was the perfect response.

Rich got a few more things out but it was obvious he was nervous. Gail saved the moment with her perky smile and noted, "That's a beautiful rose."

It broke the tension and Rich relaxed. He handed her the rose.

"That dress is spectacular."

Gail brushed the comment off with her eyes, flicking them to her side. "Thank you. And you look quite handsome yourself."

Rich had on a navy blue blazer, blue oxford button down shirt and Italian loafers, but he somehow felt under-dressed as he gazed at Gail. Maybe he should have rented a tux.

She invited him in for a round of mimosas and the tension vanished completely. Finally relaxed, Rich motioned them out the door. With about four steps taken, Gail stopped in her tracks gazing on her transportation; the 'upgrade' Alan had rented for Rich.

"I thought you had an Explorer?"

"*Had*, being the operative word." An explanation seemed in order. "I told you I had a hard day yesterday. They repossessed it."

"What? They took your car?"

"I'll get it back this week. I just kept putting off payments." Rich looked her in the eyes. "Something we've got to talk about later. I may not be the best kind of guy to get involved with." Said meekly.

Gail's eyes turned back to the rental car, then back to Rich. A slow smile formed on her face, bringing dimples.

"Any guy who would pick their date up in a car like that," gesturing to the rental, "has got to be the best kind of guy to get involved with."

Then she stared back at the powder-blue BMW Z3 coupe, top down, tonneau cover trimmed tight all around and looking like a high strung stallion, edgy at the starting gate. Alan Levine had come through for Rich.

"Just a minute though." Gail was about to excuse herself. "If we're going to drive around in that," pointing to the top down, "I'll need something for my hair."

Rich reached into his jacket pocket and produced a slim, colorful packet, bearing a Nordstrom's logo on its seal. Handing it to Gail, she opened it and did a bug-eye at the sight of the beautiful, ruby-crimson silk scarf that perfectly matched her lipstick (how did he know?) and perfectly complemented the simplicity and sophistication of her dress. Her eyes rose slowly without her head rising.

"My man has class!"

Rich helped her in and skipped around to the drivers side. They were off.

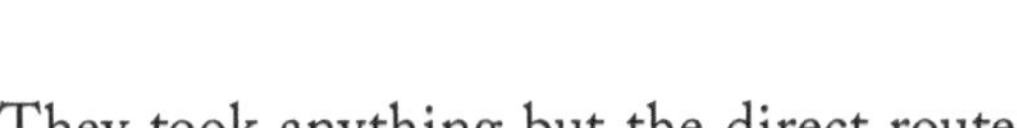

They took anything but the direct route. Heading south, crisscrossing with any number of streets, taking them through areas of working farms with ocean views, horse farms, estates and mansions abruptly contrasting with quaint little New England style town centers. Quiet, deserted country roads with spectacular scenery and fresh, robust air, ending to its south at some of the prettiest New England coast beaches around. It was at once, New England as you've always imagined it and New England as you've never imagined it. A best-kept secret. Rich knew all the roads, having cruised them as he traversed the area visiting his projects through the years.

They slid effortlessly and smoothly around every

turn, Rich seldom touching the brake. Gail would brace herself at each curve only to be surprised at the smooth passing of each. She soon relaxed, trusting her man more each minute.

They drove on, through more villages and over to Horseneck and Goosewing beaches. Approaching Goosewing, Rich asked if she wanted to pull over, take off her shoes and run through the sand. He was kidding. She did and she wasn't. Rich stared in disbelief at the glee she had in the prospect. He pulled over, took off his jacket, tie and shoes while she took off her scarf and shoes and they were off.

Running half the length of the beach they darted in and out of the hilly dunes. Rich would beat her to the top and pull her up. After the third peak, they rested and stared out at the waves and the hazy ocean. Rich wanted to tell her about his incredible situation and what he might be in for, but the time didn't seem right. Maybe this is just an afternoon out for Gail and after this, it's sayonara. Rich could see himself joining a legion of those who had gone before him, pledging their devotion and undying love to Gail only to have her think, "I only wanted an ice cream."

So Rich waited. They walked back to the car, hand in hand, brushed off the sand, put their shoes back on and headed for the Society bash of the summer! No one would notice the sand between their toes.

In less than ten minutes they were cruising down Potomska Road. As they rounded the bend leading to the cove and the bridge, the magnificent Wellington

Cottage loomed before them, breathtaking, rising like a monument out of the bay. It would stop all but the most hurried of the occasional drivers wandering by as driver and passengers would gape in amazement.

CHAPTER 16

Sunday - The Wellington's Bash

Driving down the semi-private gravel road to the Wellington's was an experience in itself. Rich had been here a hundred times, but the pomp and circumstance of today's activities was overwhelming. Six large white and green striped tents had been erected around the grounds. Flags and banners were flying; a hot-air balloon had been hired offering complimentary rides to guests. A brass band played off to the far end and a chamber music group was tuning up closer to the main dining area. Uniformed traffic guards merrily directed cars to sectioned-off areas where jacketed valet attendants would take your car. As Rich and Gail were assisted out, Rich looked across the sea of shiny prestige cars flowing endlessly on. It occurred to Rich that his was the cheapest car in the lot. And he couldn't afford it. He smiled at Gail and quipped, "I'm going to have a good time."

As they walked toward the first guest home, a white-jacketed waiter sought them out with a tray full of champagne in stem crystal. Walking beside them about ten feet away, was a face Rich recognized but couldn't put a name to, although he should have been able to. Rich had seen him a hundred times. An actor. Movies, not T.V.

"Gail? Is dot choo?" The actor calling out. Teeth. Big teeth.

"Oh, my god! Arnie! How are you?"

He and his wife, Mary or something, were genuinely glad to see Gail. They hadn't seen each other since some movie they both worked in somewhere in New Mexico. Rich was introduced but the attention was on Gail, then they separated with promises to get together sometime.

They walked a few steps in silence, then Rich had to comment on how impressed he was. Gail quickly reminded him that they weren't going to ogle over any of the celebrities and Rich quickly fell in line.

They hadn't taken more than three steps when…,

"Gail! How're you doin'?" One of the waitresses. They used to work at Rosie's together. Seemed they had a few long standing inside jokes and Gail was resurrecting each one with gusto. Then, a man's voice from fifty feet away…

"Gail, S'that shue?" The gardener, who was

supposed to be done and out of here by now but was tending to a last minute emergency. Gail gave him a big hug, ignoring the sweat and peat moss.

With the first break in ten minutes, Rich found the situation amusing. "Well, we've been here ten minutes and there's hardly anyone you don't know. And I was worried you might be ignored when I get busy with the editors."

Gail shrugged it off as nothing. A silver tray loaded with hors d'oeuvres of goose pate' and endives passed before them.

"Hello Gail." Rich knew this one. What architect wouldn't recognize one of New York's biggest contractors and property owners?

"Donny! What are you doing north of LaGuadia Airport?" *Donny?* Not, Don, or Donald. But *Donny!* Rich was introduced, cards exchanged and promises beyond Rich's wildest dreams were made pertaining to some high-rise properties in Manhattan that needed renovation.

Another local celebrity, two politicians and four food trays later, Rich and Gail had worked their way to the main outdoor bar where they observed the mass of humanity gathered around the Wellingtons themselves. John and Anne were reveling in the attention to their new home. Rich opted for a drink while waiting for his opening.

Bringing Gail to a bar anywhere in the area is akin to using honey as an insect repellent. The little buggers will just swarm. And swarm they did. Most of the crowd didn't know her, but of those that did, all wanted her to make their drink. All bartenders know _how_ to make drinks. Gail knew how to _make_ drinks.

Gail appeased a few, made Rich his special martini and grabbed a Bud Lite for herself. Fighting her way back to Rich, steadying the martini as best she could, they looked for some corner of solitude. Hopeless as that was, they settled for a vacant area near one of the main tent stays.

"So," Rich began, "you and the world, I see you've met."

Gail pursed her lips with a half smile, flicking her head to the side as she does. "Yeah, well, you know." No he didn't. "I know a lot of the locals from the bars I've tended. Twelve years, two shifts, six days - you meet a lot of people. Then if you spend any time at all out in Hollywood, you know half the celebrities by the end of the first week. They all run in the same crowds."

That's funny, Rich thought. He spent a month in Hollywood for a client and he never met one celebrity. But it wasn't Gail knowing so many people, it's that she was so affectionately remembered, that impressed him.

Rich cast a glance toward the crowd surrounding the Wellingtons hoping to find a break. He couldn't. Observing the Wellingtons, Anne was ever gracious and John needed reintroductions to everyone he had met some time in the past, a perpetually quizzical look on his slightly trembling face.

"I've got to keep an eye out for a break in the crowd around the Wellington's," Rich, explained to Gail.

"You want to talk to the Wellington's? Come on, follow me, I'll get you through," flicking him another, 'this is nothing' glance.

Like Charlton Heston parting the Red Sea, Gail led the way. As they approached, John Wellington looked up, his eyes meeting Gail's. His perpetual half smile turned full as this wonderful vision came nearer to him.

"Gail, my goodness!" John was opening his arms for a hug. "I didn't know we'd be seeing you today."

Rich was awestruck. They knew each other? And John Wellington remembered?

Gail bent to give Mr. Wellington a warm embrace, then stooped down to be eye level as they talked about whatever the two main attractions of an event like this talk about. For that was exactly what they were. No man would be more sought out than John Wellington, and from all appearances, no woman more sought than Gail. Anne Wellington would finish a close second today.

"Richard," Mrs. Wellington's voice, "don't tell me the guest you asked to bring is our favorite adoptee, Gail!"

"I had no idea you all knew each other," Rich explained. "She never mentioned it."

"Oh, Gail never admits to knowing anyone." Anne was beaming. "But every time we dine at the Mattapoisett Inn, at least one of our guests will know her. She's a popular one." Then, in Rich's ear, "And a fine catch." She winked.

"Hello, Gail, my precious." Anne was greeting her.

"Mrs. Wellington!" Gail rose and hugged Anne. "Your house is fabulous! Incredible! Knock-your-socks-off stupendous!" Then, turning to Rich, "But you had one of America's best designers do it for you. Isn't that cheating?"

Anne lapped up the attention given her new cottage. Gail was right on target.

"Oh, well thank you, that's so nice of you to say, and yes, we did cheat a little by contracting the best." She smiled coyly at Rich, who wanted to change the subject.

"How have you been doing, Mrs. Wellington?" Rich asked. "Up bright and early as usual? This is your big day!"

"Oh, Rich," Anne grabbed her heart and feigned fainting, "the most horrible thing happened! Joseph and Mary never woke us up this morning and on this, of all days, we overslept! Didn't open our eyes until almost nine o'clock when the baker rang our bell!"

That confirmed it; Tom didn't do his running today.

Well, everything seems to be going just great." Rich looked around, admiring the grand scale and efficient smoothness of the whole operation. "The extra sleep will serve you well for this day."

John Wellington engaged Gail in more conversation, giving her more attention than he had given any of the previous guests that had tried to hold his ear. Many of them had come from the west coast in their private jets, some from foreign countries via jets or yachts. Gail lived less than seven miles away, but she was the one holding court.

Anne was bending Rich's ear about the horrendous raid that had taken place at one of their neighbors just the day before. In spite of her excitement, Rich needed to get her attention on his purpose for being here.

"Mrs. Wellington, I should try to see as many of the editors and publishers that you've invited as possible. Are there any special arrangements?"

"Yes there is." Anne was glad for the reminder. "At three o'clock, if you wouldn't mind coming to the billiard room, I've asked all of them to come and meet you. You can give them a tour and answer their questions well before dinner is served."

"Sounds like a plan," Rich approved. But it was time for his "plant".

"Mrs. Wellington," Rich was bending close to her ear, almost whispering. She likes that. "I know why Tom Cochrane didn't wake your dogs this morning."

Her hand to her heart and a mischievous look to her eye, "Do tell." Also said softly.

"Tom and Debbie are moving up. Up and out.

They came into a truckload of money somehow and their lives are changing."

So far, of mild interest, but the surprise of hearing something like this from Rich made Anne warm all over.

"I know they're trying to buy up as much land in the area as possible. Then they're looking to buy the biggest sailboat available and sail off for a few years. Around the world." Rich had her attention, now for the hook. "Tom's trying to beat Carlo Bartelli out of some land deal first. I figure if he does, he'd *better* sail around the world."

This was very good, Anne thought. She stared at Rich in appreciation, pleasantly surprised that he was finally giving back after all these months. Rich knew he had planted the seed, time to move on.

Gail wrapped up a session of guy-talk with John Wellington and a group of "the boys", then excused herself. As they walked away, Rich remarked to Gail, "I didn't know you knew the Wellington's! You never mentioned it."

"They used to come into the Inn quite frequently when I worked there. I wouldn't say I know them well."

"Anne called you 'adopted'."

Gail smiled her acceptance of such an honor. "All I really know," she said, "is that they're good tippers."

Rich did two double takes.

Walking about the lawn, Gail became enmeshed in a croquet game with a small crowd of fans and observers. She was the only female playing and was quickly ahead of her five opponents. Soon, bystanders were wagering on the game, the ones betting on her wearing the biggest smiles. No small stakes either, as Rich discovered other people handle thousand-dollar bills too.

Standing next to one gent who was holding two, Rich asked, "I thought the government was calling in all those?"

"Exactly." the blonde, pin-stripe trousered and vested man explained. "Had a customer turn four in at my bank this week. I snagged them before the head teller sent them off into oblivion. Make great conversation items." Then he added, "See?" waving his hand between them, like, that's what we're doing.

"Where's your bank?" Rich was curious.

"Chase. New York."

Chase! Wasn't that the Rockefeller's bank? Well, it used to be. Who knows nowadays? Rich watched as his blonde, blue-blooded friend collected two grand on Gail's double hoop shot.

Rich grabbed Gail after her last victorious stroke and made their departure. Walking away from the finely groomed croquet lawn to the immaculately groomed walking lawn, Gail pointed out a familiar face across the way. Carlo Bartelli. Rich also recognized the face of the older man with him, but couldn't place it.

"Chicago mob boss," she said calmly.

Chills shot down Rich's spine. Did Chicago get called in on the missing money? Then the scene changed as Anne Wellington could be seen working her way to Bartelli and the other guy, Chicago.

"What's Chicago's name?" Rich asked.

"Vito. Vito Gentilianni. Looks like he got his nose straightened."

As Gail and Rich talked and walked, Rich kept casting glances back towards Carlo and company. He could see Carlo intently following Anne's gossip, changing moods. Whatever Anne was telling him wasn't setting well.

"You seem interested in them." Gail observed.

"Oh, just intriguing guys." Rich covered his real motive. "I know Bartelli a little. Never heard of Gentil…, the other guy."

Rich turned away mentioning he'd like to talk with Bartelli.

"Oh, that will be easy…" Gail was about to explain why, but she was interrupted.

"Gail, Gail, honey!" A rough, guttural sound like from a sleazy bum that had no business being in this place. It was followed by a throaty, gurgley laugh. Rich looked around and saw no one. Then he looked down a foot or so and recognized the source.

"Why Dan! Who invited you?" Gail loved this guy, you could tell. "Who in their right mind would invite a Palanga like you to a place like this?" she asked as they embraced, though the reach was a challenge for him and must have been weird for her.

"Arn told me he ran into you earlier. Ghheees, what a surprise! Who's the tall guy?" looking up at Rich.

Gail beamed, her teeth lighting up the whole area. "Dan, meet my Man. Richard Lewis."

They talked a while and Rich noticed it was three o'clock. The billiard room waited. Gail would be in good company with Dan. Rich excused himself and laid plans to hook up at dinner if not earlier. They had assigned seats and Rich asked if Gail knew where they'd be?

"Yes, table eleven over near the pool. I don't know most of our table guests. Just Carlo and Vito. I was about to tell you that we'll be sharing a table with them, so you'll get to talk with Carlo."

Finished with the interviews, Rich headed toward table eleven as an announcement had called everyone to their seats. Carlo, Vito and a redhead were already seated, along with two other couples. Gail had just arrived noting that one seat was vacant on each side of the Bartelli clan.

Rich would have split up with Gail thinking since they were the ones who were late, it wouldn't be proper to make others move. Gail has slightly different thinking patterns.

"Hey you Palangas! Move over!" She was addressing Carlo and Vito, feeling comfortable because she knew them both. "Let a couple of lovers sit with each other." Then she laughed and the two world leaders in crime, corruption and murder obediently moved over, enjoying a laugh to themselves. Gail did another one of her pucker smiles and offered a childish, "Thank you." The redhead wondered what just hit.

Gail sat next to Carlo. Introductions were made around the table. The redhead, Jackie, hit it off well with Gail but not the other two women at their table.

Vito remained quiet, no doubt a cultivated trait in his trade. Jackie was to his right and she and Gail got in deep about the latest fashions and 'what's this world coming to' and all that. Rich tried to keep the other three guests entertained fielding their questions about the Wellington's fabulous house as well as other properties Rich had been involved with. Rich was dying to engage Carlo in conversation, but he would need to bide his time for the right moment.

The food persisted relentlessly, from choices of Parmesan Tartlets, Goat Cheese Quesadillas or Roast Beef Grissini with Remoulade to Moroccan "Gazpacho", Fresh Tomato Risotto with Basil and on and on. Through a whole lot of food, Rich couldn't manage the opportunity to engage Carlo in conversation. With the table cleared, coffee, teas and espresso were offered along with the deserts. By now, Rich was getting nervous. What if he missed his chance with Carlo? Would Mrs. Wellington's tidbits be enough to do the job?

"Richard." Carlo was bending backward to talk around Gail.

"Richard," Carlo continued, "I don't want to touch a sore subject, but your ex, Debbie. Are you in touch?"

Bingo! Exactly what Rich wanted.

"No, not hardly." Play it coy, Rich thought.

"She did a bit of work for me a few years ago when you two had your contracting business." Carlo was continuing. "But I haven't seen her since. Is she doing well? If you don't mind me asking."

Rich acted hesitant. Big put-on.

"Not at all, she's doing fine as far as I know. She got the better end of our divorce you know, but that's nothing new."

Carlo nodded in agreement. He'd never been divorced but had several friends who had.

"But I guess she's taken that up a few notches." The plant. "Heard she and her husband have big plans."

Carlo grunted an acknowledgment indicating he appreciated the information, then leaned forward and returned to his espresso. Rich panicked, thinking he lost him. There was silence as Rich started a slight perspiration. What can he do to get Carlo back?

"Do you think it was her business or her husband's?" Carlo asked quietly while sipping his espresso with a twist of lemon.

Rich felt the nibble, but wasn't quite certain. "Excuse me?" he asked.

"Debbie's doing well, you say. Do you think it to be a result of her business doing well or her husband's?"

That was a pretty substantial bite thought Rich.

"It couldn't be hers. She runs a gallery. No way she can make the kind of money they just came into."

Carlo spilled some of his espresso. Rich felt the tension build two seats away. Carlo turned slowly to him, fighting to control his voice, and asked:

"What kind of money might that be?"

"Oh, I couldn't say, but just in the last few days I've been hearing all sorts of wild things."

There was short, controlled pause.

"Wild things? Like what?"

"Oh, you know… trips around the world, buying boats and land. Land, that's a new one. Tom was selling real estate and struggling at it, now he's buying everything in sight! Then I saw him in a Ferrari last week. Test-driving I think, had a dealer's plate on it. You know, things like that."

Carlo turned to Vito, who hadn't a clue of what this was about. Carlo would color the picture for him later.

"Maybe the Cochrane's had investments that paid off?" Offered by Carlo as calmly as he could struggle to manage, an effort to eliminate other possibilities.

"I doubt it," Rich taunted, "there's never been any kind of investment disclosed on her financials in divorce court, and Tom never had anything."

Carlo was furious, but had to control his temper in present company.

"Tom Cochrane?" One of the proper ladies sitting across had picked up on the name. "Is that who you're talking about, Mr. Tom Cochrane, of Padanaram?" Said so politely and full of respect.

Carlo was too enraged to respond. Rich politely looked her way and affirmed it was.

"Oh, what a nice gentleman Mr. Cochrane is." She turned to her husband Phillip and continued, "He's the gentleman our Cindy told us about." Her voice just reeked of sugar and sweetness. She continued, "Our little daughter, Cindy, graduated from Julliard last year, second in her class, and took a position here in Providence with the Trinity Ballet Company. Well she somehow met Mr. Cochrane and he interviewed her to manage a new dance troupe that he was thinking of starting." Then, turning to her husband again, "Isn't that right Dear?" Her husband smiled broadly in agreement, nodding up and down proudly.

Rich, Gail and Carlo stared at their desserts drawing the same picture of Tom and Cindy. With the conversation ended for now, Rich could only hope he set the hook well into Bartelli's jaw.

With the tables cleared Gail and Rich had a little solitude. It was obvious things were moving fast with Gail, but how wise was that considering Rich's position? He thought it best to put the brakes on. Trying for a smooth transition, he thought he might just ask, 'Does it matter to you that I'm broke, might go to jail, have no business and might get us both killed?' and that might loosen her up a bit.

But they were interrupted.

"Gail? Gail, I thought that was you!" A distinguished and familiar New England voice.

"Eddy! What a surprise!" Gail began to get up.

Rich couldn't believe this scene. He was looking at a political icon, a face he grew up with in the news. A national, no, international figure and would-be president. And to Gail, it's "Eddy!" Not, "Ed", Not "Ted". But "Eddy"!

"Eddy, I want you to meet Rich. Rich, this is Eddy."

They made their greetings, Rich impressed more than he had been all day. His role as designer was brought up and cards were exchanged again. Rich will likely be going to Hyannis in a month to quote an expansion.

As the conversation was winding down and they were beginning to say their good-byes, Eddy asked on a whim,

"Gail, will we see you next month at the wedding?"

Gail wasn't sure at first what he meant, but then remembered his niece.

"Oh, no. I doubt it." Then brazen and hussy-like,

"I never got an invitation, you Palanga. How do you expect me to go without an invite?"

Eddy rolled in laughter. He apologized for the family neglecting her but assured her that she wouldn't need one. Then he looked to Rich and made certain that he was included. Then, leaning into Gail's ear and speaking barely loud enough for Rich to hear,

"Johnnie's coming up from New York. He'll be glad to see you."

That did it. Rich was reeling in the celebrity-like aura that followed Gail. They finished their conversation, Eddy left and Rich tried to regain himself. Gail just looked at him with a "What can I say?" type of look.

"You were saying something before? Were you about to ask me something?" Gail wanted to move on.

The mood was gone. Why trouble her with his problems? Why depress someone who obviously has the world by its tail?

"Yes," he was bailing. "What's a 'Palanga'?"

CHAPTER 17

Sunday - Late Night

Cruising home, they took the non-direct route again. Winding through the countryside, top still down on a perfect summer night with almost a full moon glinting off the water, they approached a deserted stretch of beach.

Their relationship was zipping into overdrive, Gail being a fast mover and Rich a hungry man. But he was also sensible and knew what he had to do before things developed even further.

"There's something you've had on your mind all day, Rich. I can tell." Gail, being Gail, was on target again.

"Actually, I've been trying to tell you all week," Rich replied. So he started in. From A to Z, ending with his jail prospects for any number of reasons.

"You're not going to jail. For what!?" He had yet to find someone who took him seriously the first time he told them. Then, typical Gail, "I won't let them take you. I know too many judges," a little smugly, "just stick with me."

"You know judges? You mean as in: Influence them? That should probably add ten years to my sentence. Excuse me, I mean, sentenc*es*." Rich knew she was kidding. Well, he thought she was kidding.

"What kind of trouble are you in that could lead to jail? What did you do, kill Tom Cochrane?"

Ask me that on Wednesday, Rich thought.

"No, but now you're tempting me."

She cast a sideways glance.

"No, it's nothing that romantic," he continued. "Taxes, contempt. Oh, and stealing millions of dollars." Then he added, "From the mob."

She looked at him with a smirk, not believing it for a second.

"If you had millions of dollars, you wouldn't have the other problems now would you?" Rich remembered thinking the same thing at the beach, leading him to take the money.

"Well, if I stole millions somebody would sure be ticked off, wouldn't you think? Like, maybe the somebody that no longer had the millions? And if that somebody were to be a well known mob boss,"

Gail blinked as he said this, "can you see where I may have a problem?"

Flashbacks ran through Gail's head recalling his earlier interest in Bartelli and Gentilianni, wanting to talk with them. She waited for Rich.

He opened up and told her the whole story from Horseneck Beach to the news reports to giving Tom the money. He was surprised he was telling her all this.

"So when I say I've got problems," Rich rolled his eyes, "going to jail may be good news. It would mean I escaped getting chopped up into fish bait."

Gail pondered the whole story. She asked calmly what he would do, her composure incredible.

"I have a plan. I think it will work. That's why I set Tom up with the money."

A plan? This, Gail had to hear. Not because she didn't believe a plan could be concocted that would save someone from the mob, that was a piece of cake to her. She needed to know if the plan was any good. These things she knew.

"Let's walk." Rich said, nodding to the shore. They took off their shoes, held hands and made footprints.

The plan was laid out in every detail. Gail listened intently, absorbed in every detail. He finished as they arrived at some rocks jutting out into the ocean. Rich helped Gail as they hiked to the furthest, then sat opposite her.

"It's risky, Gail. But I've got to do it. I've no other choice."

Gail hadn't made a sound for the last ten minutes. As she contemplated all Rich had said, her head began to shake slightly, as if to say, "No." And that's exactly what she was thinking.

"No, Rich. It's not risky." She said it in all seriousness and with full conviction. "Your plan is perfect. What you've done already should convince you. It all went off without a hitch. And what you're planning around Bartelli - you've got him figured perfectly. It will work."

It wasn't what Rich was expecting. He thought Gail would be beside herself with anxiety, but she was confident. It had the same effect on Rich.

"Rich," she explained, "we all have talents. We all do something good, maybe better than anyone else. My thing isn't bartending. My thing is knowing people.

"My whole life, I've had no problem figuring people out and guessing their reaction to my moves." She was as serious as Rich had ever seen her. "I became quite the manipulator, using people like condiments at a barbecue. I'm not like that anymore, but this plan you just laid out is as good as I've ever seen. You'll do all right, Mr. Lewis. You'll do just fine."

Rich scoffed. He had never manipulated anyone in his life. He always let his talent do his bidding for him.

"So am I wrong to go ahead with my little plan? Should I forget my idea for Bartelli."

"No," Gail affirmed. "You've got too much riding on this. You've got no choice."

Surprised at her encouragement, Rich realized what was happening here. She was building his confidence in a way no one else could.

"Can I help?" Gail asked, breaking his meditation.

That evoked a sudden reaction. "Are you kidding? This is serious stuff! I wouldn't be doing it myself if I had any other options. No, no. I won't involve you."

Gail didn't need to say anything. Her stern demeanor shouted that she had better get involved.

"Gail, I'm serious. Forget what I told you tonight, just forget it!"

"Phhhhh." She blew it off. Literally. "We won't get in that much trouble. We can handle it."

"No. No, no. 'We' won't get in that much trouble because there will be no 'we'. I'm not going to involve you." Rich continued, "I need a few days to get the last details done, until then, 'we're' not involved. Only me."

Gail gave him a hard look, but knew he was serious. She could have objected, tried to put pressure on him, but frankly, it made sense to her too. Rich would feel better about himself if he worked himself out of his dilemma. Then he could start over. With her.

"I understand," she conceded. "You're on track,

so why should I complicate things. But promise me one thing."

Rich waited.

"If you get in trouble, if anything doesn't seem to be working, come get me. I mean it."

Rich mulled it over, smiled, and agreed. "But when I pull it off by myself, I'm celebrating with you. I might even buy you a drink."

She sealed the deal with a kiss.

They drove on toward Gail's house via the Padanaram Bridge. Driving through the village, Gail asked him to drive by his old house. She had heard a lot about it, but never saw it. Little did she know he was headed there anyway. With his plan unfolding, he needed to check on Debbie's welfare, of all things. If Bartelli was reacting too soon, they might all be in trouble.

"Come to bed Tom, it's late!" Debbie was calling to Tom who wasn't very tired having slept late, what with no jogging.

"I will, I will. But let me make a phone call first."

"At two in the morning! Who you gonna call at two?"

"A client just beeped, what can I say?" While Debbie pondered what kind of emergency a real estate man might have at this time of night Tom was headed toward his study.

"Well, I'm turning in Tom. I'm beat." Debbie had worked all day, Tom slept.

In his study, out of earshot from Debbie, Tom dialed the number that persistently beeped him. As the phone rang, he poured himself a scotch.

"Tom, where've you been?"

"What's the big emergency that you have to keep beeping me in the middle of the night?" Tom felt in control.

"What's up with your source? I need to connect, man!"

"It's a weekend for crying out loud! What am I supposed to do on a stinking Sunday when the biggest source in southeastern New England just went down the tubes? This is going to take a little time."

Bob was furious. He knew very well it was the weekend, but he just missed the two best nights of the week and didn't have any honey for the bees.

"Look, you made me miss two nights and I paid you all ready." Bob's voice was uncontrolled, and this was a man who made his living by controlling his voice and mood. "Why can't you hook up somewhere else? Do you expect me to believe that these guys work nine to five, weekdays only? Give me a break Tom. Or get broken." Bob thought that was pretty clever for an off-the-cuff quip.

Tom didn't need this stuff any more. Two days ago he'd be shaking in his boots to think he may be losing a client. But now, it was of passing interest. If it were anyone but Bob, he'd tell him to take a flying leap. But Bob was helping Debbie and he wouldn't want that relationship messed up, so Tom tried to appease.

"Look, give me a day or two. By mid-week, you should have your wings back."

Bob didn't know where else to turn. If he had another profession he wouldn't be so sensitive, but an attorney had to be careful about their suppliers and he knew Tom would never snitch on him. Never. Because Tom was implicated in a few of Debbie's scams and Bob could turn the screws on a moment's notice.

"I'll give you until Wednesday." Bob slammed the receive down.

Tom cussed the phone and hung up. He slugged down the last inch of scotch and rose from his chair. Glancing down the hallway, he could see the bedroom light was out, so he quietly went out to the garage.

He slid the garbage can out and lifted the cover. Two green plastic trash bags as he had left them. He peered into each as he took them out, confirming they were the right bags. He released a cord and lowered the front half of a canoe that hung on the ceiling. As he was about to stuff both bags into the canoe, he simply couldn't resist. He opened a bag, took out a wad of cash, and then tied it back up. Something about having money in his hands made him feel better.

He then placed the bags inside the hull, hoisted the canoe back up and wrapped the cord secure again.

It was around two o'clock when they pulled up to Gail's home. Rich hopped around to Gail's door and aided her out.

"So if I don't come by for a while, you'll understand?"

"No." Gail was honest. "I won't understand. But I'll respect it."

They stared at each other for a moment, then Rich kissed her lightly on the forehead and said easily, "I love you."

Gail blinked her eyes twice. Rich was about to turn to leave, but Gail asked, "What did you just say?"

Rich was kind of surprised himself, now that he thought of it, but it had just rolled off his lips. "I said, 'I love you.'" So there, he thought, no big deal.

Gail shook her head amazingly. "Before I told you?"

"Before what…?"

"You told me that you love me before I ever told you." Through the faintest smile, Gail said, "That's never happened to me before."

That seemed incredible to Rich! A woman who jets off to all parts of the world, hob-nobbing with the rich and famous, modeling, acting, partying, yet the dignity of being recognized for who you are, the need of being told that someone loves you, it was never there! That's when it hit him that he did in fact have something to offer this super woman. Humanity.

With endorphins running amuck through his brain, Rich raced home never remembering feeling this good in his life. Ever.

CHAPTER 18

2nd Monday

An odd bulletin was waiting on Captain Hernandes' desk as he arrived Monday morning. He placed the Dunkin Donut boxes down first, poured himself a coffee and rummaged through the boxes until he found his two creme filled. He'd have his others during the briefing. Plopping down in his seat, he picked up the bulletin from the United States Treasury Department. Nothing earth shattering, but how often does the Treasury Department put out bulletins?

There had been a rash of thousand-dollar bills turned into banks up and down the east coast area from Boston to New York. Not illegal, but most unusual. There was a Photostatted image of two versions of the bills and Hernandes studied them having never seen any before. The earlier version had an image of Alexander Hamilton and a blue seal. This series was printed and issued from 1918 to 1927 and there were precious few still in circulation even among collectors. The later version, the better-known series, sported the image of President Grover Cleveland. The Cleveland series, known as the Green Seal Series of 1928, would be more prolific. Last printed in 1945, new bills continued to be released up until 1969. Since then, thousand-dollar bills have no longer been printed nor put into circulation.

A footnote explained they were unattainable through the Treasury Department or banks, so only dealers or numismatics would have any. These bills were collectors' items worth more than face value. Exchanging them in a bank at face value didn't make a lot of sense.

The bulletin ended with a composite description of the man turning them in. He was described as being a white male, around six feet tall, medium build, brown hair, in his late thirties and professional looking.

Jane Homboldt arrived to set up the briefing room. She had brought in the doughnuts and was eying a box that didn't look full.

"Jane," he quickly diverted her attention. "Take a look at this bulletin."

Jane read while she continued setting up. When it looked as though she was finished, Hernandes inquired, "What do you think?"

"Think about what?" she asked.

"Why would somebody do that? Doesn't it sound strange?"

Jane pondered a bit, but ended up just shrugging her shoulders. "Can't help you there, Captain. If they were counterfeit it would make sense."

"If they were counterfeit, I wouldn't be asking."

They let it go, but something else was on her mind: The description of the man. It reminded her of someone.

Carlo hardly got any sleep all night. He missed his Carmella, but it was his seething at Tom Cochrane that had him tossing and turning.

If Vito wasn't visiting, the deed would have been done; Tom would have coughed up any money he had stolen. But Vito was a hard sell on the drive back from the Wellington's. Carlo and Vito had argued all the way home as to how Cochrane should be handled. Vito wasn't buying the fact that Cochrane was their man just because he's spending. But he knew Carlo was a latent volcano, ready to go off unpredictably. It was probably good he was here to keep a lid on him.

Juanita was pouring a second juice for Carlo when Vito arrived at the breakfast table. The "C" was hanging around in doorways, observing.

"Good morning, 'C'."

The "C" nodded back to Vito. That would be the most he'd say all day.

"Paisano! How are you this morning?" Vito was hoping Carlo had slept off his anger.

While he cracked a walnut in his bare hand, he smiled gracefully to Vito. "New day, new mind." Then he smiled, as if to say, 'see?'

But he was just as bitter, just as enraged. Tom Cochrane had to be the rat they were trying to smoke out.

"My friend," Vito said encouragingly, "this morning we will be meeting with our associate. It's his money more than it is ours, so let us wait until we hear what he has to say. Perhaps he has some enemies that we are not aware of. Perhaps he has contacts that we do not know of. Perhaps his snitches know what ours don't. We will wait for our meeting before we run off with guns blazing"

Carlo had his money and his life on the line. The money worried him more.

"You act as though the meeting with Montero were like some family dinner party." Carlo was skeptic. "What makes you so sure it's not an ambush?"

Vito took a sip of espresso. "For the same reason that we are not going in with guns blazing against them." He paused for one more quick sip. "Because there is too much money at stake."

Deferring to Vito's seniority, Carlo asked, "How are we going in?"

"We will go in alone. Unarmed of course." Surely,

Montero would have it no other way. "The 'C' will come around to the back door and position himself out of sight before we make our entrance. My two *bechinnos* will remain out front at the door. No problem if they're seen, it may be to our benefit. And the driver will remain in the car, the motor running."

Somewhat more sedate than anything Carlo would have thought of, but it was acceptable to him.

"And how much do we tell Montero?" Carlo was still submitting.

"Everything."

Carlo nodded his head in acceptance. "And what shall we tell Montero of Tom Cochrane?" Two walnuts cracked in Carlo's hand as he completed the question.

"We will go very slowly on that one." Vito wasn't going to be bulldogged by Carlo into a rush to judgment. "We don't know for sure about his involvement."

Carlo conceded with a grimaced nod.

"We don't know what Montero knows." Vito was going on. "I think he very well may have his own ideas. One of his own men maybe. I'm having a hard time believing that a stranger from out of nowhere just happened upon the scene and took the money that easily." Then, looking straight into Carlo's eyes, "Were your two men so incompetent that they would let a stranger witness their deed?"

Carlo's eyes dropped. No, that wasn't possible.

To admit otherwise would be to admit what a colossal fool he was to have hired such imbeciles.

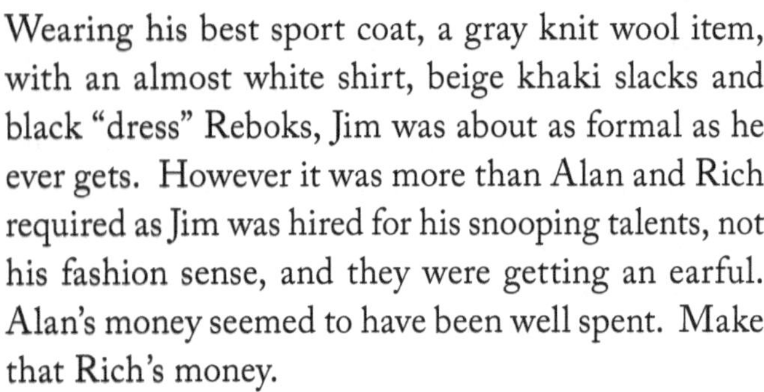

Wearing his best sport coat, a gray knit wool item, with an almost white shirt, beige khaki slacks and black "dress" Reboks, Jim was about as formal as he ever gets. However it was more than Alan and Rich required as Jim was hired for his snooping talents, not his fashion sense, and they were getting an earful. Alan's money seemed to have been well spent. Make that Rich's money.

"The three banks that showed up are all out of South Carolina, Myrtle Beach and a smaller town just south called Murrels Inlet."

Rich understood why. "That's where her parents live. Or lived. Debbie's mother died."

Jim was way ahead of him. "Part of her died. February 16, 1985."

"Part of her? What's that mean?" Rich was almost getting a little tired of Jim's elusive manner of speaking, but reminded himself that Jim was effective.

"Well, she really died, we know that. But some of her bank accounts live on." Jim tossed several piles of printouts onto Alan's conference table. "The bank's computer still thinks she's alive."

Alan and Rich perused the pile. From the statements, it looked as though the accounts were fed regularly from 1983 up until her split with Rich in 1997. From then on, it was mostly withdrawals, especially in the fall of '98 when Debbie was opening her gallery.

"How'd you find these?" Rich wanted to know.

"These were the easy ones. I just kept following the leads and these popped up. At first I didn't think much of them because they were in her mother's name and social security number. I almost tossed the information." Jim was on cloud nine. "Then I came across the interesting piece of information that her mother died! That didn't make sense, so I took a closer look at these statements and compared them to the joint accounts you had with Debbie. Withdrawals from your joint accounts would match perfectly with deposits to her mother's. You reported the income, paid the taxes, but she took the lion's share of after-tax money."

"And she just took over her mother's accounts? Is that what you're saying?" This was new to Rich.

"Exactly," Jim continued, "and made a smooth transition. Even took over her mother's balance of a few thousand in each account when she died."

Alan was quiet, taking this all in and thinking how best he could use this new information.

Rich was still confused as to how Debbie was able to pull this off. "Didn't the I.R.S. or the bank figure out that her mother died? Don't they keep records on who dies?"

"Yes and no. It's not all that hard, especially since Debbie had been helping to do her mother's banking the last years of her life. And Debbie did all the tax filings for both her parents."

That rang true with Rich. He remembers the frequent trips she would take to aid her parents. Once Debbie's mother passed on, she continued doing the banking and tax filings for her father.

"Wouldn't the father catch on?" Alan finally asked his first question.

"He was in the dark about taxes his whole life." Rich beat Jim to this one. "He always let Debbie do them, and before that, he hired tax people."

"Exactly," Jim was filling in details, "and when her mother passed away, she filed in her mother's name, still filing jointly with her father, giving her an extra deduction as well. Whether her father signed without reading or whether she buried everything in a pile of other forms, who knows? But he signed every one of them. And Debbie signed for her mother."

Alan didn't think it was that easy. Too many checks and balances. He came up with several arguments, but Jim always had an explanation or a way around it. Bottom line, Debbie pulled it off.

"So we have her, don't we?" Rich was asking Alan.

Shaking his head affirmatively, "Yes, yes. This shouldn't be to hard to prove from what I'm looking at."

Rich was beaming. If Debbie had been hiding assets, likely the entire case can get reopened. He remembered Alan saying that she'd have two strikes against her and he'd be throwing his best stuff. Well, here comes the 0-2 pitch and Alan's on fire! He flashed a great, big, friendly smile to Jim and was about to shake his hand.

"Like I said before," Jim wasn't quite through, "this was the easy stuff."

Rich and Alan were staring at Jim with wonder and awe. What else could he have?

"I found an offshore account."

"Grand Cayman! I knew it!" Alan just knew it.

"No, Bermuda."

"Bermuda. I knew it." Alan just knew it.

Rich never knew it. He sat dumbfounded, shocked to learn Debbie had been stealing from him all along. He and Alan had one question. "How much?"

"Around a million."

They both hung in their stares waiting now for their brains to comprehend.

"Didn't I tell you in court last week?" Alan was catching on. "She took a million from that one project alone, where was it, Bahamas?"

"Hawaii." Rich answered as if he were still lucid. He wasn't, he was in a daze thinking of how brazen she had been all those years.

"She was up as high as one point three million, right around the time of your break up. But it went steadily down, especially when she opened in Newport. But it's still holding steady around nine hundred thousand. $935,750.63 as of last month."

Rich was in disbelief still.

"How'd you find that out?" Rich asked.

"Ahem." Alan cleared his throat and put his head down. Rich picked up immediately.

The three sat in silence for a minute as they absorbed the feast of evidence piled before them. Most of it admissible, too, but what wasn't admissible could still help. Given sufficient evidence that the Bermuda account existed, a search warrant may be in order leading to the discovery of even other accounts.

Rich sat with mixed feelings. Joy, from seeing there was enough evidence to turn the tables, pain from seeing how Deb had done him in.

"So, what do you think?" Jim was proud of his work and was confident of his next question. "Was this all worth the six thousand dollars I'm charging you?" As he was saying that, he placed two simple invoices on the table in front of them. Both read, 'For Services Rendered: $3,000.00'

Alan picked up the phone and asked Marge to make out a check for Mr. Phillips in the amount of $ 3,000.00. Rich reached for his wallet and took out three, thousand dollar bills.

━━◆━◆━◆━━

"La Cantina" sat at the top of what is known as Federal Hill in Providence. A landmark in this Italian section of town, it's long been rumored to be a favorite meeting place of mob and underworld figures. There's probably no truth to that at all. Carlo Bartelli, Vito

Gentilianni and Louis Montero were meeting there for lunch in spite of the persistent rumors.

The three men shared a table by themselves to the back of a private room. Montero had at least three men in the room, two at a nearby table and one stationed very obviously in the middle of a hall doorway. Carlo suspected one of the waiters to be a plant since he used two hands to carry his tray.

It started off well, no one was shot. As customary at any business meeting, niceties led off the conversation. It was in the second sentence that they got down to brass tacks.

"Are you ready to tell me where my money is?" Montero, obviously furious, shot the words out through almost clenched teeth.

Vito took the lead. "I believe that would be *our* money. Until the transaction is completed."

"You got the disk. You probably got the password too." Montero was still clenching his teeth. "And I like to think that you picked up the merchandise by now because I don't stinking need twenty tons of goods hanging around waiting for me to be connected with. I brought it in for you and want it out of my life, out of my ocean!"

So now he has an ocean.

Montero reflected to himself the plan he had devised for bringing in such a record amount of cocaine in one shipment. It was brilliant to his way of thinking: Package the endless bales of cocaine in waterproof bags, net them all together and tow them behind a large oil tanker. The bales were dropped in a sandy part of the Atlantic, oddly enough within view of Bartelli's bedroom. Scuba divers could easily retrieve the bales, although it would involve several long days, once the location was known. The exact location was encoded on diskette, safe and secure.

But with the bungled exchange, Montero was out the cash and the drugs and was facing his own horror story back in Cartegena should he return without money to pay his contacts. Montero was none too pleased that the exchange went south.

"We do not have the disk." Carlo admitted, fidgeting a little. "We placed the disk in the jacket pocket of your courier. Didn't anyone claim the body?"

Montero slowly swiveled his head to look at Bartelli.

"His mother claimed the body. *Su madre'*. Shall we go rough her up?"

Carlo had enough of this. He wasn't going to sit here and put because of Montero's stupid plan.

"Mr. Montero. We're sorry for the screw up. We're sorry for your courier passing away like he did, puking on my new shoes and all. We're sorry that the exchange didn't go as well as expected. We're sorry that you haven't gotten your money yet, or that we haven't gotten our merchandise yet." Then, out-staring the Colombian, Carlo added, "But we really don't give a fat cat about your little computer disk. I always thought it was one of the screwiest ideas I ever heard of in any deal. I almost told you where to take your little computer disk. But then I thought, 'Give the Colombian a break. He's disadvantaged enough without confusing him with a real plan'."

Montero was seething, his hand drawing close to the inside of his vest.

"Gentlemen, gentlemen. There is no reason for anger or insults." Vito, the peacemaker. As he had told Carlo earlier, there is too much money involved. No one's life is worth 28.8 million. If it were a smaller amount, a million or two, then the whole room could get shot up and it wouldn't matter. The survivors would walk away with bragging rights and that "feel good" sense that comes from a hard days work. But if that happened now, the money would be gone.

"We must face the fact that we need each other." Vito was continuing. "The deal can still be done. We have only experienced a slight setback. But we need each other. We need to cooperate and stop insulting one another."

Eyes darted back and forth. What Vito just said was true and they each had to admit it.

Montero softened first. Like lead is soft. "My contact in the Police Department assures me that my courier did in fact suffer a heart attack. There were no marks or bruises and the autopsy indicated congenital heart failure. I can accept it for what it is, a most unfortunate occurrence that messed up an otherwise brilliant plan." The last sentence was directed at Bartelli.

"But the second unfortunate occurrence that befell

me this week is not so clear." Montero was continuing, morphing into cold steel again. "I'm not convinced that the raid on my home was entirely instigated by a police surveillance operation. So I have to ask myself, 'Who might want to cause trouble for me and remove me from the scene?'" Again, directed coldly at Bartelli.

Slowly and softly, Bartelli responded. "Are you a complete imbecile? *We're* out the money, *we're* out the drugs and *we're* the ones that have had a great big spotlight turned on because of some bodies that have turned up." Then, returning the icy cold stare to Montero, "What possible reason would we have for shutting down your cheap, penny-ante, candy operation? How would that fix anything?"

The realization began to form that they were not each other's enemy. Somebody else out there is!

"I am willing to give you the benefit of the doubt." Montero had to save face. "I will accept for now that I must be the unluckiest man on the planet, having two quirks of fate work against me in one week." He gave no thought to the strewn bodies of the week. How lucky were they? "But I'm still holding the biggest shipment of goods ever attempted and I want to get it off my books! Our deal was made and I want my money, not the shipment!"

Carlo and Vito were home free. Montero still wanted the money, not the drugs, meaning he didn't have another buyer lined up. They would walk away today, as Montero would need them alive.

"Do you have any ideas," Montero asked, "as to who might have taken the money?"

"We have a good idea." Carlo wanted to blurt out Tom Cochrane's name, but Vito had to be placated. "We are just waiting for confirmation." Carlo shot a glance at Vito who nodded approval.

"Will I grow to be an old man before you have this, 'confirmation'?" Montero was stoking the flames.

"Neither you nor our suspect shall grow to be an old man before we act." A note of finality carried in Carlo's voice. "Which brings us to your second unfortunate occurrence this week. Why do you think it was more than a normal police sting?"

Montero was willing to shift gears for now.

"Too coincidental. And I don't believe in coincidences." Montero had been assured by Officer Ryan that it was just a fluke, that there was no rat. But Montero was from Colombia where there was always a rat. It made life easier to have a rat every time something went wrong.

"And who might your suspect be?" Carlo had no qualms in being forward.

"A client." Montero said the word with a loathing. "From Padanaram."

Carlo and Vito both recalled Officer Ryan mentioning that Montero had two suspects from Padanaram, one obviously Bartelli. But who would the other be?

Vito took charge. "It's been said that it is a small

world we live in. Could it be so small that we suspect the same citizen of Padanaram?"

Montero looked surprised. "Your suspect is from Padanaram?"

Vito and Carlo both nodded affirmative. Nothing was said as the three stared in bewilderment. Carlo waited for them to offer a name. They waited for Carlo to offer a name. Great minds being what they are and thinking as they do, it was almost predictable that they would all feel the urge at the exact same moment to utter the same name.

"Tom Cochrane."

CHAPTER 19

2nd Tuesday

With his shower going, Rich never heard the knocking on the front door. As Rich shut off the water, the knocks rang out for the sixth time. Rich yelled out to wait a minute, then quickly toweled off, threw on some clothes and went to answer the door with his hair askew.

"Who is it?" Rich glanced at the clock. Eight o'clock!

"Agents Johnson and Dupuis, Mass. D.O.R." came the answer.

Rich hung his head in disbelief. Will his troubles ever disappear? He opened the door and motioned them in.

"Are you Richard Lewis?"

"Yes, I am." A smiling Richard Lewis.

"Mr. Lewis, are you aware of the outstanding taxes that you owe the Massachusetts D.O.R.?"

This was too much like the other day with the I.R.S. Rich remembered his words to Alan to the effect that you're most powerful when you have nothing to lose. So why wasn't he feeling very powerful?

"Yes, I am." Rich looked at both men. "I wrote, didn't you get my letters?"

The two men had already entered the apartment and were now looking around the crowded kitchen. Paint buckets, brushes, drop cloths, trash can overflowing, a large painting covered with a blanket, typical of how most broke people live.

"This is a summons to appear in District Court on the seventh." He said. His voice was calm, not antagonizing at all, just doing his job.

The other man now spoke. "We have the authority to seize your assets."

"Well," Rich explained, "any other day and that would mean my car. But Fabio beat you to it Saturday."

They each looked at each other. "Who's Fabio?"

Rich waved it off as not mattering. He accepted the summons and Johnson and Dupuis turned to leave. As they were going down the stairs, Rich wondered if he should have asked for identification. Then he thought, who would impersonate D.O.R. agents? So he just asked, "Who's Johnson and who's Dupuis?"

Neither turned around, both raised their right hand and waved as if to say, "That's me."

Tom was still in his robe by ten o'clock as Debbie was trying her best to get out the door. Jule's was only going to put up with so much and if he had to watch the entire shop alone for much longer, he would surely be asking for a raise. So all decked out, looking smooth in her two piece, robin's egg blue suit and cream colored silk blouse and jewelry out the wahzoo because it wasn't a court day, Debbie stood poised with hand bag and keys in hand as she tried to bring this latest argument to a full conclusion.

"My accounts are secure, they all pay good interest rates and they've never been traced! So what's wrong with putting most of the money there?"

"Interest rates, what a joke!" Tom knew better than to settle for mere interest when an entire world of finances lie at his beck and call. He had money now. "The stock market is at an all time high and everyone predicts up, up, up! I've been fooling with it for years now, not with real money but, you know, like a dummy account? I know how to pick winners. I know what to look for. And the returns can be phenomenal! I'm not talking about three to seven percent interest, I'm talking doubling, tripling, quadrupling your money! In a year or two!"

Tom heard somewhere that someone did something like that, if he remembers right. So, there you go.

"Tom, take some of the money and fool around all you want in the stock market. But we've got to hide it too, don't forget." Debbie was beside herself knowing that Tom wouldn't know what to do with any amount of money. "Don't forget, Tom, a million dollars hidden from taxes is the same as a million and a half that's not. How's that for capital gain?"

Tom was over his head talking investments with Debbie, but knowing what she had done to Rich, he wouldn't be so stupid as to entrust his fortune to her. Besides, the thought of being in the stock market appealed to Tom.

"I see it just the opposite." Tom was lecturing, "Why don't you take a small amount, maybe a few hundred thousand, and deposit it into a *joint* account, and see how it does?"

"Tom, my accounts are already set up and they're not traceable." This made so much sense to Debbie and Rich always went along with her, she didn't understand this resistance Tom was giving her. "The bulk should go into my Bermuda account. I was fortunate to get it set up the way I did, you'll never be able to get such a sweet structure."

"All right." Tom was about to concede. "On your next day off, let's count up all the cash, it's too much for me to do on my own. Then, I promise, half can go into some of your accounts." Debbie was softening as Tom's words were flowing out. "But I should at least have access to those accounts. Get me on as a co-signer or something."

Nothing that can't be handled, Debbie thought. She'll put his name on but put a limit on his transactions and he'll never know the better - unless he tries to pull a fast one.

"Now you're making sense, Tom." She flashed a smile, walked over to Tom and gave him a hug and a kiss. She said good-bye and bolted out. Tom headed back to the bedroom for some more shut-eye. Only three days since he retired from early morning runs and he's already made the difficult adjustment in sleeping schedules.

Driving through Padanaram, Rich dialed Alan's number while trying to handle the car and failing. He narrowly missed two pedestrians and a Yugo as he fumbled with his phone but regained control as Alan came on.

"Alan, have I thanked you enough for renting me the Z3?"

Alan laughed. "Maybe forty six times, but then we've only talked twice since the rental office."

"Your good Alan. Thanks." Rich was coasting over the Padanaram Bridge now, enjoying the sight of a hundred sailboats dotting the shoreline. He took a deep breath of the fresh sea air as he continued with Alan.

"Alan, the time has come, you've got to call Bartelli."

Alan stiffened. "Rich," he said somberly.

Oh-oh, Rich thought. The tone, the voice, the

one word 'Rich' with the long pause, was he backing out?

"Do you know what you're doing?"

Rich paused a few seconds. Of course not. He was as much out of his element as a surfer in Nebraska. And dealing with the mob? Of course he didn't know what he was doing.

"Alan, I've got to go through it. But don't worry, you're covered. All you're doing is putting together a land deal. I'll cover any bill." Rich swallowed. Did he overlook something? Could this whole thing backfire and get Alan killed? No. No he didn't. If Rich had any doubts about that, he just had to recall Gail's assurances.

"Rich, I'm not worried about me. It's you. Will you be all right?"

"Absolutely." Rich said. Maybe, he thought. "I just need to position Bartelli at a certain location and time."

Alan had no idea what Rich was up to and Rich wasn't about to involve him more than he had to. Then it occurred to Rich to throw Alan a bone.

"Alan, if things go exactly as planned, you won't even need to sit with Bartelli. The meeting will never happen."

That got Alan's attention. "Why? What do you mean?"

"I really can't say, other than I think something will come up for him at the last minute."

Rich couldn't imagine Carlo sitting through a

closing when he's just found out where his twenty-eight million dollars was.

"All right, all right," Alan would just be glad when this was all over. "What do I do?"

"Call Bartelli now. Tell him he has to meet you in your office first thing tomorrow morning." Rich curled his toes awaiting Alan's reaction. "At 7:00."

"SEVEN O'CLOCK!"

That would qualify as a reaction.

"Alan, I know it's tough. I know you sleep late, but it has to be then. Has to be."

"But seven! He's not going to go for that. Why? What possible explanation can I come up with for him to meet me that early?"

"Tell him you have ethical responsibilities to Tom Cochrane and if the deal isn't completed by nine, you have to go to Tom first. He'll buy that."

"Why would he buy that?" Alan didn't think this was going to work. "Who makes real estate deals at seven in the morning?"

"Alan, you mention Tom Cochrane's name to Bartelli and his logic systems will break down. He'll fall all over himself to get to you wherever you are, whenever you want. If I'm wrong on that, this whole plan will likely fizzle anyway." And me with it, Rich thought.

"All right. I'll call Bartelli and have him meet me in my office tomorrow at seven, on the dot. We can't do this at my house?"

"At your office, Alan. Your office." Rich was

asking a lot, but the geography didn't work going to his home.

"You've got it Rich. I'll call Bartelli now."

As Rich drove on, he remembered the word Alan always admired in others. Chutzpah. Now Rich admired it.

Carlo and Vito departed the bocce' court and headed to the outdoor bar for a pop. Carlo nodded to The "C", busy doing some hedge trimming, then broached the subject he was avoiding all day.

"We will put the word out at our meeting tonight. All we need is something. Anything more substantial than what we have now. And Montero is doing the same with his men. Who can escape a net like that?" Vito was confident

"And meanwhile we do what?" Bartelli was not given to patience. "Twiddle our fingers and grow old?"

"You should be happiest to grow old, my friend." Vito looked caringly at Carlo. They had been like brothers and it would be most unfortunate if Carlo didn't survive this little mess up.

Juanita came out carrying a remote phone and alerting Carlo it was Alan Levine. Carlo took the phone and sat on a pool chair under an umbrella.

"Hello, Mr. Levine. And how are you doing?"

"Hello, Mr. Bartelli. I'm doing fine and I have some good news for you." Alan, the quintessential professional. Nervous as a coffee shop owner at an audit, but calm and collected to all appearances.

"Is it land I smell?" Carlo's day just brightened.

"Yes, yes it is. That parcel we had discussed is ready to move. We can do the deal tomorrow."

"Great! Tomorrow should be fine."

"There's one unusual detail." Now it was Alan's turn to breath deep. "If we can't do the deal by nine, I have ethical responsibilities to Tom Cochrane. I hope you can understand."

"I'm sorry, so what are you saying? We have to hook up before nine tomorrow?"

"We have to be done by nine and you never know if something may come up." Alan was surprised Carlo seemed to be taking it so well. "We should get started in my office not later than seven."

"What time?" Carlo thought he said seven.

"Seven o'clock." Alan said.

"Sev… What are you talking about? In the morning? Or tonight?"

"Seven in the morning. Mr. Bartelli, it's not that bad."

Carlo decided not to pursue it. What does he care what time. He'll be beating Cochrane out of a sweet land deal, hopefully just before he beats Cochrane out of everything else. Carlo confirmed it would be no problem, thanked Alan for keeping him in mind, and hung up. When Carlo told Vito, Vito just laughed. Vito would be letting Carlo out of his sight after all as there was no way he'd be accompanying him.

Carlo could be trusted knowing that the net would be spreading wide by tomorrow and Carlo wouldn't miss the catch for anything. Maybe the net would hold Tom Cochrane. Or maybe it would hold someone entirely unsuspected.

It was six o'clock as Hernandes pondered over the events of the past week. He had no idea what was related and what wasn't, but something else was odd.

Following the bulletin on thousand dollar bills, Hernandes contacted the Treasury Department, asking for a printout on the banks that were involved including dates and times the bills were exchanged. The Treasury faxed a long printout, over ninety banks in four days! The biggest surprise: The spree began right here in Dartmouth.

"Man, I miss you so much."

"Well come on down and visit. You don't have to stay late." Gail wasn't used to pleading with men to come see her. She usually pleaded for them to go.

"I still have some things to get done." Rich looked at his sign, thinking it came out pretty good. "I won't bother you with any details, but everything's on schedule."

"I won't pry. I know you think I'm better off not being involved, so let's leave it at that." Then Gail added something she's never told anyone, let alone a man. "I've got to learn to start trusting other people."

CHAPTER 20

2nd Wednesday - Early

He didn't need the alarm clock. At three o'clock, Rich was up. His eyes felt terrible, like sandbags with leaks in them. He sensed something different this morning and as he stepped out of the shower it dawned on him. It was raining. Bad omen or good omen, Rich didn't care, he had his work cut out for him. He put on a rain slicker and carefully, quietly, carried the sign down to his Explorer. It wouldn't have worked with the Z3. He returned for his other items and set out.

He drove through the deserted streets of New Bedford on a mission. Good or bad, it ends today. He would go no further without putting some control into his life. He had nothing to lose - a powerful position to be in.

He was in Padanaram in ten minutes, weaving his way over to Carlo Bartelli's street. There were no police cars, his biggest fear. Padanaram was a small village and the monied residents insisted on tight patrol. He and his Explorer were known to them so he could only pray they wouldn't be parked where he needed to "work".

At the corner of Franklin and Rockland, Rich pulled over. At five-thirty he had to wonder why he got here so early? If he set the sign now, someone would see it and get suspicious. His first mistake. He decided to drive around for a bit and kill an hour. Why didn't he realize that in his planning? What else did he overlook?

At six-twenty, Rich parked next to the roadblock he had encountered when he visited the Wellington's. No one was around. He got out, popped his rear door and loaded the two roadblock barriers and the arrow-sign. He got back in quickly and headed for Rockland Street.

At six twenty-five, Rich was back at Franklin and Rockland. Again, there was nobody. This was the drop off that worried him the most. Putting up a fake D.P.W. sign could be dicey, especially since it was going to pose an inconvenience for some of Padanaram's most elite residents. It would surely be reported in a short time, so the timing had to be flawless. Carlo should be leaving soon. Carlo was always punctual, which means he was early.

Rich popped the rear door and quickly set up the roadblock barriers and the arrow-sign pointing to the right. With the coast still clear, he went back to his Explorer for the main sign. He was glad for the rain as the cloud cover gave him more darkness and it would keep people home. He positioned the sign perfectly, removed the blanket and threw it back into his car. He headed toward Debbie's home.

As his old house appeared, Rich slowed. It was a great house. Not ostentatious, well designed. He missed it. He missed Padanaram. But why lament, he thought, get on with it. He placed the merchandise carefully, strategically. He stood back admiring his work.

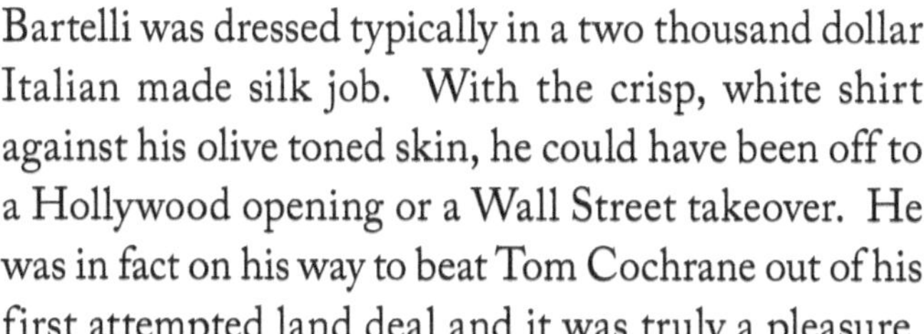

Bartelli was dressed typically in a two thousand dollar Italian made silk job. With the crisp, white shirt against his olive toned skin, he could have been off to a Hollywood opening or a Wall Street takeover. He was in fact on his way to beat Tom Cochrane out of his first attempted land deal and it was truly a pleasure.

He ignored the rain completely, being above earthly phenomena that affects mere mortal men. He marched out to his Lincoln Continental on his way to show Cochrane who's boss in this world. A determination showed on Carlo's face that would send chills down most peoples back.

With his wipers and lights turned on, Carlo pulled out of his wide, circular driveway. Even his driving emanated a purpose that could not be denied. There was an attitude to it. Rich noticed it from his Explorer parked deep into some trees on the side of the road.

At the end of Rockland Street he intended a left turn down Franklin but noticed the roadblock. As he slowed, he had difficulty reading the sign through the rain soaked window. He powered it down half way and read:

DETOUR
FOR DARTMOUTH STREET
CONTINUE DOWN MOSHER STREET

A slight inconvenience, nothing to get upset about. His mood had improved knowing he was beating Cochrane today.

Turning down Mosher would bring him by the Cochrane's, or Debbie's house. So now he could see what the ratfink was up to. Would there be a light on or is this fish still sleeping? Carlo had no good feelings for this *giadrule*.

As the Cochrane's house came into view, the grimace on his face tightened. He hated Tom Cochrane with all his life, Tom had his money and he could feel it. He could smell it. There wasn't room in this world for the two of them. Carlo's grip on the steering wheel tightened. His heart raced. As he approached the house, the trash caught his attention as it was placed thoughtlessly too close to the edge of the street, almost on it.

Steering to avoid the trash, something caught his eye on the curb, something in the trash. It passed by quickly and into his blind spot, but Carlo was almost sure. He took his foot off the gas to coast, slowing to confirm what he saw. He shot a drilling stare out to his right side view mirror. Nothing yet, then it drifted into sight. Carlo's eyes bugged out, his grip on the steering wheel incredible.

Shouting profanities, Carlo slammed on the brakes. The car lurched to a stop. He threw it into reverse and squealed the tires as he backed up, turning the car around in a skidding, sliding mess of a turn. The back of his Lincoln made contact with two garbage cans sitting on the curb sending them crashing into the two unmistakably obvious Samsonite, "Voyager" suitcases that were put out with the trash for pick up.

❖ ❖ ❖

Carlo peeled out in a rush of smoke and squealing. He grabbed his cell phone and found Alan Levine's number. He speed dialed and was almost screaming as Alan picked up.

"Mr. Levine, this is Carlo Bartelli." Even Alan could sense the hatred, the hostility. He thought of Rich and hoped he was all right. "I apologize, but

I must cancel this morning's meeting. Something's come up."

Alan panicked. What could this mean? Was Rich in trouble? Was this part of his plan?

"But, Carlo! We have to do this thing now! Now or never!" Alan was trying his hardest. Then he thought of the magic phrase that worked before. "If we don't, Tom Cochrane will beat you to the deal"

Carlo literally spit. Then he turned back to Alan on the phone, "I don't believe Mr. Tom Cochrane will be buying anything this morning. Something's about to come up for him as well."

CHAPTER 21

2nd Wednesday - Morning

Rich pulled out of a neighbor's driveway where he had taken refuge as Carlo screamed by doing about seventy. Satisfied with the reaction elicited, he calmly proceeded back to the corner of Franklin Street where he pulled to the side, popped his rear door and waited for a white Volvo to pass. He sprinted over to the fake sign and returned it to the Explorer. He let a red Saab pass, then scooted over for the two roadblocks and the arrow sign.

He drove back to Edgeworth Street where the D.P.W. would have preferred the roadblocks and simply heaved them off to the side. Rich figured kids would get blamed as he always did when he was a kid. He headed home for a quick change.

Carlo didn't have to raise Vito. The noise and fuss from screeching into the driveway, slamming doors, spewing venom and spit was enough to wake up the dead.

"Paisano! What? What?" Vito stood with both arms outstretched, palms up.

"The weasel Cochrane!!! I told you, I told all of you! He's a weasel, a maggot, a… a… an insect!"

The "C" came running in smiling, sensing action at hand. He stopped in the doorway, his favorite spot. The two *bechinnos* appeared next and hung in the opposite doorway, a little more crowded. Cold stares hung between them and The "C", sensing they would soon be vying for a privilege. Jackie appeared last, wondering what this ruckus could be in the middle of the night.

Vito was gesturing Carlo into silence when he turned to the four spectators. "Please, may we have some privacy?" Reluctantly, they all obeyed.

"Carlo, Carlo, calm down." Vito spoke. "What are you carrying on about?"

"That little flea, Cochrane! I told you he was the one. I told you!"

"Did you hear something?"

"Hear something! I've got eyes my brother!" Carlo was holding his two fingers out, "V" style, pointing to his eyes. "I saw what I had to see to nail that, that worm. That wart! That wart worm!"

"You saw what?" Vito was finding this hard to believe, checking the clock at the same time. It's not even seven o'clock! "What can you see at this time?"

"Ahhhhh! Ahhh, Ahhh!" Still pointing to his eyes. "What did I see? I saw Tom Cochrane's fate! And he'll see it too, before this day is over!"

Vito did a quick shake of his head wondering if Carlo lost it. Carlo sensed he had been ranting.

"Forgive me." Carlo hung his head, shaking off his high-strung antics. "Vito, I saw the proof we need. Tom Cochrane has our money!"

"What proof did you see, my friend?"

"The suitcases! The two suitcases we put the money in and buried with Fowler, the screw-up courier."

Vito's eyes widened, but he wasn't yet convinced.

"Suitcases. That's it?" Vito's eyes were peering up. "Don't other people have suitcases?"

"Vito. Vito." Carlo was finally smiling. "Not like these. These were special, these were classy, and these were very rare!"

Rare suitcases? Are there suitcase aficionados out there? Vito seemed unconvinced.

"Vito, these cases are unique, nobody else would have one of these, let alone two! They were two-tone, leather edged, brass trimmed. When's the last time you ever saw two suitcases like these?"

"Last time I visited Italy! My grandmother has them. Everybody's grandmother has them." Vito was losing faith.

"No, no. Not like these, these are new! A reproduction! I picked them out myself!"

Vito was almost back to believing. "And you're sure about this?"

"One of them was even open. The lining was the same. Everything was the same. And there were two of them! Two!" Holding up the two fingers again. "And they were being thrown out! Who would throw out two new, perfectly good suitcases?"

Even Vito was smiling now. The proof was convincing.

They formulated a plan. They would act swiftly, this morning. But first they would contact Louis Montero. The gesture would be appreciated and Carlo suspected Montero had his own score to settle with Mr. Cochrane.

⬦⬦⬦

"You're up early today." Tom was surprised to see Debbie up and around at eight.

"I couldn't get back to sleep after that awful squealing and screeching. Did you find out what it was?"

"Evidently a few bums using our trash day to get rid of some things. I rushed over to the window as fast as I could, but they were gone. Never got a look at them. They left some suitcases with our trash though and I could see the tire marks they left."

"What's this neighborhood coming to?" Debbie was shocked. "Did you call the police?"

"No. What's a couple of suitcases, the garbage guys will take them." It wasn't that Tom was magnanimous, but he doesn't talk to police. "If it happens again, maybe you should call."

"If it happens again, we're moving. I don't think this neighborhood is what it's cracked up to be." Debbie didn't really care for the house other than that it had good value.

"Move out! What, are you kidding? This house is beautiful!" Tom never had a house in his adult life. It was always apartments. Once a condo, but that was a girlfriend's.

"If Rich is paying the mortgage here and we sell the house, what happens about that?" Tom wouldn't want to lose that value or the fun of having Rich pay.

"Then he'll owe us." Debbie had looked into this. The way the Agreement was written, the value of the house was solidly Debbie's, Rich would have to pay until she received full value. "He'll pay us the fifteen hundred a month instead of the bank."

A smile came to Tom slowly. He liked that. Debbie liked it too. In life, people really do get what they deserve, Debbie believed.

"Where will you be this morning?" Deb asked Tom.

"The Yacht Club. I'm meeting a client there to talk about a piece of property, then I want to start looking into some sailboats." The money was burning a hole in Tom's pocket. "How big of a boat do you want?"

"Nothing under sixty feet."

On that note Tom left, shaking off the earlier disturbance and happy that Debbie was behind him about the boat. Debbie headed for their exercise room for an hour of stretches, crunches and lifts, then fifteen minutes of tanning. After a relaxing Jacuzzi, she was ready for a shower and her business suit.

It was after eleven as Debbie dabbed the finishing touch of her mascara and then put on her jewelry, ready for a rainy, soggy day at the gallery. She gathered a few items, slid them into her Gucci brief case and reached for her keys. That's when she saw the reflection in the mirror of an odd shaped man standing in the doorway to her hall. It was The "C".

❦

"Humboldt, how busy are you?" Captain Hernandes asked.

"Right now? I'm on the fly. Just got a call in. Some kids were messing with the detour signs down on Franklin Street in Padanaram. D.P.W. people aren't working today on account of the rain so we've got to go fix it." Humboldt was a real trooper. How many other women would go out on a day like this to move around heavy detour barricades?

"You and who?"

"Ryan." They weren't usually partners, but this was the way the draw had fallen today.

Ryan popped his head out from around a cubicle. He gave the high five salute to his Captain, indicating he was almost ready to go.

"Ryan," Hernandes barked, "I just promoted you. I want to talk to your partner, so let me ride down to Padanaram with her and you can have her when we get back."

"Sure, Captain. What should I do in the mean time?"

"Like I said, I'm promoting you. Do my job."

Ryan looked down the hall to where Hernandes' office was. "You mean, desk and all?"

"Of course, desk and all. Give it to 'em good."

Hernandes just made Ryan's day. Now Hernandes was hoping Humboldt would make his by agreeing with his little theory. As Hernandes walked down the corridor with Humboldt, Ryan called out to him.

"Hey, Captain. Are you gaining weight?" It's not often that Hernandes walks down corridors. He's usually stuck behind his chair where no one notices his girth.

"Nah. Impossible!" Hernandes was brushing it off. "I work out every morning, first thing when I get here." He turned to Officer Humboldt while exaggerating a chewing motion with his mouth. She recognized his reference to the Dunkin Donut routine.

Once in the cruiser, Humboldt drove and Hernandes talked. "Jane, let me run this by you and you shoot it full of holes wherever you can." Hernandes was about to start, then added, "But be kind." She smiled.

"This silly little bulletin about thousand-dollar bills being turned in, all by the same man who takes the time to drive up and down Rte. 95, hitting all the key exits. Eighty some odd banks in what, four days?"

Humboldt nodded in agreement. "Actually, three days, he only hit a few on the first day."

"I've got to ask, why?" Hernandes was peering out into space, like this was the first time he was pondering the situation. "Why does a guy go through that kind of effort and all that driving? Like it's some sort of covert operation. He's just turning in bills for crying out loud! Why not call one local bank, make the arrangements and get the job done?"

Humboldt shrugged her shoulders.

"There's only one reason a guy would go through all that trouble and that's if the money were dirty." Said as a statement, the bonafide end of the matter. He looked to Humboldt for acceptance. And got it.

"You know that gut feeling I had about Dartmouth being the center of all these weird incidents in the last week?" Jane nodded, yes. "Well, here's another weird incident, and we're right in the center of it again."

"Center! Tony, Dartmouth's not in the center of Boston and New York."

"It is when the exchanges start here." He had her attention. "The first bank used was in New Bedford. The next three were in Dartmouth. And each day, before nine in the morning, another Dartmouth or area bank was used. The trail to the other banks led out from Dartmouth!"

They looked at each other, Hernandes was proud of himself, his chest sticking out almost as far as his gut.

"How do you know all this?"

"Called the Treasury. Had them fax me the particulars." Tony was nodding his head up and down, enjoying the view out his window. He was contemplating whether he should inject the next piece of the puzzle or let Jane figure it out. He didn't have to ponder for long.

"And you're connecting this with whatever it was that was dragged out of the burial site out at Horseneck?"

He turned back to Humboldt, admiring her quickness.

"The first few banks were hit the very next day. All in New Bedford and Dartmouth areas." It wasn't really a "hit", but that's cop talk. Humboldt nodded in agreement, so Hernandes went on.

"I think there's a John Doe out there who witnessed a mob or gang burial. Not a murder, but a burial of a body and some cases or boxes or something. Full of money." Hernandes had no explanations for the why's of these details, but who knows the minds of criminals? This scenario fit. "He took the money, reported the body and ran. For some bizarre reason, there were a ton of thousand dollar bills in the cache and he needed to exchange them. It all fits."

It did fit. Jane tried to find holes but there were none. They discussed it from different angles but Tony's theory stood firm. Jane agreed, no one can figure these mobsters out. If anyone were to horde stashes of thousand dollar bills, it would be these guys.

"So if we can find who our 'John Doe' is that was turning in the Clevelands," Jane was summing up, "we'll find our tipster too?" As she said this, her mind kept going back to the vague description of the 'John Doe' that had come across the wire and wondered again if it could be who she thought.

"That's right. And it shouldn't be that hard." Tony had thought this through and it seemed pretty easy.

"Where would you start?"

"The first bank John Doe went to, First Federal, down town New Bedford." Hernandes felt a confidence building. "My guess is, he started at his own bank."

They arrived at Franklin Street where Humboldt braved the rain and the muck and returned the roadblocks and signage to their places. Hernandes sat dry in the cruiser as he had forgotten his yellow rain slicker.

⸺⬥⬥⬥⸺

The "C" and the two *becchinos* were very proper and respectful in handling Debbie in her home. Though Debbie was petrified, had turned a ghostly white shade and had given herself a sore throat from her one piercing scream upon noticing The "C", none of the three men made a threatening move. The trembling Debbie immediately capitulated to even the least gesture or motion from any of the three would-be abductors, eliminating a charge of "forced" abduction.

Emilio took the lead and asked Deb where Tom was. The Yacht Club. He next asked if Tom was alone. Yes, No, meeting a client and then looking at boats. Debbie was still trembling, still white. Then he asked where the money was. In the closet. Bedroom closet. This was going better than any of the three had imagined.

The "C" immediately headed for the bedroom and the closet door could be heard opening. After a few shuffles, The "C" returned with a paltry pile of money in a green garbage bag. Emilio and Valentine looked at each other in disbelief, then at The "C" who was wearing an unbelieving expression himself. Their attention all fixed on the trembling, tearful, totally frightened Debbie.

"Where's the rest?"

Debbie looked at Emilio, puzzled. Then her trembling increased visibly so. She tried to form some words and ask "what rest?" but her shaking overpowered her. She cried into the back of her hand as she raised it to her mouth. Debbie realized in less than a second that Tom hadn't shared all the money with her. Wherever the rest was, she had no idea. She would probably die for not knowing.

Even Emilio and Valentine were feeling sorry for Debbie. The "C" took it in stride. He didn't see this as having much effect on the final outcome anyway, so to his way of thinking, what was the difference?

Emilio approached Debbie, trying to calm her with his hands assuring her he meant no harm. Debbie recoiled, thinking he was going to attack her or beat her. Emilio placed his right hand on Debbie's shoulder and with the left directed her to a chair. It registered in Debbie's head that he was being polite. She sat down, a quivering white mass of tears and fears.

Emilio crouched next to her and rubbed his forehead, wondering how best to handle this. By now, The "C" had emptied the trash bag on the sofa and even without counting all three men knew this was not the mother lode.

"There's more money." Emilio said calmly to Debbie. "Tell us where it is."

Debbie moaned, a quivering, sickening moan. She didn't know. Why didn't Tom share it all with her? She would turn it all back and these men would leave and Debbie and Tom could get on with their lives. Separately.

Valentine motioned for The "C" to follow him through the house as they made a cursory search for the remaining money. Neither held out any hope but they went through each room, tearing through all closets, pulling out all drawers and then tipping over the bare frames of any of the chests or bureaus to check behind. The mattress was sliced as well as the sofa and two large upholstered chairs. With nothing to show for their destructive binge, Valentine and The "C" returned to Emilio gesturing frustration.

"You're sure Tom is at the Yacht Club?" Emilio asked calmly, not even knowing what the Yacht Club was.

Debbie nodded affirmative. A shaky, almost epileptic motion, she still couldn't speak. Her whole body was sweating and mixing with the tears, she was soaked.

The three men looked at each other, then around the strewn room. Emilio looked at his companion Valentine.

"To the Yacht Club." He said, then assisted Debbie up and escorted her out. Gently.

⸻ ❧ ⸻

To any driver happening by, the three men and Debbie would look like four mourners leaving for a funeral. The men, dressed in dark suits, with crisp white shirts and well chosen ties, huddled around and assisting the grieving woman having difficulty in managing her steps on the way to the waiting, deep burgundy Cadillac. But the driver of the BMW Z3, parked a hundred feet up the road and nestled into the trees, knew better.

Rich had held onto the rented Z3 for a few extra days. It occurred to him that maybe someone would have seen his Explorer earlier and recognize it. The Z3 made more sense. He would have had the top up regardless of the weather.

The Cadillac pulled out and Rich waited a respectful several seconds, then slowly pulled out himself. He had almost abandoned his entire plan. Ten minutes earlier, hearing the sickening, gut-wrenching scream from inside the house, Rich thought of rushing out of his car and bursting in to attempt a rescue of Debbie. After all this time and all she had put him through, he still didn't want her hurt. But then he realized they wouldn't hurt her yet. Her life and welfare were safe until they either had Tom or the rest of the money.

The burgundy Cadillac wound its way around the tight, almost herringbone streets of Padanaram and pulled in to the driveway of the Yacht Club a few blocks later.

⊷⊷◆⊶◆⊶◆⊷⊷

The mood was entirely different inside the Yacht Club, almost festive. Though the weather stunk, boaters and lunch guests were crowded inside deeply enmeshed in "land sailing", the only kind most of this crowd would think of on such a drenching day as this. Festivity and merriment were in the air. Tom was in his element.

He never saw the two men, Valentine and The "C", coming up from behind him. Sitting at an outdoor table sheltered from the rain by an overhead canopy, and twiddling with the straw in his iced coffee, Tom was engaged in conversation with an artsy brunette sporting about twelve obvious facial piercings and leading him to muse over other, not so obvious ones. She was an illustrator having trouble finding work.

So, quick thinking Tom was in mid-sentence: "I was thinking of opening a very upscale tattoo parlor in Providence, maybe Providence Place, but I would need a …," when he was encouraged to stand, turn around and exit with the two gentlemen offering the encouragement through their coercive, under the armpit persuasion tactics. So persuasive were they that Tom nearly floated out of the establishment, his toes barely making contact with the ground except in little pigeon toe type steps, missing about one out of three.

They forced Tom into the back seat of the Cadillac and confirming they were not the police: They failed to duck his head for him. The head bruise, though throbbing now, would shortly feel like a tickle compared to the venue planned for the afternoon.

Tom was even more surprised when he saw that it was Debbie he was sliding next to. He took one look at her pallor and realized this was not a joke. The time of reckoning had come to Tom Cochrane. His mind was racing as he tried to think of exactly which infraction this might be for.

CHAPTER 22

2nd Wednesday - Afternoon

With Emilio driving, Tom and Debbie sat crunched between Valentine and The "C". Rich could only imagine the terror going through their minds by now. He knew he had to keep distance or the driver may spot his Z3 tailing him.

Rich took to tailing like a natural. He stayed back as far as possible on straight stretches. If the Cadillac made a turn, Rich would speed up to the limit of the Z3, which was pretty impressive. In no time he'd be up to the turn-off and be able to see if it was making any other turns. With the car in sight again he would pull to the side, let the distance build and follow again. He didn't dare lose them.

The procession proceeded north to Route 195, and

headed west. In Fall River, they headed for the Bragga Bridge but exited at the last exit before the bridge. Heading north, they past the Battleship Cove area. The "USS Massachusetts" loomed off to their left dwarfing a full-size replica of "The Bounty" docked just north of it. The area was packed with hordes of summer tourists. The Cadillac kept away from the crowds by keeping to the main highway until past the Cove.   Winding through streets and buildings that dated to the Industrial Revolution, they soon ended up in an old factory area. Large warehouses loomed before them.

They wound their way into a deserted area to a large brick structure with countless large windows lining the sides, all barricaded with painted plywood. The Cadillac pulled to a set of brown anodized metal doors, apparently a recent addition. Rich pulled behind a large dumpster.

Rich spied the Cadillac and quickly noticed the Lincoln. Bartelli was already here. A third car, a Jaguar sedan was parked at an angle to Carlo's. Then Rich noticed for the first time that it had stopped raining. His mind was so occupied he wondered if there was anything else he didn't notice.

The front door of the Cadillac opened and Emilio got out. The rear doors flew open. The "C" exited dragging Debbie behind. Valentine exited, Tom behind him. They all hurried up the front stairs and through the glass doors.

Rich grabbed his cellular phone, his lifeline. He

ran toward the building looking for an alternate entry. Half way down he noticed bay doors along the side. He headed straight for the first door, only to find it locked. The next was locked as well and he thought of returning to the main doors. Time was of the essence, but the main door might be suicide. He ran to the end of the building and found access. An old bay door that looked like it had been jimmied more times than it was ever opened in the name of legitimate business. Local drug gangs, no doubt.

Rich pried the door up just enough to squeeze under, hoping he wouldn't be walking right in to a gang council meeting. Everything looked clear. Through the empty bays and loading docks, graffiti everywhere, Rich journeyed deeper into the dilapidated structure. There was just enough light from old, dirty and broken windows to see his way around. The halls were filthy and the rooms bore unmistakable signs of being living quarters for some indigents. Rich pressed on. So did the squalor and smell.

Following his instincts toward the main entrance, Rich came to a huge open area, then a door that he surmised would lead to the main area. It did. Down the hallway he could see light emanating from one of the rooms. As he entered, he sensed noise for the first time. Voices. Groans. Then a bone-chilling, blood curdling scream. It was Tom.

Quietly, Rich approached an open door leading to the area the scream had come from. Preparing himself for a ghastly sight, Rich peeked in down to the large open factory floor one flight lower. Carlo and Vito stood out immediately in their immaculate dress. Three goons were tying up Debbie and Tom. Louis Montero and one of his henchmen were there, Rich recognizing him from his news picture. Tom was all right, but they were tying him up, hands high above his head. Debbie was being tied, but to a chair. She was pale, shaking, crying and thoroughly distraught.

Rich grabbed his cell phone thinking this had gone far enough. He was ready to call the police. Thinking the dialing beeps might alert someone, Rich scurried back down the hallway and into the other large open area. A second ghastly scream echoed from Tom. Rich dialed 911.

Nothing. Again, 911. Again, nothing.

He checked his power level, which was fine. He shook the phone. Nothing. Shook it again. Nothing again. He tapped it. Nothing. He hit it. Nothing.

Suddenly there was something, his memory. He remembered he sent the check out only two days ago. His service had been terminated.

***

"Oh, I remember the day very well. Cindy exchanged it. She was so excited, never saw one before!"

Linda Thayer was the head teller, thus the logical place to start for Officer Humboldt.

"But she's gone." Linda was still smiling, glad to be of such significant service to the Dartmouth

Police Department. Even though they were sitting in New Bedford.

"When will she be back? After lunch?"

"No, I mean she's gone. Quit. Left and moved." Linda was just so gracious. She was still smiling broadly, though Jane's smile had suddenly ended.

"Moved? Where to?"

"Arizona. Scottsdale. Just left on Friday."

"Well, did anyone else see the man? Did Cindy mention who he was?"

Linda shrugged it off. It couldn't be that important, New Bedford would have sent their own investigators if it was.

"Oh, no. We handle so many accounts a day, who could remember?" But she was still smiling.

Humboldt knew it had begun too easy. With over eighty banks involved, what were the odds she'd hit at the first one?

"Did Cindy leave a forwarding telephone number?"

Linda stopped smiling. She wasn't appointed the Head Teller for nothing, even though she was the president's wife. There were untold responsibilities and incumbencies that required the discretion of a responsible head such as she. It was a position of extreme trust and not to be meddled with. Or so her husband, Morton, had taught her.

"Well, that information is confidential." Then Linda smiled.

"Oh, I understand," Jane went on, "I just thought, for a police investigation, you know, maybe a few exceptions could be made." She was smiling, but it was forced.

"Not without proper authority." Linda was good at her job. "Maybe a search warrant?"

Jane cringed.

"Any chance that I can take a look at a listing of your depositors or customers?" Still smiling.

Wide-eyed, Linda answered, "I'm afraid that would be confidential as well."

Humboldt didn't think this should be such a big deal.

"Well, if I tell you who I think was exchanging the bills," Jane thought this has to work, "can you just tell me if he's a customer at this bank?"

Linda pondered the many ramifications. Still smiling.

"Maybe I can help you with one name, if you have someone specific in mind." Linda was leaning into Jane, speaking quietly. She took a pen and a pad of paper, turned them to Jane motioning with her hand. "If you can just write his name." A wink.

A wink? Officer Humboldt took the pen and paper and wrote a name on it. She slid it back to Linda, who read the name and looked all around her, for spies. She nodded her head affirmative.

Cheeese and crackers! thought Humboldt, leaving the main lobby of First Federal Bank. Pity the bank robber that tries Linda's window!

She got back into the cruiser, the passenger side, as Ryan was driving. Since he was never told why

Humboldt had to get to this bank, he had no interest in what had just transpired inside. He did have an interest in what he had just heard on his scanner, however.

"Strap yourself in. An emergency call was just flashed for all officers in the area to respond north of the Battleship Cove section of Fall River. Two hostages, mobsters, drugs, the works!" Ryan was more than excited, he seemed nervous. It could only be Bartelli or Montero, and he was the favorite snitch to both of them.

"Fall River? That's not for us! Even if Dartmouth were included, we're in New Bedford! How are we going to get there in time to be of use?"

Her door wasn't even shut before Officer Ryan peeled out, lights flashing and siren screaming. He headed straight for Route 195 via streets that weren't laid out to get one there, but he made it work. Daring to glance at the speedometer, Humboldt saw how they would get there in time.

⸺⬢⬢⬢⸺

Huffing and puffing, Rich made it back to his bay door. He had run an easy two miles in a zigzag search for a phone, only to find the wires cut on all. Kids. He had noticed a young punk with green hair driving a BMW 321I and using his cell phone. Rich had literally thrown himself in front of the car and the punk actually noticed. Rich ripped the phone out of his hand, pressed "end" and then "9-1-1". The kid just stared in bewilderment.

When the Fall River police answered, Rich hastily described what was happening. The kid listened enthralled, thinking it was all so cool.

Rich popped into the back seat and directed the kid back to the warehouse. As they arrived, the imposing building cast a foreboding gloom and the kid wanted out. He dropped Rich and peeled away. Rich ran the last hundred yards at full speed.

As Rich entered the building the screams could be heard. Grisly, macabre intonations, each one sounding as it would be the last. Again, it was Tom.

Rich stumbled through the hallways, returning to where he could peer in. Just then he heard the worst scream yet. He peeked in and could see much the same scene as before, but suddenly he heard surprising words.

"POLICE, FREEZE! THIS IS THE POLICE. EVERYONE FREEZE, STAY WHERE YOU ARE!"

Shots were heard in the rear of the building. Bartelli and his entire company jumped to attention while Debbie stirred with a slight glimmer of hope. Within seconds, police were storming the room, guns drawn.

In the next instant, Rich heard running footsteps behind him. By the time he reeled around, four officers were on him, guns trained at his heart. The four officers motioned for him to stand facing the doorjamb with his arms in the air and his legs spread as they frisked him. Then they asked him to step out, motioning toward the stairs.

"Listen," Rich said, "I can't go out there."

"Move it! Now!" The officers were shouting.

"No, listen." Rich knew he should comply and was expecting a whack across the head or a billy stick to the kidney, but he had to make his case. And fast.

"I'm the guy that phoned this in! Richard Lewis is my name. If I go down there, they'll know that I blew the whistle. Please, can't we just wait until the two Dons are gone?"

Dons? The four officers holding Rich knew there was abduction in progress but had no idea who was involved.

"What do you mean, 'Dons'? Who's down there?" One of the officers peered down to see.

"Carlo Bartelli, the Mafia guy!" they knew the name, Rich didn't need to explain, "And Vito Gentilianni, the Chicago boss. I don't know the others," Rich continued, "but except for the man and woman tied up, they're all mob or drug figures. If they get wind of the fact that I dropped the dime, I'll be history."

The four officers nodded to each other. It made sense.

As this was happening, the faint sound of a squad car siren was building in volume, culminating outside with a screech of tires. North Dartmouth Officers Ryan and Humboldt came charging in, uninvited and unwanted, but Ryan had a personal interest at stake in protecting his two meal tickets, and nothing was going to keep him away. Humboldt had no idea of Ryan's connections, but she had a nagging curiosity that was being satisfied by being here.

Ryan was shuffled off to the Commander who demanded an explanation of his presence. Ryan made up a story about having had Bartelli and Gentilianni under surveillance since Gentilianni's arrival last week, but they had been given the slip heading earlier. When he heard the bulletin over their radio and the phrase, "organized crime figures", he assumed Gentilianni and Bartelli were involved.

The Commander accepted Ryan's explanation and allowed him to remain. It would prove to be the biggest mistake of Officer Ryan's soon to be terminated career.

With everything unfolding so fast, Carlo, Vito and Louis were still huddled close to each other as Tom Cochrane came out of his daze and spotted Officer Ryan through his blurry eyes. He launched into an almost delirious tirade.

"Ryan! Ryan, tell Montero I had nothing to do with the raid on his house!" In his daze, Tom had no idea the room was filled with other officers. He continued.

"Tell him the word came down strictly from the stakeout. I had nothing to do with it. Tell him, Ryan! They're going to kill me!".

Ryan tried to gesture Tom quiet. As Tom

continued his non-stop oration, Ryan became a little more forceful with his efforts, grunting out a guttural, "Shut-up", then, slightly louder, "Shut-up, you'll ruin it for all of us."

Tom continued to rant. He vaguely recognized now that police seemed to fill the room, but in his state of mind it didn't matter. Turning to an officer, he went on, "Ryan's their snitch. He keeps them abreast of everything. Ryan knows I had nothing to do with setting up the raid on Monetro." Then back to Ryan, "Tell them!"

Ryan was flushed with embarrassment. All he could do was to mockingly laugh it off in the hopes that no one believed Tom. But Tom's next zing was a real killer.

"Ryan buys from me! He's one of my best customers. He set me up with Montero as the supplier, then buys from me at a cut rate!"

This didn't make sense to one of the officers just behind Tom, who then tapped Tom on the back of the shoulder, asking, "Why would he buy from you if he's snitching for Montero? Why not have Montero supply him?"

"One of Montero's rules," sobbed Tom, "he never supplies anyone on his payroll! Never."

The scene was set for the next harangue of charges, which developed into a two way lamb-blasting between Ryan and Tom. Each accused the other of dastardly deeds, each then coming back topping the last charge. In two minutes they spewed about a dozen felonious charges that would eventually stick as the officers all froze in their positions listening in disbelief to the self-destruction of two small time wanna-be's.

Carlo, Vito and Louis remained huddled together, another big mistake. As Carlo and Vito watched the spectacle of the two men spilling the beans on each other, they each thought what amateurs these two are! Carlo and Vito both were mulling over the value of their heritage, silence at all costs. Never would two Sicilians be barking accusations at each other publicly such as this. An old woman would do such a thing, if she were touched in the head, but never a man. Settle your scores privately, not in public! To die or serve for life in prison would be more honorable than to cry like these two whiny Anglo wimps.

It was too bad that Louis Montero wasn't raised in this same culture, for he would have understood the depth and dependability of such breeding. And it was really too bad when Montero leaned slightly and whispered into Carlo Bartelli's ear…

"Should their ranting give you ideas, know this. At this moment, three of my best men sit in a second floor apartment at twelve Marlboro Street in Boston as they hold hands with a most delicate of ladies named Carmella."

Carlo turned a slow, icy stare back into Montero's gaze. Though handcuffed, Bartelli was all over Montero, kneeing him, head-butting him, smothering him. Montero didn't know what hit him as he doubled in three waves of excruciating pain and it wasn't over. Wave after wave, blow by blow, the attack was incessant. The police acted too slowly, taken by surprise over Carlo's animalistic behavior.

Through broken teeth and bloody lips, Montero spit out something about the killing of an Asian man. Bartelli thought of spewing out charges of Montero's drug operation, but his Sicilian upbringing countered his tendency to retaliate. Montero then referred to Carlo cutting up Marty and Tony and scattering their parts for fish bait, all because of a drug deal gone bad.

Amazingly though, no one, not Cochrane, Ryan, Bartelli, Gentilianni or Montero, ever mentioned the missing money. Officer Ryan never knew about it, while the others knew that only by avoiding the subject would they have a chance of recovering it one day, each fostering their own secret designs along those lines. Tom was still fingered as the rat that walked off with it.

The police eventually regained control and rounded everyone up and out. Their heads were still spinning from all the accusations that would be relatively easy to prove now that there was open hostility among them.

Rich was finally brought down as Debbie and Tom were being assisted out. Debbie barely noticed him as she was still in a deep shock. Casting a hollow stare in his direction, she was taken out on a stretcher.

Rich hesitated to look at Tom imagining despicable gashes for every blood-curdling cry he had let out.

Rich cast a quick glance anyway, bracing himself. He saw nothing, not even bruises. He looked closer. Nothing.

Rich nudged one of the officers near Tom. "Wasn't he tortured?"

"Nah," the officer responded. "They showed him a bat though. Really scared him."

Rich looked on in disbelief, shaking his head. 'Hero, Tom', he thought.

Rich was asked to make a statement at headquarters, but he never fell under any suspicion and was promised complete anonymity. An hour later, he was driven back to his Z3 and was soon cruising home. Rich tried numbering the different problems that had just been resolved.

⸻ ❖ ❖ ❖ ⸻

Gail was mixing some margaritas and engaged in conversation with two older factory-working women and a young Brown University girl. An odd mix, but routine for Gail. She had them in stitches over some of her latest blonde jokes.

She noticed Rich come in and excused herself from the trio of women, leaving them on their own. As she sauntered down to Rich, he had one hand in his pocket and was fingering a thousand-dollar bill. He wanted this to be the night he'd leave her one as a tip, but he was far from out of the woods. He let go of the bill, saving it for another day.

"I thought you wouldn't be back for a few days." Gail didn't think he'd be able to stay away, especially knowing what he attempted to pull off today. "So how'd your day go?" she asked. "Get a lot done?" He must have, he was alive. She knew all his plans, but his rule stood: She was not a participant.

"Same old usual," Rich replied, trying to downplay it. He was turning his head to a TV playing in the far end of the bar. He nodded to the screen, hinting to Gail that the reports coming on the news would confirm his success today. Gail picked up on it, smiling and flashing him an 'I told you so' wink. She had never doubted the outcome.

The news reported the arrest in Fall River of two of the country's top mob bosses along with a reputed drug kingpin from Colombia. A wild day in area news.

Same old usual for Rich.

CHAPTER 23

2nd Thursday

Alan looked in disbelief at Rich as he was going on.

"Wait, wait." Alan managed, "You mean to tell me that you were there?"

Rich had been interrupted in the middle of a description of the old warehouse and the haunting aura it took on with the screams and wailings of Tom Cochrane echoing through.

"Well…, yeah." Rich was puzzled, wasn't Alan following him? "I set it up, more or less."

Alan shot up out of his seat like he does.

"You set it up!? More or Less?"

"Alan! I've been telling you how I got Bartelli to think Tom was the one who took his money."

"Rich, you had me so scared! Bartelli calls full of venom over something and canceling his appointment. I had no idea what went wrong. And I couldn't get in touch with you!" Alan shook his head back and forth as he paced the room. "But let's back up a bit." Alan needed help. "How'd you get Bartelli to think Tom Cochrane took the money?"

"Not just Bartelli, everyone! I set Bartelli up first so he'd target Tom and get him out of the way." Rich saw the horrified look in Alan's eyes, so quickly added, "No, not like that. Out of the picture, get Tom so scared that he'd take off with the focus on him, not me."

"But fooling around with Bartelli! Who messes with him?" Alan thought this whole scheme was just too risky.

"Well, I guess I do when my life's on the line." Rich went on. "I knew Gentilianni was visiting, but I had no idea he'd be with Bartelli. So I never expected to bring Bartelli and his organization down! Good night! All I wanted was to get the spotlight off the money situation. Next thing I know, I'm in the middle of this huge Mafia take-down." He shuddered thinking about it.

"How did you set Bartelli up? How'd you get him to believe Tom took his money?"

"By painting my own, 'Mona Lisa!" he replied proudly. Rich settled back and explained everything. Alan was smiling, in disbelief.

"So, I helped in setting up Carlo Bartelli, crime

lord of the Northeast, Mafia Don! Nice, very nice. And if this plan of yours didn't quite work the way you hoped..."

"Alan, I'd never put you at risk. But if it makes you feel better, I'll never involve you again in any plans to bring the mob down."

That passed over Alan's head. He sat with mixed emotions, proud of Rich for pulling it off, but also thinking of all the money.

"You passed 28.8 million dollars on to Tom?"

"Not all of it. You know the situation I was in financially. So I held back what I needed and set Tom up with the rest."

They pondered the situation. A slow smile came to Alan as he thought of Tom getting his due after thinking he was set for life.

"What happened to all that money? Any idea?" Alan was sick thinking of it.

"No idea." Rich had expected it to be recovered and the authorities do whatever they do with it, but there was never a mention.

"Did they hurt Tom bad?" Alan was genuinely concerned.

"Yeah." Rich was still in disbelief about this one, "Completely dismembered his ego."

Alan knew there was more coming, so he waited.

"They never touched the guy! All this screaming and moaning and it turns out, all they did was threaten him! Can you believe that?"

Yes he could. Alan knew Tom.

"What about Debbie? She's all right I trust?"

"Shook up, but never hurt physically. I heard at the station she was going to be held in the hospital for a night or two, but she'll be fine."

Rich looked at Alan to get his reaction on this next one.

"Something else I heard at the station when they were getting my statement."

Alan was waiting for Rich.

Smiling, Rich said, "Because Tom was implicated in so many felonies, they're issuing general search warrants for the whole house and property."

So the elusive search warrants would be issued after all. Debbie's records were sure to turn up and with Alan's savvy, they would make it to court next week.

———————

With the parking lot full at St. Mary's Hospital, LaFleur grabbed a doctor's space and threw a sign in his windshield claiming, "Attorney". Beginning his second billable hour, LaFleur entered Debbie's private room.

"How's my favorite client doing?" Said sincerely.

Debbie looked like a changed person. She wore a blank stare and emanated a hollow aura. LaFleur could see police brutality charges in addition to the abduction, kidnapping, duress and twenty or so other charges he would be filing against the very deep pocketed Carlo Bartelli, Vito Gentilianni and Louis Montero.

"Debbie, you look good. I was so shocked when I heard what happened. Are you going to be all right?"

First there was a blank stare. Then Debbie's mouth formed a few words.

"It was awful." A pause. "I thought I was going to die." Another pause. "Tom…", then a shake of her head.

"Tom called me last night," LaFleur picked up the slack, "his phone call from the holding cell. He wanted me to represent him, but I'm not sure, there may be a conflict of interests." Being highly ethical, LaFleur needed to investigate the appropriatness of representing Tom. "Does he have any money of his own?"

Deb stared off blankly. LaFleur's last question didn't seem to register.

"Debbie," LaFleur thought to change the subject, "I've spoken with the doctor and he assures me you'll be fine. You'll be going home tomorrow and resting. I was hoping we could use him to get a continuance for the hearing next week, but the doctor wouldn't go along."

It was doubtful any of that registered with Debbie. LaFleur needed to slow his pace even more and not worry about how high the charges ran.

"Debbie, do you remember we have a hearing next week?" He waited and she finally nodded affirmative.

"Rich and Alan Levine may be on the attack. We've got to hit first. Deb?"

She waited two seconds, then nodded again. "He was there, I think." Said slowly, almost as if toward space.

"Who was where?"

Debbie was puzzled, but not perplexed. Something was coming back to her, something that the mention of Rich's name was bringing back to her.

"At the warehouse. Rich was there." Still spoken very slowly. "I think."

It couldn't be, thought LaFleur. Debbie must be having false memories. Debbie began a slow nod up and down. Then she was sure.

"Yes. At the end. He was there talking with the police."

LaFleur was upset. Why would Rich be there?

"If Rich was there, he must have been part of the conspiracy! He must have been party to the abduction! Debbie, we'll nail him for criminal charges. Of course, that's it! Rich was behind all this!"

LaFleur was getting excited. More charges, more motions, more hearings and even a full-blown trial! And kidnapping! A capital punishment crime! If only they were in another state, one that had it.

"No." Again a long pause. "It wasn't like that. He was being patted on the shoulder. Like he had something to do with stopping it." Then she drifted.

LaFleur knew he had better drop it for now. He'd

look into the charges brought on to all the perpetrators, then see how he could tie Rich in.

"He does, you know." Debbie had something on her mind.

"Excuse me?"

"He does." Still very slowly paced. "Tom."

"All right..." LaFleur was trying to humor her. "Tom does what?"

"Have money."

Bingo. LaFleur was so glad that he stayed.

"Oh, that's interesting. How... What money does Tom have?"

"A bag full." The pace would not quicken. "But more too."

"A bag full," he repeated. "What would that be? Hundreds? Thousands?"

Debbie took a breath, she was just relaying information at this point. She had no personal interest.

"Thousands." She said, vacantly, envisioning the money pouring over her in bed when Tom first brought it home to her. "Many thousands."

"Thousands?" The single word piqued his interest. To an attorney like LaFleur, that would be known as a good start.

"And more." She was still vacant. "That's what they wanted."

"Who wanted?" LaFleur couldn't keep up.

"Those men, yesterday." Debbie shuddered.

LaFleur couldn't keep up, but he got the money part. "Tom will need representation. I see no conflict of interest here. I'll check into the charges against him and contact him this afternoon." He was smiling for the first time.

"I'm divorcing him."

LaFleur stared in disbelief again. Divorce - a good, lawyerly word.

With Debbie spacing out, he gracefully departed, mulling over the work at hand. He was a rainmaker and Debbie his cloud. As he approached his car he discovered yet another expense she'd need to cover. A parking ticket.

CHAPTER 24

July 1st - Early Morning

As Marge led Rich into the conference room his heart sunk. Seated around the table with Alan were four men he had met in his apartment: Two IRS agents and two Mass DOR agents.

"Rich, come on in." Alan seemed just too chipper. Especially for 7:30 in the morning, the second time in a week.

Rich hesitated a split second, then nodded a greeting to everyone and entered.

"Rich, you've met these four gentlemen previously I believe." Alan was still smiling and happy. What was wrong with him, Rich wondered.

"Mr. Lewis, how are you today?" It was from the tall IRS man.

"Fine. Surprised to see you all, but I'm doing fine."

Alan was still beaming. Was he glad to be getting rid of Rich as a client?

"Rich," Alan beamed, "I've had an 'Offer in Compromise' before both of these departments for the last week. I didn't tell you about it before now in case it all fell through, but I'm glad to say that both departments have seen their way clear to accepting our offer."

Rich had no idea what was just said. An offer in what? And why are these four agents almost smiling? Isn't that illegal?

"That's good?" Rich asked.

"That's very good." Alan was answering. "Let me explain. First, let's take the IRS. With back taxes for three years, fines, penalties and interest, you owe the total of $ 213,249.35."

Rich swallowed hard. He was next expecting Alan to proclaim that he's convinced them to drop the thirty five cents and declare a major victory with the IRS.

"But their department has looked at your financial situation, including the lack of any property or assets, and they've agreed to accept a one-time, final payment of $20,000.00." Alan was proud.

"And the Mass. DOR is owed a total of $ 47,016.48. They have graciously agreed to accept a final pay out of only $4,500.00. Rich, you'll be totally free of all your tax debt for only $24,500.00! Isn't that wonderful?"

It was. It truly was. Who would have thought these two departments would compromise so deep. Alan had really done a marvelous job. But what makes Alan think Rich has that kind of money?

"Now Rich," Alan continued, "I've spoken with the bank manager at First Federal, and they've agreed to advance you this sum and issue the checks directly to these two departments. I have all the paperwork filled out for both the loan as well as the acceptance of these offers."

Rich was amazed. Alan seemed to be back in form. Marge was called back in and she brought a ten-inch stack of documents. They were passed, signed, copied and filed. With the deed done, the agents rose simultaneously, nodded their thanks and good-byes, and filed out leaving Alan and Rich to their little victory.

"I didn't think those departments compromised like that." Rich was thanking Alan, still amazed.

"There are rules and guidelines." Alan could have dissertated for hours on this subject. "If you owned assets, you would never qualify. But with all the financial reports you've had to file for the courts, they were convinced you're broke."

"Lucky me!"

"You are." Alan knew how important it was to get the tax people to agree this morning. "At least for now. Rich, in another hour we go into a hearing that could change all that. I think we have enough evidence to completely turn this settlement around and you may be awarded a few assets. It was critical that the tax people sign before the court makes you whole again."

Rich got the picture and had to smile. He had put his trust in Alan in spite of the mishap of the divorce, and here was the first sign of legal brilliance playing in Rich's favor.

"But won't they get upset if they hear about any change in my status from the hearing?"

"Never." Alan was reassuring. "First, they'll probably never know. Second, it's all legal. And third, they're just agents, they really don't care."

"Not to put a damper on anything," Rich had to ask since he wasn't used to legal successes, "but what happens if it goes badly in court today?"

"Well, you'll still be better off having this tax thing gone, right?" Rich had to agree with that. "And I don't think you're going to have a bad day in court today. Didn't I tell you I'd be throwing my best stuff this time?"

<hr>

A dark pall hung over the law office of Attorney Robert LaFleur on this otherwise bright, sunny, first day of July. While Debbie had managed a string of wins in court for two years, today LaFleur needed to prepare her for a radically different outcome. How quickly things can change.

"Debbie, how are you feeling this morning?"

Debbie looked a long shot better than she had in the hospital, but it wasn't the same old Debbie.

"I'm fine, Bob. How are you?"

Don't even ask, thought LaFleur. He decided to just skip the answer to that question.

"Debbie, I was reviewing Levine's motions and I could see that we're in for somewhat of a rough ride today."

"Why is that?"

"Because of that stupid husband of yours, Tom! The search warrants issued while you were in the hospital turned up everything but your dirty laundry! They found account records, bankbooks, safety deposit box keys, an extra set of books for your gallery… and cash. A lot of cash."

Debbie just shook her head. She went back to how LaFleur was feeling.

"Debbie, I had a rough time yesterday with your soon to be ex. I don't really want to go into it now, but it wasn't pretty."

"But how? What went so wrong with Tom?"

"Tom's a snake. A real low-life." LaFleur was wound up. "All those months I supported him by buying from him. Now he's threatening me! Threatening! Can you imagine?"

Debbie was puzzled. An almost perpetual state lately, but she wanted answers.

"Buying from him? You mean houses?"

"C'mon, Debbie." LaFleur looked around like all felons do. "I was one of his drops. I partied on weekends and Tom supplied me."

Debbie looked puzzled.

"Debbie," he hesitated just a second, "you must have realized that Tom was running a small drug operation."

"No." Simple answer. Then she shook her head slightly as if to buttress her answer. "I should have guessed, but no, I didn't *know* Tom was running drugs."

"Well, he's in a pack of trouble because his entire circle of contacts were arrested last week. The Dartmouth Policeman arrested was a customer, Officer Ryan. Now Ryan's spilling his guts trying to plead a deal."

That's what he could tell Debbie. What he couldn't tell Debbie was that Tom was holding this over his head. If LaFleur wouldn't represent Tom pro-bono, Tom would blow the whistle on him. LaFleur had no choice. And to protect Tom, Debbie was going to have to take a fall. LaFleur needed to change the subject.

"Well, the cash is a problem. Tom told me the whole story, as bizarre as it sounds. But if you testify that Tom came home with it one morning having seen some eccentric burying it, you'd be implicating yourself in a crime. You both should have reported such an incident."

Debbie agreed, she always knew they were taking a chance.

"But worse than being implicated in a crime," LaFleur should have her with this one, "Carlo Bartelli will nail both of you for the money. You know it's his, don't you? That's why he abducted the two of you."

She nodded yes. She had learned most of the details in the warehouse.

"Debbie, you can't let it be known how Tom came across the money. Bartelli or his men will track you wherever you go. If they can recover the money, they will, if not, they'll make an example of you. Either way..." he didn't have to complete the statement.

"Won't the police think it was part of Tom's drug dealings?" Debbie was hoping there would be a way to tie Tom in with it and make his troubles worse.

"That's not what we want anyone to think. For your sake, Debbie." LaFleur surprised himself how sincere that just came out. "If Tom's linked to a drug ring, it will be hard for you to prove you weren't involved. Especially when you had a bag of cash right in your closet!"

Debbie saw where this was going. She was going to have to concur with Tom's story, whatever it was. Neither of them could afford to tell the truth.

"Debbie." Looking square at her eyes, LaFleur continued. "You've got to say the money had been from your marriage."

"With Rich? But if it was, I should have disclosed

it! I'll be in trouble, won't I? I'm not taking the fall for Tom's stupid antics!"

"Debbie, they've found all of your records. They know about all your hidden accounts. So, Deb…" he tried to slow the pace down, "you're going to have to answer for that anyway."

Silence ensued as Debbie realized for the first time what she was in for today. LaFleur continued.

"This is serious, I don't mean to mislead you. But Debbie, hiding assets and failing to disclose the accounts is only one charge. Saying the cash was part of it isn't going to effect your sentence at all."

SENTENCE! The word stabbed through the air, directly into Debbie's heart. She looked to LaFleur with total disbelief.

"It's the only way, Debbie." LaFleur had thought this through and knew what had to be done. "If you're charged with not reporting the cash Tom found or if you're tied in to Tom's drug world, it will be worse for you. And your legal troubles will be nothing compared to your Mafia troubles."

A resolve washed over Debbie's face. She'd be going down today, and alone. Though LaFleur guided her in all this, knew everything about her hidden accounts, there was no way to tie him in, he had been too clever.

LaFleur could see that Debbie was accepting her fate without a murmur. This session had gone much better than he had ever anticipated.

CHAPTER 25

July 1st - 9:00 A.M., Bristol County Probate Court

Descending upon the courthouse from two opposite directions, Rich and Alan arrived at the front walkway only steps ahead of Debbie and Attorney LaFleur. Debbie had no venom in her look today as she acknowledged Rich, a first in at least two years. Rich nodded back, actually feeling dread for her sake.

Polite silence hung in the air as first Rich and then Debbie filed through the metal detector and were met by their respective attorneys who simply passed by to the side of the detectors. Courthouses are the last bastions of society where lawyers are trusted more than average citizens. As more LaFleurs are launched into the profession, that will change.

Checking the docket board, Alan was the first to see they had been scheduled before Judge Santos again. Rich smiled. Today the slate would be cleared and the tables turned. At least this was the dream Rich was holding on to. The next hour would tell the story.

Filing through the doors just behind them were two police officers from Dartmouth, Captain Hernandes and Officer Humboldt. The two had all the pieces by now and had drawn their conclusions.

Alan led Rich into Courtroom #2 and directed Rich to a seat. After a few minutes LaFleur and Debbie arrived and settled in on a side bench. A side door opened and a guard came out muttering something. Without hearing the exact words spoken, Rich knew the drill. All rose and gave their attention to the door. Here comes the judge.

❦

With the formalities over, the parties took their seats. Judge Santos looked them all over and for the first time in two years, he wasn't shooting darts in Rich's direction.

"Mr. Levine," Santos was getting the ball rolling, "You've filed some very interesting documentation in support of your motions. Would you care to enlighten me on some of these details?"

"Certainly, your Honor." Alan was calm and relaxed, as if he had nothing to lose. Rich figured it was because Alan had nothing to lose, it was Rich that had everything to lose.

"Over the past several weeks, we've come across information indicating that the marital estate in the matter before the court was never divided equitably or fairly. It was never evaluated properly because huge amounts of money had been hidden in various bank accounts, some..."

"Objection, your Honor!" LaFleur, naturally.

"Mr. LaFleur, you'll have your chance to respond." Judge Santos was trying to nip this stuff in the bud. "I will allow Mr. Levine to make his full statement first. Afterwards, if you have objections to any evidence he puts forth, I will hear it."

LaFleur would be much more subdued today as he'd want to keep a professional distance between him and his soon to be guilty client.

"Thank you your Honor." Alan was sensing an entirely different mood already. "I'll make my presentation very brief your Honor. The records that I've submitted disclose five separate bank accounts maintained by the defendant that were never disclosed prior to, nor since the divorce. Together, these accounts total over $1.2 million dollars!"

The onlookers reacted. Hustle and bustle ensued and Santos quieted everyone down with three raps of the gavel. Debbie hung her head.

"Through the last two years we've made every

effort to discover the exact value the defendant had taken out of the marital estate before leaving the plaintiff. Until just recently, we were stymied in all of our efforts. But the much publicized and unfortunate incident occurring in Fall River last month, involving the defendant and her husband, led to a police search of her property and the disclosure of all these accounts."

The crowd almost got into it again but a look from Santos dispelled their inclination. He wasn't a happy man.

All attention went back to Alan as additional explanations were expected. But Alan thought he had said enough for now. Let LaFleur commit himself and see what issues would be argued.

LaFleur was surprised to be called upon so soon. He was expecting a barrage of accusations and charges.

"Your Honor, I would first like to point out the impropriety of much of the evi…."

"Impropriety!" Santos was livid. He had evidently been yanked around for two years, being led down a yellow brick road paved with false allegations and phony representations staged by LaFleur and company. "What could possibly be improper about evidence obtained in a police search, executed by a properly issued warrant?"

"Well, sir, I would have to see the terms of the warrant and the …"

"Terms of the warrant!" boomed Santos. "You had the briefs served in sufficient time to do your research.

Did you or did you not find any improprieties in any of the documents offered for evidence?"

"Uh, well, uh, at first glance…"

"First Glance!! I don't care if it's first, second or third glance, counselor, did you find any improprieties?"

"No, no, your Honor." LaFleur scanned his notes for his next point. He continued. "Yes, uhm, there seems to be some inconsistency in the deposit amounts …"

"Inconsistencies! We're talking about large bank accounts that have existed for years in the defendant's name that were never divulged to this court!" Santos was all over LaFleur more than he had ever demonstrated with Rich or Alan. "Why should we care about some technical inconsistencies in a few transactions that might take a C.P.A. only two minutes to clarify for us? Who cares?"

LaFleur was on the ropes. "Point well taken, your Honor." With another glance down to his notes he began again. "Many of these accounts are not in my client's name…"

"No they're not in her name! But she did all the transactions, she made the deposits and she made the withdrawals. And this person whose name is on the accounts, isn't this person actually deceased as we speak? Hasn't she been deceased for the last two years?" Santos was giving it to him, and it was as if LaFleur had been cut above the eye, he was blinded and struggling to find his feet.

"Well the Bermuda account is confidential in nature…"

"Confidential! It exists, doesn't it? Records were obtained legally, weren't they? What's confidential about that?"

"Well, uhm, there may have been some oversights…"

"Oversights!? Is that how you pronounce p-e-r-j-u-r-y, counselor? OVERSIGHT?"

LaFleur was taking a good beating, but he took solace in the fact that it wasn't him going down, it was his client.

"Well, there may have been some impropriety on the part of my client that I was not aware of…"

"Objection, your Honor!" Alan beat Santos to his next tirade. "I believe there is evidence that Attorney LaFleur did indeed know about these hidden assets but purposely and willfully failed to direct his client to disclose these assets." Opening a manila folder in front of him, Alan removed copies of two checks. "I have here facsimiles of two separately processed checks in the amounts of $25,000.00 and $15,000.00, dated February 23, 1997 and April 14, 1998 respectively. Both checks are made out to Attorney LaFleur and bear a notation, 'For legal fees'. They are drawn on the Bermuda account in the name of Deborah Lewis. Your Honor, Mr. LaFleur clearly knew about this account, yet failed to disclose its existence."

That was Alan's fastball.

It was clear that Santos was about ready to make

a ruling. But first there would be one attempt at clearing an issue that was on everyone's mind.

"The report from the Dartmouth Police Department notes a sizable amount of loose cash found in the defendant's home and garage. It lists here a sum of $887,550.00. Would Mrs. Cochrane care to explain the existence of such a large amount of loose cash?"

Debbie snapped out of her empty daze and turned to Judge Santos. LaFleur indicated with a gesture that she should stand, and then some weird body language exuded from him in an attempt to remind her to stick to the plan discussed. Please don't pin the money on Tom, he thought. LaFleur held his breath as she answered.

Debbie stood with a hollow face and cleared her throat. Then she asked Judge Santos to repeat his question.

"I want to know where almost a million dollars in loose cash came from? In trash bags, at that." He smiled, but it was forced.

Debbie sighed. She started to say, "My husband Tom..." and paused. She gritted her teeth and continued... "Well, Tom likes cash. He insisted on saving money like that, said it made him feel more secure. Most of it was from an account I had closed out before the divorce and some we added by way of a savings."

LaFleur breathed easier. He would be going down for impeding discovery, but not for drug charges.

Santos shook his head in disbelief but had no reason to doubt that the money was a pre-marital asset. So he was ready to rule.

Opening with a stern lecture on the sins of perjury, Debbie was reamed out as a very naughty person. She was sentenced to thirty days in the House of Corrections. It could have been much longer, but considering the reversal of fortune she was about to suffer, it seemed to Judge Santos to be the humane thing to do.

LaFleur was then reamed out. He obviously was implicated in failure to disclose significant marital assets. The matter would be investigated and taken up with the Bar Association. Further legal action may be taken pending the findings. Sanctions were imposed on Attorney LaFleur in the amount of $30,000.00 to Attorney Levine covering Richard's costs for all the frivolity of the last two years. An additional $20,000.00 was to be paid directly to Rich as punitive damages.

LaFleur went limp. There was no fight left in him.

Then Santos went on, modifying the settlement. Santos basically reversed Rich and Debbie's positions. All of the non-disclosed bank accounts were to be closed down, fees and taxes paid and the money transferred to Mr. Lewis. LaFleur feebly tried to object but Santos had a great answer. He pointed out that since these accounts never existed according to their side, how could their side be hurt by giving them to Mr. Lewis?

The loose cash of nearly a million dollars was awarded to Rich. No objection.

Finally, in a total surprise, Judge Santos ordered Debbie out of the house in Padanaram and ordered the property to be turned over to Richard. Debbie was going to be allowed to keep all of her possessions, her car, furniture, jewelry and her business. All these would await her upon her release from incarceration.

With that, the case was closed. Santos cast Rich a glance and a nod as if to say, "Sorry for your troubles." Rich didn't need an apology. He was just awarded the entire shooting match, an apology would have been overkill.

Rich looked Santos in the eyes, something he could hardly bring himself to do before today, and a respectful smile broke through. Then Judge Santos returned the sentiment through a smile of his own.

Court Officers escorted Debbie out the side door. Rich felt bad for her and thought he might send her a check in a few months. She would need something to get started again. But then, inexplicably, Debbie turned backwards briefly, her eyes meeting Rich's. She threw him a sour look that would turn milk blue. So much for the check, he thought.

Alan gathered his files and brief case, grabbed Rich and headed out. Exiting the door, beginning to congratulate Rich, they were interrupted.

"Mr. Lewis."

Rich and Alan looked around. Behind them were Captain Hernandes and Officer Humboldt.

"May we have a word with you both?"

<hr>

The foursome proceeded downstairs to one of the private conference rooms. Without even sitting down, as soon as the door was closed behind them, Hernandes started right in.

"That's a tidy sum of cash that was laying around in the Cochrane's home."

Rich and Alan nodded quickly. It sure was.

"This court drew the conclusion that Debbie had taken most of that money from your marriage along with all those other bank accounts." Hernandes was doing all the talking. Again, Rich and Alan could only nod in agreement.

"Well, Officer Humboldt and I know better." Hernandes paused for drama. "We know where it really came from."

Alan stiffened. Rich sighed. They both looked at Hernandes and signaled him to go on.

"I'm sure you'll recall a few weeks ago, an incident down at Horseneck Beach? There was a body found buried?" Two sets of nods came back to Hernandes, who then continued.

"Well, a series of strange occurrences seemed to follow that incident, not the least of which was the fiasco in Fall River where your ex-wife was about to be murdered." Hernandes was looking directly at Rich now. "She and her husband Tom were taken there to be murdered because of that money."

Alan was squirming now. He was thinking of his disbarment hearing, hoping it might be after LaFleur's.

"You see, the body found in Horseneck was buried with cases or something, and removed before the body was reported. Those cases were evidently full of cash." Now Hernandes was back to including Alan in his view. "It had to be a lot of cash. Including thousand-dollar bills."

Rich was surprised of the accuracy of all these conclusions. How could they have figured all this out?

"Shortly after those cases of cash were removed, thousand-dollar bills started showing up in banks between here and New York. Did you know they don't even make thousand's any more?"

Rich nodded. Yes, he had heard that somewhere before. Alan was too stiff to move.

"Well, it was an odd enough occurrence that the Treasury alerted us to look for anything suspicious in conjunction with thousand-dollar bills." Then, looking at Humboldt, he added, "That was a first for me.

"Anyway, we looked into it because when we obtained a printout of the banks and times of the exchanges, they started right here in our area. A description of the man exchanging the bills was obtained and Officer Humboldt here started to do a little digging of her own."

Alan was stiffer than ever, but forced a slight smile. Rich was used to things like this. Hernades then turned the show over to Humboldt for the privilege of wrapping it up.

"I visited the first bank that the suspect went to. I couldn't get a positive ID, but I was able to confirm that a suspect fitting the description, did in fact bank there." She was looking at Rich head on. "At First Federal."

Rich hung tight. Alan's hands were sweating.

"It was then that the call came in about the Fall River abductions, so I wasn't able to pursue my search any further. But when the Cochrane's home was searched and all this cash showed up, including a fair share of thousand-dollar bills, we knew we were on to something."

Hernandes interrupted at this point. He was stealing the spotlight after all, but it was his baby and he was the Captain.

"Mr. Lewis, your wife didn't get that cash from your marriage." Alan stared down at the floor. Rich stared back at Hernandes squarely. "Tom Cochrane found it. He found it when he happened on the body at Horseneck Beach and never reported the money. He reported the body, anonymously, and tried keeping the money for himself."

"That's why he and Debbie were about to be killed

in Fall River," Humboldt interjected, "it was mob money and the mob was determined to recover it."

Humboldt and Hernandes waited for the reaction and were proud as they witnessed two huge sighs of relief issue forth. They looked to each other, smiling and proud, well rewarded for their hard investigating work.

"We wanted you to know so that you don't go through life thinking your ex-wife took you for a million more than she had." Humboldt explained. "What she tried to get away with was terrible, but the cash wasn't part of it."

Alan and Rich kept nodding away. They could accept all of this, yes, this is a very good explanation. Soon, Alan's senses began returning and the attorney in him prevailed.

"So, what will become of the money?" he asked.

The two officers looked at each other, then Hernandes spoke for them both.

"We're the only two that have put this all together. Everyone we bring it to thinks we're crazy, so who cares? Even the gang from the Fall River warehouse, Bartelli and them, no one is talking! I think there's even more money, money that Tom Cochrane buried or hid. The mob is waiting until they can get it out of Tom. Anyway, it would be more trouble than it's worth for us to make a stink about. Even if we got people to believe us, where would the money go? Probably get absorbed into some useless department budget or stolen internally, even though I'm not supposed to say that. Forget it! It's yours. Keep it and spend it in good health!"

Humboldt indicated her agreement and the two officers beamed a pair of proud smiles. How often do they get to do such a good deed for a deserving individual?

Hernandes wasn't done with his good deeds yet. It gave him even greater pleasure to lay this next gem onto the table.

"Rich, there are a lot of thousand-dollar bills in that stash. They're collector's items, worth who knows how much. So be discreet. You may be able to parlay your little fortune into an obscene fortune." Hernandes winked at Rich, fully behind him in this.

The four all shook hands and began to head out. Jane Humboldt stopped, turning to Rich with something she's wanted to say for a long time.

"Mr. Lewis, I've been hoping to run into you for a while now. I just wanted to say what a beautiful job you did in designing the Wellington estate! You did the whole community proud."

❖❖❖

As Alan and Rich were finally making their way out of the Courthouse, Alan's head was still swirling over what just took place.

"I heard the bullet whistle by," Alan was saying, "can you tell me how it missed us?"

Rich was alert to the other people milling around.

As there was a gap among them, he leaned into Alan's ear and explained his version.

"This was never part of my plan. Just a bonus I guess."

A couple started to pass them and were within earshot, so Rich held up. When they passed, he continued.

"I guess when I set Tom up, it worked better than I expected. Even the police suspected he was the one that found the money with the body."

"Yes, but they had a description of you turning in thousand-dollar bills at the banks!" Alan couldn't explain that one.

Rich laughed, knowing exactly what happened.

"Alan, do you know how many times I've been told that Debbie left me for a younger version of me? To people that don't know either of us well, Tom and I are considered twins."

Alan looked bewildered, but he could see it. A little.

"Only," Rich added, "I'm much better looking."

They both pondered their great luck as they passed through the old wooden planked hallway and outdoors to the Courthouse lawn. Alan pulled up short as they gained a little space. With their newfound privacy, Alan looked at Rich most consolingly.

"Rich, you had a great day. You deserve all the spoils Santos awarded you. But I'm sorry for all the rest of the money. I guess Tom hid it somewhere and it may never be found." Alan grimaced thinking of almost twenty eight million dollars that just vanished because of a dope like Tom. "And the police are letting you keep it too, what's left of it. They don't know how much is missing, do they?"

Rich took a deep breath of the outdoor air. He smiled to the sky, then looked Alan straight on.

"No, they don't know." Rich was glad for that. "And it's not missing."

CHAPTER 26

After Court - A New Beginning

Rich led them away for about a block to ensure privacy. Alan was a bundle of nerves trying to figure out what was going on but Rich countered every one of his questions with a one-forefinger answer, meaning to wait a minute.

They stopped on a quiet corner, one block east of the Courthouse. Rich started in answering the questions Alan had been shooting out along the way.

"Alan, I kept almost all the money. I planted less than a million for Tom to find."

Alan was bewildered. The three sacks full? How was that?

"All those trips to the bank that the police figured were by Tom, that was me and it was a lot of work!

I exchanged almost a quarter million worth of the Clevelands into smaller denominations." Rich had worked hard to get to all those banks, wondering all the time if it may blow up in his face. But he wasn't about to set Tom up with more than a million dollars, under any circumstances.

"Do you know how much room a quarter million dollars takes up when it's all in small denominations?" Rich asked Alan. "Especially when it's all fluffed up and not in neat bundles. It was incredible Alan! But it wasn't enough to set Tom up; I had to throw in a bunch of thousands. It hurt at the time, but as they say, all's well that end's well."

They both laughed over the whole scenario. Alan chuckled at what Tom must have felt finding the money. He would never count, he probably thought he had a billion dollars.

"But Rich," Alan was serious again. "That's an incredible amount of money. Maybe the police let you off the hook for now, but you can't hide that kind of money!"

Rich shrugged it off.

"I'm serious, Rich." Alan went on. "I've built a career around people who tried to hide money and it seldom works. It's like a time bomb, ready to go off. It's usually the IRS that discovers it, and you just ended your troubles with them."

Again, Rich was shrugging it off wondering why Alan was making such a big deal of it. Alan should know, more than anyone why it wasn't going to be a problem.

"Alan, you know I can't do anything about it if I wanted to. We had this discussion in your office. If I report it, the mob comes down on me and I'm a dead man."

Alan had forgotten about the mob. Rich was right, his life would be over if he reported it. So here he was with his client now worth who knows how much, and Alan really had no advice for him.

"You know," Alan looked two ways as if he didn't want anyone to hear this, "like Captain Hernandes said, thousand-dollar bills are worth more than face value. A lot more."

Rich nodded that he knew. Suddenly, his thirty million had gone off the scale!

"If you were to use anonymous dealers," Alan was saying, "you can drive up the value, gradually. Who knows what they can eventually be worth?"

Tripled, quadrupled, quintupled! Cash registers continued to ring in Rich's head.

"So how are you going to hide that kind of money?" Alan was deeply concerned, his eyebrows furled.

"Oh, I don't know," Rich had this one all figured out, "Write a book I guess. You know, about everything that happened. I'll call it a 'fiction', it will become a big hit and everyone will just assume that I made all my money on royalties."

Alan was really concerned now, looking at Rich

incredulously.   Small beads of sweat were starting to form.

"And what would you call it?" Alan asked, "*Padanaram Village*?"

Rich shrugged it off. "Nah. Who can pronounce it?"

Alan didn't know if he was kidding or not.

"Relax," Rich assured him. "I'm kidding."

"But seriously," Rich continued. "It just became public record that I've been awarded all of Debbie's accounts, and together they're worth over a million. Then the cash, almost a million more, plus the house, which is practically paid for. And don't forget, there's everything everyone always seemed to assume I had to begin with. Publicly, I'm worth an easy two or three million dollars."

It wasn't helping. Alan still had his eyebrows furled and light perspiration forming. With a short laugh he continued.

"An *old*, wise friend," emphasis on the drawled out 'old', "once told me that when it comes to hiding money, 'after the first two or three million, who notices?'"

Alan recognized the words. He had uttered them on the same city street just a few blocks away. He never meant it as tax advice and was surprised Rich had even remembered. But as he thought about it, he thought maybe it wasn't such bad advice. Alan had been around all sorts of money and all sorts of characters with it, and the words rang true. How differently would a man live on two million than on thirty? Or whatever eventual worth Rich would come to have. Who would know the difference?

With relief slowly replacing his anguished look, Alan nodded his head in surrender and said, "You mean, a _wise_ friend told you," emphasis on 'wise', and the reference to 'old' being discarded completely.

Rich smiled more broadly, still staring straight into Alan's eyes.

"No." Rich responded with a slight pause. "I mean... a *friend*."

Silence hung in the air for a few seconds. Then they embraced.

Four minutes after departing Alan, Rich walked through the door at a most unusual moment. A moment when Gail wasn't talking. With her back to the bar, she was busy crafting two Rusty Nails, a Tom Collins and a Basil Hayden in a snifter. Without seeing him enter, she sensed it.

Today was the day. Rich had wondered if he'd return to Gail in victory or be carted off unceremoniously to a County provided suite, feebly clutching his toothbrush that would serve as his closest companion for the foreseeable future. At least he genuinely hoped it would be his closest companion. But he didn't want Gail there. It had been his battle, his dilemma, his resolution. He would sink or swim on his own. Before even seeing him Gail sensed his entry.

Her head swiveled around searching for what her senses were already screaming, Rich was here somewhere. As their eyes met, they both froze, expressionless for about three seconds. Gail broke first, gradually forming a slow, beaming smile, with her trademark two dimples. Her respiratory system had still not kicked in. Rich let out a silent sigh and flashed his own Hollywood smile as the slightest nod of his head told her everything went well.

Gail released the glasses in her hands, grabbed a fistful of air with her right hand and yanked it in low toward her waist yelling out, *"YES!!!"*

The patrons took notice wondering what had just happened. Through the silence their attention quickly riveted to Rich as he calmly unrolled a thousand dollar bill and placed it on the bar, still smiling. It was as if no one had ever seen Grover Cleveland before.

"I'll buy every Palanga in the place a drink," he said calmly.

This time, three seconds of total silence, then every Palanga in the place grabbed two fists of air, yanked them in and harmoniously yelled, *"YES!!!"*

To a chorus of cheers and laughter, the crowd having no clue as to what they were celebrating, Gail floated over to Rich for a light kiss on the lips. Rich slid another thousand dollar bill her way and it was understood there would be no change required. A tip from the Great Palanga that was buying.

OTHER BOOKS BY JACK BURBANK...

- **Cutting Teeth**
  A collection of early short stories, mostly of mystery/suspense genre.

  ORDER: https://www.amazon.com/dp/ B08MW2JNZY

- **The Paperhanger**
  Finding clues to a decades old missing beauty queen, paperhanger Mark Sinara might be able to solve the crime, or die trying.

ORDER: https://www.amazon.com/ dp/1977068359

– **The Sentence**
An attorney who never won a case hooks up with his double-murder convicted client in a wacky scheme to get him out. Good idea?

ORDER: https://www.amazon.com/ dp/1976961890

AND MY NEWEST, First of the Yo Becham series…

– **Trouble**
Having left for Thailand just hours after a local church burning and mass killing, mystery writer Yo Becham comes under suspicion while getting into another problem in Thailand.

ORDER: https://www.amazon.com/dp/ B08FTWD9MM

All available in either paperback or eBook.

Did you enjoy this book? Learn more about the author and his other projects. Offer comments or even write a review.

Go to: www.jackburbank.com

Thank you,

Jack Burbank